ANGUS LIBRARIES
38046 01 0391

C000071793

www.angus.gov.uk/anguslibraries

Please return to any Angus library

Please return or renew this item by the last date shown.
You may apply to renew items in person, by phone,
by email or online.

1 7 APR 2014   2 9 DEC 2015   − 2 MAY 2019

2 4 MAY 2014   1 5 JAN 2016

                     2 7 AUG 2016   ANGUSalive

−5 JUN 2014   − 6 JAN 2017   Withdrawn from stock

1 4 JUN 2014   2 8 MAR 2017

−4 JUL 2014   2 8 NOV 2017

1 9 JUL 2014   5 NOV 2018

3 0 JUL 2014   1 9 APR 2019

−5 AUG 2014

1 9 AUG 2014

                     − − MAR 2014

Buried
in the
Past

The Mike Nash Series

Buried
in the
Past

Bill Kitson

ROBERT HALE · LONDON

© Bill Kitson 2014
First published in Great Britain 2014

ISBN 978-0-7198-1230-9

Robert Hale Limited
Clerkenwell House
Clerkenwell Green
London EC1R 0HT

www.halebooks.com

The right of Bill Kitson to be identified as author of this
work has been asserted by him in accordance with the
Copyright, Designs and Patents Act 1988

2 4 6 8 10 9 7 5 3 1

For Val

Wife, lover, best friend, critic and editor.

Typeset in 10½/14 Palatino
Printed in the UK by Berforts Information Press Ltd

ACKNOWLEDGMENTS

My grateful thanks to my readers, Angela Gawthorp, Andy Wormald, Cath Brockhill and Jan Ozkurt for their appraisal of the original draft manuscript. Also to fellow Robert Hale author, Peter N. Walker (Nicholas Rhea) whose book *Murders and Mysteries of the North Yorkshire Moors* provided my inspiration for part of the plot.

Thanks to Gill Jackson and the team at Robert Hale Ltd for their work in producing this, the latest Mike Nash adventure. As always, to Derek Colligan for his superb cover, and finally to my wife, Val, whose hard work and skilful proofreading and copy editing makes life much easier for me.

chapter one

1986

The car was being driven well within the speed limit. The road was unfamiliar and Hendrik was unused to driving on the left. In addition, there was no lighting, neither town nor village to bring relief, only the car's headlights to pierce the blackness of the night. Hendrik muttered something extremely unflattering to his companion about the backward state of the British nation.

'At least this road is so lonely there are no other cars for you to worry about,' Rutger pointed out.

'I can see why. Who would drive along this road out of choice? How much further do we have to travel before we meet our man? I want to get rid of this stuff, take our money and return in time to catch the morning ferry.'

They were speaking Dutch, their native tongue. 'Only a few kilometres more. We have to look for an inn that has been abandoned and boarded up.'

Hendrik gave a scornful laugh. 'Hardly surprising the inn is abandoned. Probably from lack of customers. My only question would be, why build one out here in the first place? Are you absolutely certain we're on the right road?'

'I'm following the instructions I was given to the letter, and when you think of it, the loneliness of the meeting place is ideal, given what we are carrying.' Nevertheless, Rutger shifted uncomfortably in his seat and eased the handcuff on his wrist. The movement caused the briefcase on his knee to slide forward. He clutched it, aware of the value of its contents and the perilous nature of their journey.

Several minutes later, Hendrik pointed to a large building picked out by the headlights. It was set back from the road with a large open space in front, which had obviously once been a car park. As they got nearer they could see the boarded-up windows. This had to be the place.

There was a vehicle in the car park, possibly the first to have parked there in years. It was tucked away in the furthest corner, almost as if ashamed of its presence in the dreary location. As they swung onto the tarmac the headlights of the stationary vehicle flashed, once, twice, three times. 'That's it,' Rutger said. 'That's the signal.'

As Hendrik pulled to a halt alongside a small van, the driver got out. They could see he was carrying a briefcase, slightly larger than the one they had. The Dutchmen relaxed. This was obviously the man they had to meet, and that would be the money.

The man reached their car, opened the rear door and slid into the back seat. They heard the briefcase being opened. 'Good evening,' Rutger greeted him, his English heavily accented. As last words, they were hardly memorable. Hendrik saw Rutger slump forward in his seat, felt something warm and sticky splash his cheek. Then the knifeman turned his attention to him and he neither heard, nor saw, nor felt anything more.

The knifeman located the key in Rutger's pocket and deftly unlocked the handcuff, removing the briefcase. He carried it back to his own vehicle and passed it through the open window. 'Better check we have the right one,' he told his companion. 'It would be a shame if we've got the wrong men.'

A few seconds later, aided by the courtesy light, they both gasped in awe at the sight of row upon row of bright, sparkling diamonds, the stones winking with sinful glee at them. 'Beautiful, absolutely beautiful,' the passenger breathed.

They ignored the fact that two men had died so they could get these diamonds. Or perhaps they knew that many men had already died because of them. The passenger closed the case, and they both felt a sense almost of loss. 'Right,' the driver said, 'now to get rid of these two. You're clear what you have to do?'

'I follow you to the dump site, right?'

The driver donned a boiler suit and returned to the dead men's car. He hauled the driver from his seat, dumped him in the boot, repeated the process with the passenger and drove away with his own vehicle following close behind. This was the most dangerous part of the operation. They had to reach their destination without attracting any attention, especially that of a passing police car. The journey went smoothly, and an hour later, as the sun was rising, the radiance of its early morning light was augmented by the brilliance of the fire caused by several cans of petrol, which they had poured over the car before torching it.

They turned their backs on the vehicle until the flames died down. When satisfied that the inferno had destroyed any evidence of the crime committed within, they began the long walk down the muddy track to their own vehicle. 'So far, so good; that's phase one over with. Now we have to get on with the rest of the plan.'

'You're not worried there might be repercussions?'

'I feel sure there will. In fact I'm counting on it.'

'That means more people will die.'

'Inevitable, I'm afraid. What we have to do is make sure we're not among them.'

'Where are my diamonds?'

'Sorry, I don't understand? You have your diamonds. My men went yesterday to meet you.'

'No they didn't. I waited and waited, nobody turned up. I was at the place we agreed until after dawn.'

'Perhaps they missed the inn, or went to the wrong one. I will have to wait for them to call me.'

'Hang on. Inn? What inn? We were supposed to meet up in the motorway service area.'

'Yes, but that was before you changed the meeting place. You told me you were afraid there would be an attack. Something you had heard on, what was the word you used . . . ah, yes . . . the grapevine. So we should change the route and change the meeting place for safety.'

'Have you been drinking? I never said anything of the sort. When was this conversation supposed to have taken place?' the aggrieved customer demanded.

It was at that point that both men realized something was badly amiss.

'You phoned me yesterday afternoon, soon after you returned from a visit to your dentist, you said.'

'I told you I'd been to the dentist, did I?'

'Yes, and that was why your voice sounded odd, because of the injection.'

'You've been conned. I didn't phone you. And I didn't go to the dentist yesterday – or any day this week, for that matter.'

'You realize what this means?'

'It means that you're short of two men and seven million pounds worth of diamonds.'

'It also means I cannot report the theft, because of where the diamonds originated. If it became known that I was trading in blood diamonds I would be finished, and probably end up in jail.'

'Then I suggest you start trying to find out who took them, starting with your own men. How well do you trust them?'

'Implicitly. They have both worked for me for over twenty years. I pay them sufficient to guarantee their honesty.'

'That sounds like extremely bad news – for them, I mean.'

Near the heart of London, the surface of the narrow lane gleamed with the constant damp that came from the enclosed atmosphere. The thoroughfare, barely wide enough to take two vehicles, was topped by an enormous vaulted ceiling of brickwork, once red, now stained and darkened with over a century of grime. The arch formed what was, in effect, a tunnel, which would have been more appropriate to the criss-cross pattern of railway tracks that ran in profusion across the top of the imposing structure.

It had been constructed when Queen Victoria was still becoming accustomed to the role of monarch, principally as a support for the emerging network of railway lines that carried cargo, both human and otherwise, into the capital. However, the enterprising owners, ever keen to increase the yield on their investment had seen the commercial potential of the space below and ordered the erection of further walls, partitioning the chain of archways into individual units. Doors and a wall in the outward-facing side completed the enclosures, which were then offered to let as repair workshops, storage areas or miniature manufacturing plants.

Over the years layer after layer was added to the already soot-blackened surface of the bricks, courtesy of London pollution and grime. Nevertheless, the arches had provided an economic birth-place for many successful businesses.

Inside one such unit, illuminated in a meagre fashion by a single naked light bulb, three people were clustered at the rear of the single-chamber building. The walls were racked out with shelving, the dark timber contrasting with the ancient, peeling whitewash that had been applied many years previously. Two of the occupants were standing, the third was seated. Of the three, however, it was the man in the chair who was least comfortable. The source of his discomfort might have been the fact that he was naked, and even in the hottest of summer days, the temperature within the arches was never hot enough for naturism. Alternatively, his discomfort could have stemmed from his being tied to the chair with lengths of rope, which secured his wrists and ankles. To complete his predicament, he was gagged by the simple method of having an old piece of soiled rag stuffed into his mouth.

He was unable to call for help. He was also unable to scream as an outlet for the immense pain he had already suffered, was continuing to suffer, and would suffer until the end.

From time to time, one of his torturers would remove the gag briefly. This was no act of common humanity. The victim could not be allowed to die until their purpose was completed. The removal of the gag prevented him from choking on the blood inside his mouth. Blood, that came from the gaping holes in his gums from where his teeth had been extracted.

In effecting this removal, the sophisticated instruments used by dentists had not been deemed necessary. A pair of pliers, now bloodstained, were the only tool used to complete the procedure. The removal of the gag also allowed the captive chance to speak, if he so wished, or if he was able. His refusal to do so may have been purely an obstinate refusal to yield, even to the intense suffering he was being subjected to. Or it might have been simply because he had no answer to the questions which his torturers were asking him.

The principal torturer watched as his colleague replaced the gag, lighting a cigarette as he waited for the captive to be silenced once more. He allowed a lazy spiral of smoke to drift towards the ceiling, listening to the rumble of a heavy goods train trundling slowly across the tracks overhead. Tiny, almost invisible flakes of whitewash fluttered down, unable to sustain their resistance to the vibration that threatened to shake them loose from the ceiling any longer.

The torturer-in-chief inspected the end of his cigarette before addressing the captive. When he spoke, it was to repeat the question he had asked time after time during the course of the interrogation. 'Let's talk about diamonds, shall we? That's the reason we're all here, after all.' As he finished speaking, the torturer reached forward and applied the glowing red tip of his cigarette to the captive's testicles. He waited, holding the cigarette in place, watching the man writhe helplessly, eyes bulging, mouth straining against the gag. Eventually, he relented, allowing the pain to subside. Then he moved the cigarette to a different place and repeated the treatment.

The torturer stood back after a while and looked across at his colleague. 'I was hoping he'd play ball by now.' He laughed at his pun, then added, 'As it is, I may need you to go for another packet of fags before long. We have to do the job properly.'

He turned his gaze back to the victim, whose eyes were dulled now, either with pain or shock; or a combination of both. He admonished the helpless captive. 'You ought to know that cigarettes can be very bad for your health. Now, we're going to continue to talk about diamonds for a while, after which, I'm going to introduce you to Percy Sledge.'

He turned and picked up a large sledgehammer from a nearby shelf. 'This is Percy,' he murmured. He let the hammer fall, as if by accident onto the victim's foot. Overhead, the rumble of the train was accompanied now by the squealing hiss of the brakes, but even above the increased level of sound, the noise of bones breaking was clearly audible. Neither of the torturers seemed to notice it, or if they did, it failed to concern them. Why should it, they would probably have argued, as, although he was still breathing, in their eyes the man in the chair was already dead.

The officer was new to Bethnal Green police station in the East End of London; but not so new that he didn't recognize the name. 'Sarge, I've just taken a phone call from a woman who wanted to report her husband missing, and I thought maybe CID would want to know about it.'

The sergeant looked across at the young constable. He was a bright lad, so the sergeant didn't dismiss his suggestion out of hand. 'What makes you think the suits might be interested?'

'Thing is, I recognized the name, Sarge.'

'And the name is?'

'Max Perry.'

The sergeant stared at his subordinate in silence for a moment. 'Max Perry? As in Mad Max?'

The constable nodded.

'Too bloody right CID will be interested, perhaps even their mates at the Yard. Pass that report over and let's have a dekko.'

He scanned the few facts on the missing person report before reaching for his phone. 'Here, I've got some news for you. News that will maybe get you buying a round of drinks tonight, even with your reputation for tightfistedness. Guess who's gone AWOL? Only Mad Max. Yes, Max Perry. The lovely Corinna rang the desk a few minutes ago to report that he's disappeared. Alternatively, if you don't go to the pub, you might want to nip round to Max's flat to console her. I know you've always fancied your chances there. Let's face it, if someone's got rid of one of the most notorious gangsters around, your life's going to be much easier from now on.'

The storeroom was in the basement of the building. The back and side walls were shelved from floor to ceiling, most containing bottles, drums and tins of chemicals, the others being loaded with sheets, towels, blankets and sundry other linen, all neatly enclosed in plastic covers. Many of the containers were labelled with the skull and crossbones insignia that denoted the contents were poisonous. Others had the additional potent warning sign of a large cross, accompanied by the word *corrosive*.

The intruder closed the door carefully before switching the light on. He moved from shelf to shelf before he found what he was looking for. He scanned the contents label until he was satisfied that this was the right product for his purpose. Then he took a small hacksaw from his pocket and began to cut until he had created a slit near the base of the can. He positioned the vessel directly over the conduit that encased the electric cables that ran through the room and on to the rest of the building. He watched as the chemical began to leak gradually from the tin, to trickle along the wooden shelf, then down the vertical surface of the shelf edge, before dripping close to the conduit. Noting the near miss, the intruder repositioned the tin slightly and checked to see if the new site was achieving the desired effect.

This time the chemical was hitting its target and after a few minutes, he began to notice the change. First, a wisp of smoke drifted up from the conduit. Shortly after, the white plastic surface started to discolour, then distort, until after a while a hole appeared. The corrosive liquid was now dripping directly onto the outer casing. Soon, the inflammable substance would make contact with the mains cable supplying the building. Time to leave.

Being a careful man, the intruder remembered to switch the light off before relocking the door, then walked slowly towards the steps leading to the ground floor. He thought about what he had done and tried to remember anything he could have missed. There seemed to be nothing, because his pace increased as he climbed the stairs.

When he reached the ground floor he glanced across to the office. The sole occupant was behind her desk, as befitted her role as a secretary. But she wasn't working, for her head was resting on the surface of her desk. The sedative she had been given would ensure she slept through the fire that would shortly engulf the whole building, taking her and two of her colleagues along with it.

He continued to the first floor, where the other three occupants of the building awaited him. Two of them were as unconscious as the woman downstairs. The intruder glanced briefly at them, before turning his attention to the only other person awake. 'Everything OK?'

'Yes, they're well out of it. How is it down below? Everything set?'

'Coming along nicely, I guess. It had already reached the cable when I left. That acid's bloody strong. I think now would be a really good time to leave.'

Outside, they waited, their car parked discreetly in a corner of the car park, out of sight of all but the most careful observers. After some time, they saw the fire, which had started to take hold of the building. 'I hope their insurance is up to date,' the arsonist murmured, as he accelerated clear of the conflagration.

chapter two

Ray Perry answered the phone, recognizing the lisping falsetto voice immediately; Tony Callaghan, known to one and all as Dirty Harry after his namesake in the films.

'Ray, I've been trying to get hold of you all day. I need to talk to you. Now your Uncle Max has gone, I think it would make sense if we combine forces. We've enough competition without fighting each other.'

Ray was suspicious; the two gangs were armed neutrals at best, and he knew Max hadn't trusted Callaghan any more than Callaghan had trusted Max. Added to which, Max's murder was still fresh in Ray's mind.

'I hear you've been having a lot of trouble with the Chinks and we're getting the same. Thing is, I've a plan to get shut of them, but it needs both teams working together and we've got to act fast,' Callaghan told him. 'Besides which, I think I know who killed Max.'

It was certainly true that the Chinese triad gangs had been attempting to muscle in on their operation, equally true that Ray was looking for information about Max's murder. 'If you're up for it,' Dirty Harry continued, 'come over to Five Elms at eight o'clock tonight and we can talk it through.'

Five Elms Car Sales had grown from a 1940s bombsite; the sort of pitch started in many places after the war, later to become a respectable-looking used car dealership.

Alongside the showroom was a small office and facilities, with a large workshop behind, which covered the width of the building. The workshop rapidly gained a good reputation locally for the quality of its paintwork, becoming known as 'the Beauty Parlour', for the excellence of the spray jobs they turned out.

Ray Perry was surprised to find the showroom door open when he arrived. He went inside, and getting no response to his call, ventured towards the office. 'Callaghan. Callaghan, where the hell are you?' He pushed the office door open.

'Christ, what the hell's happened here?' He looked down at the body of Callaghan's minder. The man's throat had been cut; there was blood all over the floor, the walls, the ceiling. Ray was no stranger to violence but the sight of so much blood made him nauseous. He opened the door to the workshop. That was when he found Dirty Harry. He too had been stabbed, but in the chest; the knife was still in the last of the wounds.

Some malign influence caused Ray to pluck the weapon from the dead man's body. As he did so, blood spurted from the wound, covering his trouser leg and mingling on his boots with that of the minder. At that moment the door behind him slammed back against the wall. 'Police! Don't move; put the knife down – slowly.'

Perry swung round, stared at the advancing officers. He took two steps backwards, looking frantically for an escape route, in the full knowledge that he'd been set up.

'Perry, put the knife down. Now!' The officers began moving forward. Ray leapt over a trolley jack, heading for the concertina sliding doors at the back of the workshop. The first officer dashed after him but his foot caught on the lift arm of the jack and he fell to the ground, wincing with pain. A second officer skirted Callaghan's body and met Perry head on. Two officers grabbed him from behind and Perry lashed out with the knife as they tried to wrestle it from his grasp. In the ensuing struggle an officer was cut before Perry was eventually held face down on the floor, handcuffed and panting, listening to the sergeant: 'Ray Perry, I am arresting you. . . .'

1990

There was silence, or near-silence in the woods, and the walker loved it. Savoured it, for the complete contrast it gave to the rest of his normal, everyday life. For six days a week, up to sixteen hours a day, fifty weeks a year, he had to live with noise, had learned to

17

tolerate it. The ringing of telephones, the chatter of colleagues, the bleeping of monitors, all formed a constant background to his working day. Then there were the added, more strident, sounds. The clamour of sirens as ambulances screamed their way to the hospital, demanding a clear path, sometimes with the counterpoint of accompanying police cars.

Here, in the depths of the forest, he walked on tracks that were barely discernible, and only kept passable by the movement of deer and other woodland creatures. Admittedly, the silence was broken from time to time, but only by the rusty croak of a pheasant, the raucous call of a magpie, the gentler cooing of a wood pigeon, or even the occasional rattle of a woodpecker. These sounds were almost apologetic in tone, and once they died away the silence seemed even more absolute.

On this morning, the forest seemed particularly quiet. As he penetrated deeper into the woods, even the spaniel that was his joyful companion was silent, as if in awe at the wonder of her surroundings. The sun had risen in a cloudless sky, but here, the foliage was so dense that only an occasional glimmer broke through.

As the walker reached a gap in the thick barrier of bramble and briar, a fallow deer, possibly startled by him or the dog, broke cover and darted through the gap, hurdling a fallen tree trunk with the effortless ease of a racehorse. He watched the mottled hind quarters of the deer vanish through the tunnel formed by the scrubby mixture of evergreen and deciduous trees and followed at a more leisurely pace. He noticed the many impressions of deer slots, signalling the passage of a sizeable herd. At that moment, he felt that everything in his surroundings was as close to perfect as possible.

He had stooped to avoid an overhanging branch in the entrance to the arbour when the spaniel emerged from a dense part of the thicket away to his left, carrying a stick in her mouth. 'Here, Bella,' he called.

The dog trotted towards him and as she got closer he realized it wasn't a stick she was carrying, but a bone. A deer had died, he thought, possibly shot, or maybe expired from disease or old age. It was only when Bella was directly in front of him, her tail wagging in search of approval, that he became aware that his second thoughts had been as inaccurate as his first.

Many people would have missed the significance of the shape of the bone. But, as an orthopaedic surgeon, he knew, with a kind of sick horror, that he was looking at a femur. A human femur.

'Netherdale CID. Detective Constable Pratt speaking. How can I help you?'

'I've found a body.' The caller spoke quietly, his voice calm.

'Sorry, you'll have to speak up, sir.'

'I said, I've found a body.' He described the location briefly. 'Or rather, some body parts. They're definitely human, but they have been there for some time.'

'Can you tell me more? Is this close to where you're calling from?'

'As close as can be, a few miles away, no more. I'm at Bishops Cross. In the phone box.'

Patiently, the young officer took the caller through the routine. As the questions were answered, he was struck with a thought. The caller seemed calmer than he did. Why was that? he wondered. He set off to consult his superior.

'The call came in a few minutes ago, sir.'

'And you're sure it isn't a hoax?'

'As sure as can be, sir. The man seemed genuine enough. For a while I thought he was taking it too calmly. Most people would be upset at discovering something as gruesome, but when he told me he's a surgeon and how he came to recognize the bone as human, that explained it. Then, of course, he went deeper into the woods and found more body parts. What do you want me to do, sir?'

'I'm still not convinced. I don't want to send a whole team of officers on what might be a wild goose chase. You go, and take Binns with you. Radio in if there's anything in this tale. Oh, and, Pratt . . .'

'Yes, sir?'

'I don't want the pair of you out there all bloody day. There's a station here to run, remember.'

*

'The rest of CID will love it out here. Tramping through the woods will get their nice shiny shoes all muddy.'

The two officers were standing alongside the surgeon who had reported the grim discovery. They stared at those body parts that were still in situ. The remains they could see were purely skeletal.

'The rest of CID?' Binns asked.

'You don't think whoever this is . . . er . . . was, simply wandered out here one sunny day and decided to lie down and wait for the end to come, do you?'

'I take your point, and the implication must be that they were murdered.'

'Either that, or suicide, but again, if someone had decided to top themselves, they'd hardly take the trouble to come all the way out here to do it.'

Pratt turned to the surgeon, who was struggling to control his dog, who wanted to be free of her lead. 'You know more about these things than we do, sir. How long do you reckon the body's been out here?'

The surgeon considered the question for a moment, then shrugged. 'Difficult to tell with any degree of accuracy, certainly without conducting a detailed examination, but I'd say two or three years perhaps, possibly longer, but no more than five years at the outside. There again, pathology isn't my specialist area, but out here the body would attract a high incidence of predation, and constant exposure to the atmosphere would accelerate decomposition. On second thoughts, perhaps three years would be the approximate upper limit.'

'Thank you, sir. Now, we have your contact details. You're in the holiday cottage until next weekend, I think you said, and then you'll be contactable in Birmingham, on the numbers you gave us, is that correct?'

The surgeon nodded agreement. 'I assume you'll need a formal statement and that the coroner may want me to attend an inquest.'

'Someone will be in touch, sir.' Pratt turned to his colleague. 'Toss you for it, Jack. One of us has to go back to the car and contact Netherdale, and then wait for forensics, so that we can guide them to the spot.'

Binns won the toss, and a few minutes later Pratt watched him disappear along the woodland path together with the surgeon and his dog, now bounding excitedly around, free from restraint. Pratt turned and stared at the remains, his solitary vigil only just beginning. 'Who are you?' he asked aloud. 'And how did you come to end up here? What story could you tell, if you were able?'

All questions that would remain unanswered for many years.

2012

Margaret Fawcett enjoyed her weekly shopping trips into Helmsdale on her day off, especially on market day. That meant she didn't have to take the car. When she'd finished her shopping, she left her bags with the butcher. Lee Giles was more than happy to look after them until it was time for her to catch the bus back to Kirk Bolton. It was part of the service that made the business a local legend.

Margaret pottered around the market place, inspecting the goods on display on the many stalls, peering through the windows of the gift shops to see what the tourists were buying this summer and stopping occasionally to speak to one of the many mums with children. One of the shops belonged to the local coach operators. Margaret read the trips advertised there. In amongst the visits to stately homes, theme parks and shows in the West End, one caught her attention.

It was a fifteen-day excursion, taking in the capitals of Europe: Paris, Rome, Madrid, Prague, Geneva. Margaret read the list with growing excitement. The price was just within her means. She hesitated and thought for a moment, took her diary from her handbag and checked the date. She remembered her passport still had three years to run and stepped inside.

When she emerged twenty minutes later, she felt a guilty thrill of pleasure, as if she'd done something sinful. It would make a big hole in her savings, but it was worth it, surely? After all, she might never get the chance again. The trip was to leave in a few weeks; there was a lot to organize.

As Margaret made her plans, she was unaware that the decision she'd just made, reckless or not, had saved her life.

Many of the villages scattered round the market towns in the dale contained houses that had ceased to be permanent residences. The demand for holiday homes had pushed the prices beyond the means of locals, many of whom had moved into town, or out of the area altogether. A good proportion of the houses were let only during the summer. Bishops Cross was no exception.

Phil Miller, seated alone in the small lounge of the cottage looked up as he heard the crunch of gravel outside. He glanced through the window, his expression anxious, then relaxed once he recognized the car parked alongside his. He strode quickly across to the front door and opened it just as Corinna was about to knock. 'Expecting me?' she asked. 'Or had you a date lined up?'

He gestured to the fields. 'Of course I had. There's my harem. A different one every night.'

She glanced over her shoulder at the flock of sheep and laughed. 'You must be desperate. We'll have to see what we can do about that. Are you going to let me in or have I to stand here all bloody day? Don't tell me I've driven all this way to spend my time chatting on the doorstep.'

He moved to one side as if to let her in, but when she moved forward to pass him, he pinned her against the wall. What followed was as rough a prelude to mating as could be imagined, but Corinna, it seemed, didn't mind. Either that, or she was used to it. 'You missed me then!' She grinned as she walked past him into the lounge.

'Too bloody right. I always wondered what they meant by stir crazy until I came here. As if last time wasn't bad enough. Did you get it?'

'I did. It's in the boot.'

'Come on then, show me.'

They walked to her car, arm in arm. She pressed her car key and the boot lid opened smoothly. He stared down at the contents, ignoring her suitcase. 'Perfect,' he breathed. 'How did you get it?'

'Don't ask; just don't ask.'

Twenty minutes later, he stood in front of her, arms spread wide. 'What do you reckon?'

'You look just like a real fireman. Now would you mind explaining why you want it? If you tell me it's because you've been invited to a fancy dress party I swear I'll slit your throat.'

Chief Fire Officer Doug Curran looked at the sheaf of reports that had accumulated during his leave, before glancing up at his second in command. 'This hoax call to Netherdale Council offices. Tell me exactly what happened.'

'The treble nine came in around lunchtime last Thursday. The exact time is on the report. We sent two appliances, a tender and a van, just to be on the safe side with it being a big building. It took us over an hour to search the premises and make sure everyone was accounted for. Turned out there was nothing, it was a false alarm. So after we got back I started checking the call out. At first I thought it was just the usual – kids playing what they think is a funny practical joke – but as it turned out, it was something different.'

'What made you think that?'

'First off, we had the caller's number. It was a public phone, located in the reception area of the council offices. I thought that would give us a chance to spot the caller, lift an image from the CCTV camera footage and publish it, in the hope of either identifying them, or scaring them off from repeating the hoax.'

'I take it things didn't work out that way.'

'Hardly,' the deputy took on a sarcastic tone. 'The council were to have had CCTV fitted this year, but owing to budgetary restraints the installation has been deferred indefinitely.'

'But you do have a tape of the caller's voice. What made you think it was out of the ordinary?'

'For one thing the voice sounded far too mature to be a kid, and for another, it was a woman.'

'Your point being?'

'I can't remember many instances of hoax calls from women, can you?'

'I think you're right, but there's very little we can do about it, except to warn the emergency operators to be on their guard in case she tries it again. Even then' – Curran shrugged helplessly – 'we'd have to investigate the incident.'

'You're due for release next week. Where will you go? Back to London and your old haunts, I suppose. Your type always runs true to form, that's why you're so easy to nick. Mind you, things have changed a bit since you were out. They have cars nowadays, for one thing.'

Raymond Perry ignored the jibe. 'I don't know yet. I haven't made any firm plans. Wherever the fancy takes me, I guess. I might get the yacht out and go for a cruise round the Med.'

'Well, when you've decided which marina you're heading for, perhaps you'll let me know so I can complete your travel warrant.' Unable to get Perry to bite, the prison officer wandered away. In truth, Raymond Perry was a bit of an enigma. He didn't come across as the hard man his reputation suggested. During all the time he'd been in Durham, he'd been quiet, obedient, docile even. Had it not been for the dreadful things he was known to have done, Perry might have been a prime target for bullying, or worse. However, the other inmates of the high security wing steered well clear, or walked on eggshells around him.

They knew what evil Perry was capable of with little, or no, provocation. Why else would he have been given a life sentence, and been refused parole on several occasions, for the frenzied knife attack that had left two men dead? Not men who were easy targets either – far from it. Tony 'Dirty Harry' Callaghan, was one of the most feared gangsters ever to roam the back streets of London; the other, his muscular bodyguard. And the reason for their murders? Simply that Perry had sought revenge for the murder of his Uncle Max in a railway arch, said to be down to gangland differences. No, the convicts argued, Ray Perry was best kept well away from.

Once the officer had gone, Perry considered what the man had said. In truth, there was little or no incentive for him to return to London. Everyone he'd known there had either moved away, or passed away. Everything that had happened to him and around him there had been so long ago that it was sometimes difficult for him to remember much about it. Except for the highlights, of course, or in his case, perhaps lowlights would have been more accurate.

Even the crime for which he had served over twenty years was little more than a blurred, faded snapshot in his memory. He had been all set to tell his story, weak though he knew it to be. All set to explain about the phone call, the Chinese, Callaghan's statement that he knew who'd killed Max, everything. But then events overtook him, and the warning he received forced him to change his mind.

So Ray had kept silent, and maintained that silence throughout his trial, his sentencing, and the term of his imprisonment. He'd kept out of trouble and waited patiently for news. News that never came. Day after day, year after year, mail was delivered to the prisons where Ray was held. Nothing came for him. Year after year, visiting time after visiting time, no one came to see Ray Perry.

Now his release was a matter of days away. Release; which would enable him to find answers to those questions. To find out who had killed Max, who had really killed Dirty Harry and what had happened since then. Someone out there owed him well over twenty years of his life. And he was going to make sure they paid. Besides, there were other things he needed to know, things he had yet to discover, about the past, the present and the future. The search might take a while, but that didn't matter.

One good thing was that Ray knew where to start looking. Not in London or anywhere near the capital. He would start in a North Yorkshire town called Harrogate.

chapter three

It was a strange sensation, one almost of anti-climax; certainly not one of elation. As Perry walked away he didn't glance back at the forbidding walls that had enclosed what had been his home for so long. Nor did he look around to see if there was anyone waiting to greet him. He had long since ceased to hope that there would be anyone.

He did pause and stare as another released inmate was greeted enthusiastically by a buxom young woman who emerged from a dilapidated estate car. She hugged the prisoner with some difficulty because of the infant in her arms, the whole procedure watched from the back seat of the car by two more infants, neither of them yet of school age.

Perry turned away, this overt display of domestic affection too painful to witness any longer. He continued walking, his expression on the grim side of dour. He stopped a middle-aged woman and asked her for directions to the railway station. He had to ask her to repeat her instructions, the unfamiliar sing-song north-eastern accent defeating him.

'You're not from round here, pet?' the woman asked, then her gaze went beyond him to the prison walls. 'Oh, I see.' She gave directions and hurried away.

Perry stared after her. No one had called him pet for many years. Nor, to be fair, had he wanted them to. Not in that place.

He didn't notice the car that followed him as he made his way through the town. When it became obvious where he was headed, the occupants discussed what they should do. 'We can't afford to lose him,' Corinna said.

'I suggest I get on the same train then ring you on my mobile when I know where he's going. That way you can be there before us.'

'Won't it be better if I go on the train?'

'No, there's more than an outside chance of him recognizing you. He's never seen me before, remember?'

She laughed. 'Oh yes, I'd forgotten that.'

Perry reached the station, inquired about trains and handed over his travel warrant. The ticket purchase was conducted with only the briefest comment from the clerk. 'Change at York,' the man snapped as he handed over the ticket. He'd seen many released convicts; hence his lack of patience.

Perry sat in the waiting room; watching. He wondered idly if he'd ever get out of the habit. During the journey to York, although he stared out of the window at the ever-changing scenery that flashed by, all the time, part of his attention was taken up with what was happening in the compartment, noting all the passengers.

As the journey progressed, each stop brought new arrivals, replacing those who alighted. By the time they were nearing York, Perry noted that there were only two who had boarded the train at Durham. One, a young girl he guessed might be a student, and the other a man who had spent a considerable time talking quietly on a mobile phone.

On the York platform, Ray walked over to the monitor that gave the information he needed for the Harrogate sprinter train that would take him on the final leg of his journey. Out of the corner of his eye, he noticed that both his fellow travellers seemed to have the same destination in mind. More from habit than any sense of danger, Perry examined them covertly. To the best of his knowledge, he'd never seen either of them before in his life. Their presence was obviously innocuous. Both Harrogate and Durham were large towns, and there must be a considerable number of passengers who commuted between the two regularly.

Once he alighted from the train at Harrogate, Ray set off to walk in the direction he thought led towards his destination. As he crossed the station car park, he saw the man climb into the passenger seat of a waiting car, the young girl joining a queue at one of the rank of nearby bus stops. Perry reached the main road and hesitated, no longer certain that he was heading the right way.

Time for more directions, and this time they were easier to understand. The information confirmed his memory and he set off at an increased pace. Not far behind him, in the car that had shadowed the train from Durham, the occupants tried to plan their next move.

'What if she's here? What if he knows where she is? What do we do if he gets to her before we can?' Corinna asked.

'We'll have to deal with them both. There's no other way.'

She seemed to accept this, and concentrated on threading her way through the traffic.

Perry reflected that the houses didn't seem much different to when he had been here last. Not that he'd paid them close attention back then. His eyes had been fixed on his companion, his mind preoccupied with what was happening to them. Now, with luck, only a few minutes separated him from his objective, and when he reached it, the answer to a question that had occupied his mind every waking minute of his life behind bars.

Although some aspects of the view had changed, such as hedges and trees being much taller, he knew exactly where to go. Towards the far end of the road there was a short double row of semi-detached houses at right angles to the main thoroughfare. There was no vehicular access to these properties; the only means of reaching them was via a broad pathway.

Avoiding a couple of small boys on skateboards, who either had less than perfect control or were suicidal, Perry headed for two properties designed and built to contain two flats, one on each storey. He entered the small front garden and as he reached the door, looked for which bell to press in order to summon the occupant of the ground floor flat. Before he could do so, Ray paused, hearing footsteps behind him.

He looked round, to see an elderly man wearing dark glasses and carrying a white stick. The man was walking up the path towards him. 'Good afternoon,' Perry greeted him, anxious not to startle someone with defective eyesight.

The old man turned in his direction, his expression one of

surprise. 'Do you live here?' Ray asked.

'Aye, I do that.'

'Are you on the ground floor or upstairs?'

If the old man found the question odd, he didn't let it show. 'Ground floor. Just as well; my missus can't manage steps any more.'

'How long have you lived here?'

'Why do you want to know that?'

The old man's suspicion was now patently obvious. Ray hastened to allay it. 'I'm trying to locate the woman who used to live here. It's a long time ago, but with moving house, her address got lost. I'd heard she's moved. She's my sister-in-law, you see.'

'Blimey, you are going back a long time. That must be well over twenty years ago. We've lived here that long, and more.'

'In that case, I reckon you must have moved in here right after she left. Can you remember where she went? Did you forward her mail, perhaps?'

'Aye, for a while we did. After a bit it stopped coming. Except for the junk – that ruddy stuff never stops coming.'

'Did you keep her new address?'

'No, binned it long since. But I can tell you the name of the village if you want. It was in the dales. Close to Helmsdale.'

Perry listened as the old man recited the details, thanked him and left. Of course, he thought as he retraced his route down the walkway, there was no guarantee she would still be there, in which case his task could be well nigh impossible. Finding someone who doesn't want to be found is far harder after such a long time.

The couple watching Perry reversed their car and swung it to face the row of lock-up garages at the end of the street. Corinna, who was driving, watched Perry in her rear-view mirror. When he turned and headed in the direction of the town centre, she looked at Phil. 'Now what do we do?'

'We have to find out why he went there. Give me that credit card folder of yours. The one that looks just like a warrant card.'

'You really think that will fool the old man?'

'Didn't you notice? He was blind, or near enough. He was wearing dark glasses and carrying a white stick. He won't be able to tell the difference between a warrant card and a lottery ticket.'

Inside the flat, the old man entered the lounge. His wife was listening to the radio. Her favourite programme was on, and he knew better than to interrupt. 'I'm back,' he told her. 'I'll put the kettle on, shall I?' As he walked towards the kitchen, the doorbell rang.

'Good afternoon. DS Holgate, North Yorkshire Police,' the caller stated. He held up a small blue wallet.

The old man peered at it, then at the man holding it. He listened with increasing curiosity to the caller's tale. 'We've had several complaints about a gang of thieves who are targeting senior citizens. They operate with a front man who calls with some sort of spurious questions, which enables them to check out the property. Have you had any strangers calling on you recently?'

'Aye, we have. Only a few minutes back. I'm surprised you didn't bump into him.'

'What reason did he give for calling?'

The old man explained.

'Interesting. That's a new one on me. Were you able to tell him anything?'

'No, I said we'd only moved here a couple of years back, and he lost interest after that.'

'Best to keep your guard up, and if you get any more suspicious callers, report them. They're very cunning, these conmen, cunning and extremely plausible.'

'Aye, they are that; extremely plausible.'

As he walked back down the path, Phil Miller wondered why the old man had placed such emphasis on that final sentence, then dismissed the idea as his imagination. He climbed into the waiting car.

'Perry's set off back the way he came. What happened back there?' Corinna asked as she accelerated after Perry.

'He asked the old man where the woman who used to live there went after she moved. Obviously that has to be the sister.'

'Did you find out where?'

'No, the old man says he's only lived here a couple of years.' He paused.

'What is it?'

'I don't know, something's wrong. I'm not sure if I trust what the old man said or not. Just a feeling, so I may be completely wrong.'

'Where does that leave us? What do we do next?'

'We can't let Perry get to her, that's for sure. If the old man was lying, he could have told Perry where she lives. Whatever happens, we can't allow him to get to her first. And if we can't get there before him,' he took a deep breath, 'that'll be it, game over, and we'll be ruined.'

'So what do you suggest?'

'We have to make sure he doesn't get there – ever. I also think it's time to go visiting and try to get what we need via Perry's bastard. At least we now know where he is.'

'Look, there's Perry at that bus stop. What does it say on the stand? Can you see?'

From behind the net curtains of the ground floor flat, the old man had watched the caller get into the car. Only when he saw it drive off did he turn and complete his tea-making promise. He carried the mugs through into the lounge as the signature tune denoted the end of the radio programme. He set one down on the table next to his wife's chair. 'There's your tea.'

'Who was at the door?'

'Some conman pretending to be a police officer. Showed me a credit card and claimed it was his warrant. I've a good mind to report him.'

As he spoke, the old man bent down to stroke the Labrador lying alongside his wife's chair. 'It's a grand day outside, I needed my sunglasses. Oh, by the way,' the old man added, 'whilst I was in town I had a new ferrule fitted on your white stick.'

It was almost dark, which at that time of the year meant it was getting late. Ray Perry wondered if he would reach his destination that night, and what his welcome would be if he did. He had long since ceased to hold out any hope of an open-arms greeting; the door slammed in his face was far more likely. But he had to know for certain, one way or another; all doubt removed.

He had to find out the truth, not for his own benefit but for the sake of others. He'd had his chance and blown it, blown it in the biggest way imaginable. Now he had to discover if others had made the most of their chance in life, or even if they'd been given one.

If he didn't reach his destination, he'd have to find somewhere to spend the night, an empty barn, a hedge-back, wherever he could. He smiled, a bitter expression lacking all amusement. Even if he did reach the village, he still might have to settle for a night in the open. He wasn't used to the countryside, wasn't used to walking, wasn't even used to being outdoors.

He was so deep in thought he failed to notice the car. He was walking on the correct side of the road, facing the oncoming traffic. Not that there was much. He'd been on this country road for almost an hour, he guessed, and all he'd seen was one tractor pulling a trailer. What the trailer contained, he didn't need to guess; the stink was bad enough to give him a clue. The sound of the car engine broke into his daydream. It was the rudest of awakenings. He looked round in time to see the radiator grille, like the open jaws of a metallic monster, bared teeth ready to devour him. He tried to leap to one side, but was too late. The car picked him up and hurled him backwards, to crash against the low stone wall of the field.

DI Mike Nash was about to leave his office at Helmsdale police station when the phone rang. Even without the receptionist telling him the caller's identity, he'd have recognized the voice of his old boss, Superintendent Tom Pratt, now a civilian support worker helping out at either Helmsdale or at Netherdale HQ.

'Mike, are you busy?'

'No, as I'll be in Netherdale all day tomorrow I was about to go home. Anything I can help you with?'

'I wondered if you had anything planned for the weekend?'

'I have on Saturday. I'm going through to visit Daniel at school. He wants me to watch him in the nets.'

'He's a bit young for that, surely.'

There was a trace of paternal pride in Nash's voice as he replied, 'I thought that too, but his teacher and the cricket coach both think he's got potential.'

'What about Sunday, then? That was the day I was more interested in.'

'No, I've nothing planned that I know of, unless I'm needed here. What's this about, Tom?'

'I wondered if you'd care to go for a walk on Sunday morning. In the woods by the Winfield Estate. I'll explain why later.'

Nash was intrigued, and pressed Tom for details, but Pratt would say no more. 'OK, Tom, what time on Sunday?'

'Ten o'clock, if that's all right? I'll pick you up at your house.'

Nash and Daniel had enjoyed their afternoon. Not only had Nash been able to support him during the cricket trials he had been able to spend some time with his son, time which they rarely had, Nash mused as he was driving home. He missed eight-year-old Daniel, brought from France to live with him when his mother had died three years earlier. There was no option but for the boy to go to boarding school, not with a single parent who never knew where he would be from one day to the next.

Sunday morning was bright and clear, the sun promising another hot day. At precisely ten o'clock, Pratt's car pulled up outside. Tom had always been a stickler for punctuality, and that hadn't changed.

From the passenger seat, Nash was able to admire the constantly changing panoramic views of the dale, from the chessboard patterns of the arable fields in the lower dale, to the many-hued greens of the forests; the dark, forbidding slopes of the high moorland on the sides of Black Fell, and beyond, to the even more precipitous Stark Ghyll.

Pratt brought the car to a standstill at the side of the road, bumping slightly as the nearside wheels mounted the grass verge. The nearside was heavily wooded and it was to this forest that Tom directed him.

'This is it.' Pratt opened his door and got out. He walked round to the back of the car and opened the boot. To Nash's surprise, Pratt lifted an expensive-looking bouquet from inside and joined him, clutching the flowers by their stems. He gestured towards the forest where Nash could just discern a path leading into the dense under-growth. 'This path' – Tom gestured towards the woods – 'leads to the site of one of the few unsolved murders in this area, the only one I was directly involved in.'

They had been walking for over fifteen minutes before Pratt turned to an even less well marked path. 'Along here is where the remains were discovered.' He took him a short distance to where the bowed trunks of a variety of trees formed a vaulted ceiling over the path. 'In there,' Tom said, 'that was where it was found. That,' he added slowly, 'was more than twenty years ago. I was new to CID then. Jack Binns was on duty answering the phone whilst the duty sergeant was dealing with the overnighters. He put the call through to me.'

Nash smiled at the term that denoted prisoners locked up overnight, mostly for their own protection following over-indulgence.

'We didn't even have a station in Helmsdale in those days. Anyway, the phone call came in at about half-eight. The man on the phone said he'd been walking his dog and found a body. Or rather his dog found it, and ran back to him with a bone in its mouth. Fortunately, the man was an orthopaedic surgeon, and recognized it for what it was – a human thighbone.'

'I've read about this,' Nash said. 'Not from the time it happened, it was much later. It was a press cutting that was found at the *Gazette* offices. It was a woman's body, wasn't it?'

Pratt nodded. 'That's right.'

'As I recall the woman has never been identified, has she?'

'No, even though we exhumed the body a few years back and extracted DNA from it. We tested the sample against several possible candidates as part of a cold case review, but drew a blank. That's why I come here every year, on the anniversary of the day that call came in. Despite all our inquiries, despite the fact that we know she must have had a child, possibly children, alive somewhere; nobody has ever come forward to claim her. I know this might sound weird, but I simply want her to know there is at least one person left who hasn't forgotten about her, or that she ever existed.'

Pratt looked across at Nash and saw the faraway look on his face. He knew that expression, knew Mike too well to interrupt.

'You're certain it was murder?' Nash's tone was gentle, vague almost.

'Absolutely, why else would she have been left out here? There were some indications of violence too.'

There was another long silence, as Nash stared into the distance. The forest scenery was stunning, but Nash wasn't taking any of it in. Instead, he was thinking about the victim, wondering how she had come to end up in this remote location, unburied, unknown and unmourned. Despite the beauty of their surroundings, both men felt the desolation and sadness keenly.

'Where did the surgeon come from? To be walking his dog so deep in the woods, I mean?'

'He was staying in a holiday home on the edge of the woods.' Pratt turned and pointed due west. 'About a mile and a half that way, where the forest boundary is, there's a house that used to be an agricultural worker's tied cottage. You can walk it easily from here. Once you get through this bit, there's a ride they keep cut as a fire break. It's a grand spot for a holiday too; the house is surrounded by fields, and then there's this wood and views across to Black Fell and Stark Ghyll as well.'

Nash watched as Tom walked forward into the miniature arboretum before them and gently laid the bouquet on the ground. 'I can see why this case haunts you,' he said.

chapter four

When Nash walked into Helmsdale police station the following morning, DS Clara Mironova was already there. 'Good weekend, Mike?' she greeted him.

'Quiet, but interesting,' he told her. 'How was it here? Busy?'

'Not really, just the usual. A couple of fights fuelled by booze. Nobody seriously hurt – a few minor scratches and bruises. Uniform locked up the title contenders over Friday night, let them go on Saturday. They'll be up in court today. Probably only get their hands smacked and told not to do it again. Viv handled the one serious incident.'

'What was that?'

'It was a hit-and-run. I don't know the full details. Viv will be able to tell you better when he arrives. But it sounds awful, what bit I heard. Apparently it happened sometime on Thursday evening. I'm not sure where, but Viv will have more detail. He's dropping Lianne off at Netherdale General. She's on day shift this week and he'll be able to see how the injured man is. He's in a coma in the ICU and I don't think it sounds too good. Apparently he'd no ID on him, so Viv was going to ask permission to take his fingerprints, see if we could try to find out who he is that way. What did you do with yourself?'

'I went to watch Daniel play cricket on Saturday.'

'That sounds fun; nice and relaxing.'

'That's what you think. I never thought a parent watching his son could be so nerve-racking. He did rather well, though. And yesterday I went for a walk with Tom Pratt. You remember, I told you he'd rung on Friday?'

'Oh yes, you were curious about what he wanted to show you.

Where did he take you?'

'Just above Bishops Cross on the edge of the Winfield Estate, a lovely stretch of woodland, except that I didn't appreciate its beauty all that much.'

'Why not?'

Nash explained about the body dumped there.

'How awful.' Clara's expression was sad as she thought over the implications. 'The murder itself is bad enough, but to go all those years, unnamed.' She frowned.

'What is it?' Nash asked.

'Don't you think that's curious? From the facts Tom told you, I mean. That nobody reported her missing? Surely, if she had a family, and if she had children, they'd miss her?'

'You have a point, but look at it this way. If there was a divorce and she'd lost custody, or if they'd been taken into care, then she wouldn't necessarily be missed. Perhaps later, somebody might have wondered where she'd got to, but no more than that. And by then it'd be far too late to trace her.'

'I hadn't thought about that,' Clara agreed. 'But how typical of Tom, to care about it after all these years, I mean. There aren't many who'd have taken the trouble.'

'I agree, and it seems equally sad that the chances of finding anything out after all this time are extremely slim. It remains an open case, but in name only, I guess. Now, Sergeant, whilst we're waiting for Viv, how about I make coffee?'

Mironova eyed him suspiciously. He only called her 'Sergeant' when he was about to insult her. Despite her caution, she fell for it. 'I'll make it if you like.'

'No thanks. I know things are quiet, but that's no reason to start the week with a poisoning. I still don't think you've mastered the art of that new machine.'

At that moment Pearce arrived. His tale was short on detail, and none of it was good news. 'The incident must have happened sometime during Thursday evening. The man who was struck by the vehicle was lucky in one way. A farmer saw his body soon after the accident happened, and wouldn't have done if it hadn't been for his socks.'

Nash frowned. 'His socks? What have they got to do with it?'

'He was lying in long grass, up against a dry-stone wall. One of the local farmers discovered him. He'd been to drop some manure off and was on his way back for another load when he saw the man. Said he wouldn't have spotted him had it not been for the red socks he was wearing. He said he remembered passing him earlier, walking towards Kirk Bolton – thought it unusual as he wasn't dressed as a hiker. The farmer had his mobile, so he called it straight in, but when the paramedics arrived the victim was barely alive.'

Pearce paused and looked up from his notes. 'He's still alive, but only just. He's in the ICU, but I had a word with the doctor in charge this morning and they don't give a lot for his chances. He's got two sets of injuries, either of which could see him off. He's got internal bleeding and several broken ribs from the impact of the vehicle, plus massive head injuries. They found minute particles of stone in the wound, so they think he must have suffered these when he was thrown against the wall by the force of the collision. Lianne said if there's any change she'll let me know.'

'Where did it happen?'

'About halfway between the edge of town and Drover's Halt. Say five miles or thereabouts from Helmsdale. You know, where that big copse of trees is on the right-hand side, before the lay-by where they store grit sand.'

Nash frowned. 'But that's a dead straight stretch of road. There isn't a bend on that bit until you get to the far side of Drover's Halt. The car, or whatever it was, must have been travelling at a hell of a lick to do that sort of damage, and for the driver not to have seen a pedestrian. Unless he was blinded by the evening sun.'

Pearce shook his head. 'That's the bit I was coming to. The car was also travelling towards Kirk Bolton, so the sun would have been behind him.'

Nash's frown deepened. 'There's only a wall on one side of the road. The driver would have had to veer all the way across the road to hit a pedestrian walking towards the traffic and throw him against the wall. How can you be certain of the direction?'

'Because of the tyre marks on the grass verge. They go on for about thirty yards before and after the point of impact. I got an accident investigation team from Traffic Division at Bishopton to go out and check everything. Their report should be with us this afternoon, but one of their experts said he reckoned the driver had stopped and reversed back to where the body was before driving off, presumably because they got scared. What do you want me to do next?'

Nash pondered the implications of what Pearce had told him. 'Either the driver was so pissed he didn't know what he was doing' – he hesitated for a second – 'or this wasn't an accident. Either way, if the car hit that wall it'll be badly damaged.'

'The guys from traffic reckon the car didn't make contact with the wall.'

'It will still carry some damage. Contact all the garages and repair shops in the county; warn them to be on the lookout for any cars being booked in for bodywork or wheel repairs. We may have a few false alarms, but someone somewhere must know what they did and we have to find them. Clara said the victim was carrying no identification. That alone sounds odd. If he was that far out of town, where was he headed? And how did he get there? I take it nobody local has been reported missing?'

Pearce shook his head. 'No, but there was one item in his pocket. A bus ticket from Harrogate to Helmsdale.'

'Better check with Harrogate; see if they've a missing person who fits the description. Did you get the man's fingerprints?'

Pearce nodded.

'Good work. Check them out as well. If he was a vagrant there's a strong possibility he might be on record somewhere. You get on with that, whilst I make that coffee. Then we'll all go take a look at the crash site.'

He noticed Viv's look of surprise. 'Why not?' He gestured to his desk, which for once was free of papers. 'We've nothing better to do, and on the way there I can bore you both with a prolonged account of Daniel's cricket trial.'

When Nash returned from the rest room with three mugs of coffee, Clara was on the phone. Pearce, meanwhile, was pacing up and down Nash's office, his face excited.

'I put the victim's fingerprints into the computer and to my surprise I got an instant match. The details are even more surprising.' He handed Nash a sheet of paper.

Nash studied it for a moment. 'See if Clara's finished on the phone.'

When Pearce returned, Clara followed him in. 'You'd better have a look at this,' Nash told her. 'Meet our hit-and-run victim. See if you can explain it, because I can't.'

The two men watched her eyes widen with astonishment as she read the report. She lowered the paper and looked at Nash. 'What do you make of this?'

'I'm not sure what to make of it. This man Raymond Perry, he's been out of prison for what, three days or so? That means he was knocked down on the day of his release! The man served twenty-five years without parole for a gangland killing committed in the East End of London. Those are the bare facts, and that's all that report gives us. The question I can't get my head round is: what is Perry doing so far from his normal habitat? And what's more, he headed straight here after leaving prison. Why? During my time in the Met I encountered one or two types like Perry. They're very parochial. Rarely go outside their own patch, except if they want some holiday when they jet off to Spain. They certainly don't go on nature rambles through the countryside of North Yorkshire. I doubt if some of them would be able to tell a sheep from a cow unless it made a noise. With his accent, Perry would have stood out a mile round here, which isn't exactly what an ex-con needs. Whatever it was brought Perry here, it must have been important. He was walking, which is another thing his type never do if they can avoid it. Not only that but he was heading out of Helmsdale. Which leaves two enormous unanswered questions; well, three really. What was the purpose of his visit and where was he headed when he was hit?'

'That's only two,' Pearce commented. 'What was the third one?'

'Actually, it's more of an assumption than a question. The third is: Who was he going to meet?'

'There's no proof he was going to meet anyone,' Mironova objected.

'I said it was an assumption, but if he was walking away from town, where was he headed? What is there on his route? Four small villages little bigger than hamlets, with one pub, one church and no post offices. He might have been going to commit a robbery, but the facts don't support that theory. It would have to be something pretty special to get him so far away from his home ground, and there's nothing I can think of in that area that fits the bill. In addition to which, he'd hardly go to commit a robbery on foot. And how would he have picked his target? Unless he's been subscribing to one of those rural lifestyle magazines whilst he's been inside.

'Discounting the robbery theory, or his desire for a camping weekend' – Nash saw Pearce smile at the notion – 'we're left with the possibility that he was going to meet someone. Or he was trying to find someone. All of which remains a mystery. And will continue to remain so, at least until we get our hands on his file.'

The stretch of road was exactly as Nash remembered it. Absolutely straight, and fairly broad, for what was little more than a country lane servicing the few small villages towards the top of the dale. He pulled up before the Police Accident sign. 'Seems an improbable place for an accident, don't you think?' Mironova said as she got out of the car. 'Especially if the vehicle involved was travelling out of town, as the traffic boys suggested.'

'Perhaps the driver was too drunk to realize he was on the wrong side of the road. Either that or he lost control. Or maybe he was travelling too fast, or had a burst tyre or some other mechanical problem. Could have been the steering that failed,' Pearce suggested.

'Those are all possibilities. But there's one other: that it was deliberate.'

Mironova stared at him. 'You're not serious, are you? That would be highly unlikely, given as remote a location as this.'

'I don't know. The whole incident seems rather improbable. Let's take a closer look.'

They stared at the verge. Although there had been no rain recently, the long grass, which received only spasmodic attention from the local authority, prevented the soil from drying out. The tyre tracks were clearly visible in the middle of the six-foot-wide strip. They began, as Pearce had said earlier, well before the point of impact. From where the vehicle mounted the verge, the tracks continued in a dead straight line.

'There's no way the driver would have strayed off the tarmac, either through carelessness or intoxication,' Clara suggested. 'This has to have been deliberate, don't you agree?'

Nash felt a shiver surge through his body. Clara was right, this was no accident. This was attempted murder.

Pearce racked his brain to come up with an alternative solution, but failed. 'What do you reckon, then?'

Nash didn't answer him directly. 'Let's take a look at the crash site.'

They spent a few minutes staring at the tyre tracks close to the point of impact, before turning their attention to the wall. There was only one stone missing from the top, which surprised Mironova. She'd have assumed that, with the injuries the victim had suffered, the wall would have come off worse. A tribute to the craftsman's art, she thought.

Nash crouched, examining the lower courses of stonework. He pictured the scene; saw the car bearing down on the hapless victim. Saw the man running to try and avoid it, trying to escape the inevitable. Saw the car hit him. Then what? As he looked, at the wall and his mental film clip, he thought he knew. He pictured the driver getting out of his car. Saw him approach the man he'd knocked down, lying helpless in the long grass. And then. . . . He looked up, squinting slightly against the strong sunlight. 'Tell me what you see, what you think,' he encouraged his sergeant.

'The first thing that comes to mind is how sturdy the wall is,' Clara said immediately.

'Why do you say that?'

'Because it isn't damaged. Or not much, I mean, there's only one stone missing.'

'You're assuming the car hit the wall.'

'Well, yes, I was. But the traffic boys reckon it didn't, so that explains the lack of damage, I suppose.'

Nash didn't answer her directly. His voice was pensive, and Clara realized he was talking to himself as much as to them. 'If the car had hit the wall there would have been collision marks, traces of paint. There are none. And if the man suffered as severe a set of injuries as we know he did, how come there's absolutely no blood on the wall?'

'I suppose it's just possible the man could have cushioned the impact with his body; the bleeding was internal.'

Nash nodded agreement. 'Let's have a look at the missing piece of stone.'

He donned a pair of gloves and lifted it clear of the grass. They all stared at it. The piece wasn't very big, no more than a foot across at the broadest point. It was roughly triangular in shape, narrowing to a couple of inches at the opposite end. Nash pointed to the blood on the narrow end of the stone, then his gaze switched to the wall. He frowned. 'That's odd,' he murmured.

'What is?' Viv asked, then, 'Oh, I see.'

Nash held the stone out. 'Put that in position on top of the wall.'

Viv did as instructed, staring at the result, then at his companions. 'That doesn't make sense,' he said. 'The bloodstains are on the wrong side of the stone. But that's not possible, unless. . . .'

Clara continued for him, 'What you're trying to say is, that stone will only fit into the gap on the top of the wall one way; the way you have it. And, if that's the case, how did the victim's blood get to be on the part that was facing into the field, away from the road?'

'Unless the car driver picked it from the top of the wall and smashed the victim's skull in with it.' Pearce said exactly what Clara was thinking.

Nash nodded agreement. 'Everything about this accident site is wrong. And from what we've seen here, I think that's because it wasn't an accident. This is a crime scene.' He pointed to the wall. 'We'd better bag that piece of stone as evidence and then we'll go back to the station.'

As they were walking back to the car, Mironova paused and glanced back. 'Speaking of which, shouldn't we get SOCO out here?'

'You're right, Clara. Will you deal with it as soon as we get back? Tell them we need photos of those tread marks, particularly the deeper ones, plus the wall, taken from all angles. We must also have all the measurements they can make. I know traffic will have done the basic ones, as they would for any accident, so I want them to concentrate on the wall. They must measure the gap where that stone came from' – he pointed to the evidence bag Viv was clutching – 'and do it for height, width and depth at both sides of the wall.'

He thought a little longer before adding, 'I think it would be a good idea to have the stones in the wall for a yard either side of the gap numbered, before the photos are taken. Tell them I want the numbers indelible, and on the side facing the field, away from prying eyes. That way nobody tampers with the evidence, and we've done all we can to avoid being accused of tampering with it ourselves. Oh, and, Viv, get onto Jack Binns, tell him I want a guard at the hospital. If word gets out, we don't want someone finishing the job.'

'Is that everything?'

'Not quite.' He gestured to the evidence bag again. 'Get them to call and collect that. We need to confirm that the blood on it belongs to the victim, and that we're not jumping to conclusions because of the blood left by some luckless pheasant that was dragged over the wall by a fox.'

chapter five

Nash and Mironova were waiting for Pearce, who had called at Netherdale General for an update on the hit-and-run victim; Clara's phone rang. She listened for a minute before saying, 'OK, one of us will pop down.'

She looked across at Nash. 'There's a woman in reception called in to report something suspicious. She hasn't seen her neighbour for a few days and she went to knock on his door to ask if he was all right because she'd noticed a very unpleasant smell. She couldn't get any reply, but she's worried something might have happened to him.'

'Where does she live?'

'Warwick Lane, in one of those houses that's been converted into flats.'

Nash tilted his chair back. 'Off you go, then.'

Mironova stared at him. 'What are you going to do?'

'Nothing.'

'I see. No change there, then.'

The older woman waiting in reception looked nervous. Not unusual, Clara thought; even upright citizens were apprehensive in the austere surroundings of a police station. Clara introduced herself, shook hands and sat down alongside the visitor. The hard, plastic-covered bench was not designed for comfort. Clara wondered if the manufacturer had been given instructions to construct something that would deter visitors from lingering. 'Care to tell me what this is all about?'

The woman repeated what she'd told the receptionist, before adding, 'I haven't seen him since Thursday.' She paused, before correcting herself. 'Well, in actual fact I didn't see him then. But he was there, inside his flat. I know that because I heard him. He was having a party, because the music was very loud.'

'Did he often have parties?'

'No, this was the first one he's had since he moved in. Usually he's very quiet. But there was this hideous pop music blaring out, all screaming and carrying on, and the dancing. . . . It was more like somebody throwing furniture about.' She frowned. 'And that isn't like him; as a rule, he's very considerate. My flat's directly below his, so I'd know better than anyone.'

'Very well, accepting that you haven't seen him for a few days, could it be that he's gone away?'

'I don't think so. His car's been parked outside all weekend. In fact he mustn't have gone to work on Friday – sleeping it off, probably. It was still there this morning, which was why I got worried. He rarely goes anywhere without it. He's ever so proud of it. That's another odd thing: he washes his car every Sunday morning, whatever the weather. I've seen him out there in a howling gale, with rain lashing down. If he was at home and wasn't ill, there's no way he'd have missed out on a lovely morning such as Sunday. He thinks too much of the car for that.'

'What sort of car is it?'

'One of those little German ones, a low-slung sports car. The one with the initials.'

'A BMW?'

'That's it. Anyway, if he'd gone away I'm sure he'd have used the car. And going away wouldn't have accounted for the horrid smell. It really is dreadful, sort of sickly and cloying. And it's getting stronger, which doesn't surprise me in this weather.'

It had certainly been hot enough over the weekend. 'It may be he's gone away and forgotten something; left some meat out, perhaps. Either that or maybe his fridge has broken down.'

The attempt at reassurance was a miserable failure. 'It's much worse than that. The smell's overpowering.'

'OK, I'll have a word with my boss; tell him how concerned you are. Then we'll get somebody to come round and check the place over. Do you know if anyone has a spare key?'

She shook her head. 'The flats are all owned by a property company. The local agents may have duplicate keys, but I doubt it. As long as the rent's forthcoming every month they never bother us. They do an annual inspection, of course; at least that's what they call it. They tie it in with the fire brigade inspection so they can get the fire certificate renewed at the same time. Apart from that, we never see or hear from them.'

'I understand, but they're hardly unique in that. Let me get some details from you.'

Mironova reached the CID suite seconds ahead of DC Pearce. Nash listened to her account of her conversation. 'Contact the agents; find out if there's a key we can get hold of. There ought to be, to comply with fire regulations.' Nash sighed. 'But that would be in a perfect world, so I'm not holding my breath. If the agents can't help, get hold of the name of the key-holder from Doug Curran.' Nash pointed to the other wing of the building, which housed the fire and ambulance services. 'Failing that, give Jimmy Johnson at Helm Safe a call. Tell him we need his burglary skills again. Whilst you're on with that, I'll find out what Viv's got to tell me about Raymond Perry's condition. We could do with the file I asked for. I wonder where that's got to. Viv, can you chase it up whilst Clara and I go see what's happened to this party animal?'

'What do we know about the occupant of this flat?' Nash asked as they drove across town.

'Not very much, only what the woman told us. His name's Nattrass, Graham Nattrass. I checked him out. He's not known to us; hasn't even got a speeding ticket, which is slightly surprising given the sort of car he drives. According to her, Nattrass is in his mid-twenties, quiet and considerate. She thinks he works in the motor trade, but doesn't know where. He owns a flash car, a BMW sports, but she's sure he's a mechanic because he goes out every morning wearing overalls, and the car's got one of those plastic seat protectors permanently over the driver's seat. She told me she was worried when he moved in, which was about six years ago. She thought he might go in for girls, noisy parties, all that sort of thing, but there's been nothing at all like that, until last Thursday night.

Most of the time, as she put it, you wouldn't know he was there.'

'What did the agents say, anything useful?'

Mironova snorted. 'Nothing whatsoever, although to be fair I don't think that's entirely their fault. They only took on the account a couple of years ago, along with four other properties owned by the same company. They tend to concentrate on finding tenants and chasing those who are behind with their rent. Nattrass doesn't fit into either category. The rent is paid by direct debit and he's never missed a payment. They've no keys for the flats, so I checked with Curran at the fire service. The registered key-holder for all the properties is the company secretary in London, which is a fat lot of good to us. Curran wasn't impressed. I think he was going to write to the company, as well as having a word with the fire officer who signed the fire certificate. Anyway, I phoned the company, just on the off-chance they'd know of someone nearer. They do, but he's away on holiday. By that time I was getting a headache from banging my head against a brick wall, so I rang Jimmy and arranged to meet him there.'

The building was like many others on the outskirts of Helmsdale, which is to say, it was typical of many in market towns throughout the county. Originally, the terrace would have been built to house some of the town's more prosperous tradesmen, their families and one or two servants. Within the newly built Victorian dwellings you would find the local butcher, baker, draper, ironmonger and many similar residents.

Nowadays, most of the houses had been converted into flats for a far more diverse set of occupants. It was obvious the neighbour had been on the lookout, for as soon as Mironova pulled up, the woman opened the outer door of the property. At the same time a small van bearing the logo and name of Helm Safe pulled into the kerb behind them.

Nash greeted the reformed burglar as he jumped out of the van. 'Morning, Jimmy, thanks for coming to the rescue.'

'No problem, Mr Nash. I'll not have to be long, though. I've a couple of installations booked for today. Good morning, Miss,' he greeted Mironova respectfully.

Clara smiled. 'Good morning, Jimmy.' Johnson had been

instrumental in helping save her life on one occasion. Apart from the debt of gratitude, it was hard to dislike the cheerful Scotsman.

'Which is Nattrass's flat?' Nash asked the woman on the doorstep.

'First floor front, directly above mine.'

Nash shielded his eyes with his hand as he squinted at the building. The morning sun was strong, promising another hot day. It was shining directly in his face so it took a minute for his vision to adjust. When he was able to get a good view of the upper window his lips tightened and he glanced across at Mironova. As soon as he caught his sergeant's attention Nash glanced back towards the window of the flat. She noticed his expression as she followed his gaze. She saw the reflection of a light in the corner of the room nearest them, a light that had nothing to do with the sun, illuminating bluebottles against the glass. The conclusion he had drawn was obvious from his face and he was preparing her for what they might find inside. She nodded slightly to show she'd got the unspoken message.

'I think it would be best for you to leave it to us now.' Nash smiled at the woman. 'Either Sergeant Mironova or I will let you know if we find anything.'

Clara took the older woman's arm, guiding her towards the door of her own flat, shepherding her away from Nash and Johnson before she could object. 'Don't worry, we'll deal with it.'

The first thing Nash noticed on entering the hall was the smell. Was that because it was bad, or because he was expecting it? He was still pondering this as he glanced across at Johnson. He saw Jimmy's face wrinkle in distaste. Not just me then, Nash thought. The smell was exactly as their informant had described it to Mironova: cloying, sickly and, to anyone with experience in such matters, unmistakeable. It was the smell of a body in the early stages of decomposition. Better not to pre-judge the issue, though, Nash thought. Some animal, a stray dog or cat, could have found its way into the building, got into a dark corner and simply expired. Then Nash remembered the other circumstances and dismissed the thought. Mironova caught the nauseous aroma, saw Nash's expression and prepared herself for the worst.

When they reached the first floor, the smell was much stronger. Stomach-wrenching in its foulness. 'Just do the door, Jimmy, then get on your way,' Nash told him.

'It'll not take long, Mr Nash,' Johnson assured him. He was anxious to get out of this building, to get away from the stench. He too had guessed what lay beyond the door. Guessing was as close as he wanted to get. It was the work of a minute to deal with the mortise lock, then the Yale. As soon as he opened the door, Johnson backed away, a reflex reaction to the wave of fetid air that rushed to meet them. He stuffed a handkerchief over his nostrils, waved a sketchy farewell and dashed for the stairs. As he took them, two at a time, Johnson thought, a bobby's job? I wouldn't have it at any price.

'Are you ready for this?' Nash asked as they each donned latex gloves.

'No,' Clara replied. 'I'm not sure I'd ever be ready for it.' She braced herself mentally. 'But I'll manage.'

Nash nodded acceptance and encouragement. He pushed the door wide. There was no corridor, the door opened directly onto the flat's large lounge with a bay window overlooking the street. The room was a mess. Papers and photographs, ornaments and cushions, all manner of bric-a-brac were scattered across the carpeted floor. The filling from the cushions, as well as those from the settee and easy chair had been pulled out, the covers having first been slashed open. 'Jimmy's not the first burglar to have opened that door,' Nash muttered. 'Be careful where you walk.' He looked around. In the corner next to the bay window, behind the large plasma-screen TV, a standard lamp was burning. This, then, was the source of the light they'd seen from the street.

He gestured towards the first of four doors that led from the sitting room. It opened onto the kitchen. In there the atmosphere was marginally less nauseous. The mess, however, was just as bad. The tiled surface of the floor and the marble-effect work surfaces were covered with a mixture of substances the detectives could only guess at by the empty containers that had been strewn about in haphazard confusion. The pattern on the floor was barely visible through the profusion of tea leaves, coffee, sugar, flour, breakfast cereals, herbs, spices and other dry goods. Elsewhere, the kitchen sink and the drainer alongside it contained an array of bottles and jars, all empty. From vinegar to beetroot, sauces, milk, lemonade and a considerable collection of pickles, all had been tipped into the bowl, judging by the mound of solids still remaining there, unable to bypass the drain. Across the room, the fridge-freezer had been emptied, the contents lying on the adjacent table in a puddle of mildly offensive-smelling liquid. This was nowhere near bad enough to have attracted anyone's attention, though. Nash pointed to the floor, near to the lounge door. Clara could see several multi-coloured smudges, blurred footprints by the look of them, leading out of the kitchen. She nodded as they turned and headed for the next room.

This proved to be the bathroom, which had received similar, though less damaging treatment, probably because there was little in there to create such a mess. They retreated, and as they crossed the lounge, Nash pointed to the oatmeal twist carpet. There were several small stains, dark brown in colour, close to the next door they were about to open. As they paused outside, their nostrils told them this was likely to be where they would find a body. Mironova saw her boss take a deep breath before he opened the door.

They both recoiled from the stench released by the slight draught of air, and by the sudden movement of what seemed like hundreds of flies. Big, fat, obscene bluebottles.

There was more movement across on the bed, and as she looked, Clara felt her stomach heave. Maggots. Nash looked inside the room, wished he hadn't, then looked away hurriedly before bracing himself to look again. Alongside him, Mironova was fighting to keep from being sick. 'Oh, God!' she muttered. 'What is this?'

'Charnel house, or a scene from hell; take your pick,' Nash's reply came from between clenched teeth. 'Let's go get some protective clothing from the car.'

They retraced their steps, following the same route across the lounge as on their way in. When they reached the outer door of the flat Mironova wanted to leave it open. 'Better not,' Nash advised. 'I'd rather not take the chance of anything contaminating the crime scene. All we need is for a cat to wander in, attracted by the smell, and we'd be in real trouble. Whilst you're getting the suits and other

gear, I'll ring Mexican Pete and SOCO. Better let the lady downstairs know the bad news. Ask her if there's anyone she can go and
stay with for a day or so. In fact, suggest it!'

When Mironova returned to Nash, he was pacing up and down,
his expression one of frustration. Clara was glad to be outside
breathing in the clean air. Nobody would want to rush back into
that house of horrors. Following her brief conversation with the old
lady, who'd taken the news very badly, Clara was surprised Nash
wasn't still on the phone.

'SOCO are on their way,' he announced. Something in his tone
told her he wasn't happy. Had what they'd just seen upset him so
much? She could hardly blame him if that was the case, but she
knew he'd attended many terrible crime scenes, some far worse
than this. Or, was it something else?

'What about Mexican Pete?'

Nash shrugged his shoulders. 'He isn't answering his phone. I
got through to a snooty secretary. She told me Professor Ramirez
was too busy to take any phone calls. She didn't know when he
would be available. She did ask if she could help.'

Mironova repressed a smile. 'And what did you say?'

'I told her she could, if she'd a degree in pathology and didn't
mind the stench of a corpse that's been dead over four days in a
warm room, having been bludgeoned to death. And if that was the
case I'd be pleased to take her up on her kind offer. Failing that I
expect Professor Ramirez here ASAP.'

Clara shook her head. 'And some people say you're sarcastic. I
just don't understand it.'

'I agree the timescale was a guess, but it would tally with what
was said about the noise.' As they were talking, Nash's mobile
chirped to signal an incoming call. He glanced at the screen.
'Netherdale General,' he told her.

'Thank you so much for your help,' he told the caller. His tone
was sweet, but Clara knew he was still angry. 'That was our helpful
secretary again.' He placed the phone in his pocket. 'Apparently
Professor Ramirez will join us in an hour's time. I suppose we
should be eternally grateful for that.'

'What do we do in the meantime? Sit here, or go back in?'

Nash didn't hesitate. 'We'll wait here until somebody arrives. Either SOCO or Mexican Pete. No point in trampling all over the place. In any case, I don't fancy spending any longer in that flat than absolutely necessary, do you?'

That question was purely rhetorical, Clara knew. 'Shall I ring the station? Ask them to send a couple of uniforms to stand outside looking useful.'

Nash nodded approval.

The wait was tedious, their boredom broken only by the arrival of the uniformed men, who taped off the outside area and escorted the distraught neighbour to a waiting taxi. She had refused to set foot in the patrol car. Eventually, after Nash had received a message from SOCO to say they'd been delayed, he suggested they went back inside. 'I really want to get another look at the crime scene before the forensics guys start messing it up. You can stay out here if you prefer.'

'What about protocol? I'd far rather stay out here,' Clara admitted, 'but that's not what I'm paid for. If you can put up with it, so can I.'

Their second inspection of the scene was no less of an ordeal, more so if anything, because now they'd time to take in more. Eventually, Nash gave the signal to retreat, much to Mironova's relief. Once outside, they stripped off the overshoes and nylon suits.

Nash stood by the car making notes on an A4 pad. He was using the bonnet of the vehicle as an improvised desk. He glanced up. 'Now, tell me what you saw in there, and what conclusions you drew from it. Let's see how it tallies with what I've got written down. Start in the lounge.'

'The place had been ransacked. Whether that was pure vandalism or the killer was searching for something, I can't be sure, but I'd go for the latter.'

Nash nodded agreement. 'Anything else, before you move on?'

She thought hard, but failed to come up with anything. 'Think, Clara,' he urged, 'it's important.'

She visualized the lounge, the contents of drawers and cupboards strewn about, the ripped cushions, the spilled fillings. About the only things left untouched were the TV set and . . . 'The lamp!' she exclaimed triumphantly. 'The lamp was switched on.'

'That tells us the killer was in the flat during the hours of darkness. Which, going by what you were told, probably means Thursday night. Hopefully, Mexican Pete will be able to confirm that, if he ever turns up. Now, given the state of the kitchen, anything strike you about that?'

'There were footprints on the floor. They came from the kitchen, but they didn't go towards the bedroom. They led towards the exit. From that I'd guess the killer searched the kitchen last, after he'd been through the other rooms.'

'Good point, and from that I think we can assume that the killer didn't begin searching until Nattrass was dead. In other words, the motive wasn't anything to do with the tenant disturbing a burglar. Now, the bedroom?'

Clara repressed a shudder. 'The body was on the bed. The victim was naked, lying face up. The dead man was a young white male, and from the description I assume him to be the tenant, Graham Nattrass. He'd been tied with duct tape round his wrists and ankles. His injuries suggest he was bludgeoned to death. The bedroom had also been searched. He'd obviously been dead for some time,' she swallowed as she recalled the worst part, 'not only because of the smell, but the maggots and the flies as well.'

'Is that all?'

'What have I missed?'

'Not much. The duct tape might yield a fingerprint, although I'm not holding my breath for that. You forgot to mention the gag.'

'I assumed that was to stop him screaming whilst the killer was hitting him.'

'I think you're right. Did you spot the ashtray?'

'Oh, yes, there was an ashtray on the top of the dresser. It looked as if it had been wiped clean, although there were one or two fragments of ash still clinging to it. We ought to have checked to find out if Nattrass was a smoker.'

'You can do that later, when you take the old lady's statement. But there is another possibility, although it's one I don't like to dwell on. Mexican Pete will confirm one way or another, but it could be that the killer used cigarettes to torture his victim, which was the real reason for the gag.'

'I didn't notice any burn marks on the body. But they'd be covered up by his other injuries, wouldn't they? Mind you, I didn't look any more than I had to.'

'I don't blame you for missing the burn marks. I don't suppose you spend a lot of time staring at men's testicles, do you? Especially those of dead men.'

'You're joking? That's gruesome.'

'Tell me what isn't gruesome inside that place. If I'd to sit and think up the most horrific way to kill a man, I doubt if I could come up with anything nearly as sick as that.'

They were interrupted by the sound of brakes and looked up in time to see the pathologist's car come to a halt only inches from the back bumper of Nash's Range Rover.

'Nash, I was in the middle of conducting a post-mortem in front of a group of anatomy students when you rang,' Ramirez told him. 'What's happened here?'

'That's what you're here to tell us,' Nash said sarcastically, 'now that you've managed to tear yourself away.'

'Well, let's get on with it. I haven't got all day to waste.'

'Neither have we,' Nash retorted. 'We've wasted enough of it, waiting for you.'

Clara winced, but fortunately Ramirez didn't respond.

She followed Nash and the pathologist back to the flat. The detectives waited as Ramirez began his examination.

'Very unpleasant,' he said after a minute. His voice conveyed no emotion. He walked carefully across to the bed, warning them to avoid the teeth on the carpet if they intended to enter. Neither of them seemed tempted by the offer.

'Have you seen the torture marks on the genitals?'

Nash nodded. 'Yes, Clara spotted them, she likes looking at men's privates. We thought the killer might have used cigarettes.' He pointed to the ashtray.

'You're probably right. I should be able to confirm it later.'

'Anything else I should be aware of at this stage?'

Ramirez was examining the dead man's eyes. 'I'll be interested in the toxicology results,' he said after a moment. 'I wouldn't be surprised if he was sedated. Probably to stop him resisting. I'll do all the usual checks, but my first guess is that he's probably been dead around four to five days. The maggots will confirm the time of death as accurately as possible. When I've finished up here I'll supervise removal of the body. In this heat the sooner the better. Post-mortem tomorrow morning?'

'That'll be fine; we'll leave you to it.'

Ramirez looked at them. 'Can't say I blame you.'

SOCO arrived as they emerged from the building. 'Ramirez is waiting upstairs,' he told the team leader. 'Let me know the results of your search as soon as possible.'

chapter six

When they returned to the CID suite, Viv told them that the file on Ray Perry would be delivered by courier the following morning.

'What do you want me to do?' Clara asked.

'Get Viv to help you find out everything you can about our murder victim.'

It wasn't long before Clara reported back. 'Here's what we know about Graham Nattrass, although to be honest, it isn't much. I phoned around the motor dealers and found out he worked for the BMW dealers in Netherdale. I should have tried them first, given the car Nattrass owned. I'm due to see their MD later. Viv went and took an official statement from the neighbour. So far, he hasn't been able to contact the other tenants. Apparently, one of them works away and is only home at weekends; some sort of salesman. The other flat's occupied by a married couple. Our old lady said she saw them loading their car with suitcases last Saturday, so if they're on holiday, we'll have to wait for them to return, which is a nuisance because they'll probably have forgotten anything they might have seen or heard. She's a bit of a nosey neighbour, if you hadn't already guessed.'

'Without them, our job would be a lot harder. Anything else?'

'I remembered seeing a cheque book amongst the debris at the flat, so I got Viv to ring the local branch of the bank. He got hold of the manager who was a bit reluctant to talk at first, but Viv managed to persuade him by keeping the questions fairly general. In the end he confirmed that Nattrass had a healthy balance in his current account, and what he called a "substantial amount" on deposit.'

'That was good work. What made you think of it?'

'I was trying to work out possible motives, and wondered if the murder was a punishment beating gone wrong. From a bookmaker, a casino or a moneylender, perhaps, but the bank scotched that idea.'

'Nevertheless it was smart thinking. And you may still be right. About the punishment, I mean. It could be for some other reason we haven't got to grips with yet. On the whole, though, I'm more inclined to believe the killer was looking for something he thought Nattrass had. Either that, or he could tell him where it was. Remember the torture marks on the body? Mexican Pete has confirmed that they were made by a cigarette, by the way.'

At the station next morning, Jack Binns handed Nash a large packet. 'Delivered by courier twenty minutes ago,' he explained.

Clara was already in the office and proffered a freshly typed report. 'Any news?' he asked.

'A bit, from yesterday, for what it's worth. Nattrass's boss told me he was a good technician. That's what they're known as these days, apparently. The man nearly fainted when I used the word mechanic. Having established that there were no complaints about him on the work front, I check Nattrass's details. Strangely enough, there was no next of kin listed on his employment form. I asked if he knew much about Nattrass's personal life. He laughed and said, "What personal life?" When I asked what he meant, he told me Nattrass was a computer nerd, who spent all his spare time glued to his laptop.'

Nash frowned. 'There was no sign of a laptop or a PC at the flat.'

'That's what I thought. I asked him if he knew what Nattrass was interested in. He seemed to think that recently, he'd been trying to find out something about his family history, but he couldn't be sure. He let me have a look in Nattrass's locker. I thought I might get some clue from what was inside, but I drew a blank. Only a spare change of work clothes and a pair of reasonably new trainers.'

Nash was still thinking about the missing computer. 'Did he know if Nattrass had a printer? Because I've just remembered, in amongst all the debris at the flat there was a load of blank copier paper.'

'He must have had one, because the MD said he occasionally

brought stuff he'd downloaded and printed into work: photos, puzzles, that sort of thing.'

'So the killer took both the laptop and printer. I wonder why?'

'Perhaps he thought that if Nattrass had them linked, it was the easiest way to download anything Nattrass might have on his computer that the killer was interested in.'

The file on Raymond Perry gave Nash and his team a much clearer understanding of the man lying comatose in Netherdale ICU. Unfortunately it failed to yield the slightest clue as to what he was doing in Helmsdale, or why he'd been attacked with such violence.

'OK, let's sum up what we do know,' Nash said when they'd been through all the paperwork. 'I'll read out anything salient and, Clara, you make notes. Bullet points will do.'

Mironova pulled an A4 pad towards her and settled in her chair. This was part of their work she always enjoyed. Watching Nash pulling information together or dissecting it was an object lesson in detection.

'We'll start with Raymond Perry's background. He was born in November 1965, in the East End of London, where his father had a scrap business. When the boy was twelve, his father was killed in an accident in the scrapyard. After his death, Raymond's mother rapidly descended into alcoholism, which meant that the boy was taken under the wing of his uncle, Max Perry, his father's younger brother and partner, who now owned the business.'

Nash paused and sat back. 'There's nothing in the file to denote whether Raymond's mother is still alive or not. Possibly not, given her disease, but worth making a note to check that out. The other point that strikes me about Perry's background is that whoever compiled this report seems to have known the family well. That's unusual, especially for the Met. Whether it's significant or not is another matter.

'The report states in quite unequivocal terms that his uncle, Max Perry, was head of a criminal gang operating from a chain of nightclubs, amusement arcades and, later, casinos in the area. The operation was highly lucrative. Moving into that operation brought its own dangers. Several turf wars erupted, and the violence that followed was a long-running series of battles, against first one, then another rival gang.'

Nash looked at his mug and seemed surprised to find that it was empty. 'During my time at the Met I learned quite a lot about the history of London gangs. There was a time when they occupied most of Scotland Yard's time and attention. After the Richardson and Kray organisations were broken up, a succession of those turf wars broke out with different factions struggling for control of vacant territories.

'By all accounts Max Perry, nicknamed Mad Max, was one of the most successful of these gang leaders. He was kept safe by his bodyguard and constant companion, his nephew Raymond, who acted as Max's strong-arm man. This continued until twenty-six years ago, when Max was killed in what's described in this report as a gangland killing, rumoured to have been ordered and paid for by Tony "Dirty Harry" Callaghan, Max's bitterest rival. The report also points out that the killer or killers were able to get to Mad Max, because Raymond was on remand for an alleged assault against a customer in one of Max's clubs.

'This part of the file,' – Nash tapped a plastic folder – 'describes the events leading up to Ray's arrest. Police responded to an anonymous phone call and attended a used-car dealership owned by Tony Callaghan. The business was known as Five Elms Car Sales.'

Nash stopped speaking and when Clara looked up, she saw he was smiling. 'What's so funny?'

'I know that address. There isn't an elm or any other type of tree for miles. Anyway, when the officers got there they found the body of Callaghan on the floor of the workshop, and that of his bodyguard in the adjoining office. Both men had multiple stab wounds. They also found Raymond Perry, standing over the body with the murder weapon in his hand. During the struggle to subdue and arrest him two officers received knife injuries, fortunately neither of them serious.' Nash stood up. 'I'll make another coffee, then we'll summarize what we've learned so far.'

When they resumed, Nash said, 'You know what intrigues me? That phone call. I'll get to it in a minute. First, some facts. Raymond had been heard by several witnesses saying that "Callaghan's got it coming to him". Presumably he was talking about revenge for his Uncle Max's murder. Police never thought to look beyond Raymond for the killer. He had motive, means and opportunity and was quite literally caught red-handed. Everything very snug and watertight. But listen, this is the transcript of that phone call. "Go to Five Elms Car Sales. You'll find Tony Callaghan's body in the workshop. He's been stabbed. If you get there sharp, you'll find Ray Perry at the scene." Now, what strikes you about that tip-off?'

'The caller knew exactly how Callaghan had been killed,' Viv replied.

'That's part of it. He also knew Perry would be at the scene. How did he know? And, he doesn't at any point suggest Perry killed Callaghan. Only that he would be there. That phone call suggests an altogether different scenario. Which in turn poses two further questions: if Perry didn't kill Callaghan, who did, and why? Was their motive to frame Perry, or was his being at the scene of the crime just a massive slice of good luck for the killer? And if he was innocent, why did Perry not defend himself? Why not do something to prove his innocence? Although, to be fair, with the evidence stacked against him that would have been almost impossible.

'Anyway, that's all speculation. The rest of the report deals with Perry's time in jail. All the time he's been in there, he's reported to have been a model prisoner. Not involved in fights, no trouble at all. That hardly tallies with his reputation, which is intriguing, but doesn't shed much light on why he was almost killed in a hit-and-run. One thing for certain' – Nash closed the folder and rested his hand on it – 'there's absolutely nothing in here that gives any connection between Perry, his family and North Yorkshire, nothing to suggest a reason for him ending up here. We need more background information.'

'How do we find that out?'

'I don't know,' Nash admitted. 'I'm open to any suggestions.'

They sat in silence for several moments, sipping coffee as they considered their course of action. Eventually, Clara stirred. 'I've had an idea. Why not get in touch with the Met? See if the file on Max Perry gives any more clues, or if there are any officers who might know more.' She pointed to the folder. 'The officer who compiled that, for instance, must have known Perry quite well. It might be useful to know how Max was killed, or if anyone was ever charged with the crime. All we know at the moment is that rumour that Callaghan was involved.'

'Good thinking, Clara. The more we can learn of Raymond Perry's past, the likelier we are to get some clue as to the motive for the attack, and possibly who was responsible.'

'That sounds quite a task,' Clara commented.

'If you think that's hard, wait till you hear what I've got in store for you. Your job is to trace Raymond Perry's mother, if she's still alive. If not, find out when and where she died, even where she's buried. In the meantime I'll get on to the Met and order that other file and see what I can find out about the officers who worked the cases. Viv, you continue with Graham Nattrass's background.'

Nash picked up the phone and rang the Met. Having requested the Max Perry file and elicited a promise that it would be sent by courier that afternoon, Nash asked to be transferred to CID and his former colleague, Brian Shaw.

After some moments, he was connected. 'Mike, long time since I spoke to you. How are things in the frozen north? Plenty of farmers' daughters to keep you warm at night?'

'Not any more, Brian. I'm respectable these days.'

'Wonders will never cease. Don't tell me you're married. Settled down, slippers and pipe, that sort of thing. Mug of cocoa and in bed by 9.30?'

'I said respectable, not ancient. Anyway, you're the expert on married life, as I remember.'

'You are out of touch. That went belly up three years ago after she buggered off with an Eyetie.'

'Sorry to hear that, Brian.'

'Yeah, well I wasn't. Glad to see the back of her. The bloke she took up with owns a string of restaurants and by what I hear he's been servicing several of the waitresses who work for him. Serves her right. If I meet him, I'll shake his hand and thank him.'

'So now you're leading a lonely, celibate life?'

'Hardly, I met up with a little smasher, name of Candy. Now I've developed a real sweet tooth.'

'Your jokes haven't got any better. Has this girl any other faults apart from defective eyesight and poor judgement?'

'Did you ring just to insult me, or was there another reason?'

'I'm trying to get hold of someone to talk to about an old case.'

'How old are you talking?'

'Twenty-six years, so I suppose they'll all be retired by now?'

'Pushing up daisies, more like. What's the case?'

'I'm not sure if you know of it. It's two linked cases, actually.' Nash explained the details.

'Perry; that name rings a bell. East End gangster, murdered by one of the opposition. Son took revenge on the boss of the other outfit and got life for it. That the one?'

'Near enough. Nephew, actually, but apart from that you've got it dead right. There's not much wrong with your memory.'

'Pride myself on it. Now, give me the name, rank and division of the men you're after and I'll get back to you. Shouldn't take more than half an hour, providing I can get someone in HR to talk to me. Do you want me to phone you back or shall I email you?'

'You and technology? I'd love to see that. Makes me wish I hadn't left.'

'I'll tell you something, there's plenty here wish you hadn't. I'll get back to you ASAP.'

True to his word, Shaw was soon back on the phone. 'I've good news and bad. Three of the men have gone to the police station in the sky. One's living in Spain, drinking weak lager and eating paella. Unless your boss is very generous with expenses, that rules him out.'

'So, what's the good news?'

'The last name you gave me, DS Wellings, he's still hale and hearty. What's more, he's not a million miles away from you. Wellings went back to his wife's neck of the woods when he'd got his time in; retired as a DCI. The note on his file says he and his wife are running a boarding house. Don't forget your bucket and spade, because it's in Scarborough. Got a pen?'

Nash was undecided about whether to phone the retired officer, when Clara returned.

'How did you get on with the Met?'

Nash explained.

'That's a bit of good luck,' she commented when he told her where Wellings was living. 'Have you phoned him?'

'Not yet, I was still making my mind up about that. On balance, I think it'll be better to wait until we've had a look at the other file. It should be with us tomorrow.'

It was mid-afternoon when the promised file arrived. Clara eyed it as Nash struggled with the wrappings. 'That looks a far bigger file than Ray's.'

'It will have the murder trial stuff in it as well as Max's own track record, I guess. Drag a chair over and let's have a look at the gory details.'

Nash said it in jest, but when they opened the file, it seemed the joke was in fairly bad taste. Clara drew her chair nearer and as they read the section dealing with Max Perry's injuries, she gasped. 'That's impossible!'

Nash didn't reply. He was still coming to terms with the implications of what he'd read.

'How the hell did that happen?' Clara continued. 'It must be some sort of ghastly coincidence.'

'You know I don't believe in coincidences.' Nash shook his head, as much to clear it as to emphasize his denial. 'But how a motor mechanic in North Yorkshire dies of what appear to be identical injuries to those inflicted on a London gangster over a quarter of a century ago, baffles me. Even down to the teeth having been knocked out.'

'What do you intend to do?'

'First of all I want confirmation of what we've just read. I mean an expert opinion. And the only person who can give us that is Señor Ramirez. I'll try and get to see him tomorrow. I reckon you and I should go for a day at the seaside in the next few days.'

'A day at the...? Oh, I get you. Go see the retired officer. Wellings, you said his name was, didn't you?'

'That's right, I'll phone first to make sure it's convenient,' Nash kept his face straight. 'And in case we have some spare time, be sure and buy a newspaper and don't wear any tights.'

'What?'

'You can fold the paper up to use as a hat and you won't want tights on when you go paddling.'

Nash picked up the folder, and as he did so a photo slid out of the file onto his desk. He picked it up and studied it. 'Wow! What a stunner!'

'She's remarkably beautiful,' Clara agreed. 'Who is she?'

Nash looked on the back but there was no inscription, neither could they find any reference whatsoever to the mystery woman in the file. 'Let's see what help we can get from Scarborough.'

Nash phoned Ramirez, and explained what he needed. 'I'll have a look for you. As it happens, I have a free day tomorrow, unless you manage to find any more bodies, which is always a strong possibility. Ten o'clock in the morning OK?'

Examination of the pathology results provided the confirmation Nash needed. 'The post-mortem findings don't confirm the weapon,' Ramirez said, 'but the wounds look identical, and the diameter of each injury is the right size. The pathologist didn't suggest a possible weapon, but now I've had chance to study Mr Nattrass's injuries closely, I think you should look for a sledgehammer as the most likely to have inflicted those wounds. There are other similarities between Max Perry's case and that of Mr Nattrass. The pathologist at Max Perry's post-mortem failed to identify the marks on the genitals,' Ramirez continued. 'I find that surprising. They're quite clearly burn marks. And just the right size and shape to have been made by a cigarette. Added to that, there's the way Perry was tied up, which to me looks identical to how we found Nattrass. Do you agree?'

'Yes, I'd noticed. I think that makes it fairly conclusive.'

chapter seven

The Scarborough guest house was almost identical to those surrounding it. Set back from the road, the front garden had been covered in tarmac to provide parking spaces.

Wellings was nothing like the mental image Nash had conjured up of the retired officer. No more than medium height, slim, wiry of build, with gold-rimmed spectacles, he looked more like an academic than a policeman or a hotelier. He greeted them and led them into the dining room, where he indicated the coffee machine in the corner. 'Breakfast finished only half an hour ago, so the coffee's still fresh. Unless you'd prefer tea?'

They shook their heads. 'Right, I'll be with you in a second. I'll just pop into the kitchen and put a jug of milk in the microwave.'

When they were seated round one of the tables, Wellings stirred his coffee. 'What's this all about, then?'

'An old customer of yours,' Nash told him. 'Well, two to be exact. Raymond Perry and his Uncle Max.'

'Ray Perry? I haven't heard that name in a long number of years. Not that I've wanted to. Nasty piece of work; sliced up Tony Callaghan good and proper. What's your interest in him? Don't tell me he's come to Yorkshire?'

Nash nodded.

'That's a first, I'll bet. I don't think Ray's willingly been north of Watford Gap all his life. What's he done?'

After Nash explained, Wellings responded, 'Can't say I'll shed many tears.' Wellings took a swig of his coffee. 'Ray Perry was a bloody nuisance, not to put too fine a point on it. Caused us a lot of problems, one way or another, even before he did for Callaghan.

Then he became more than a nuisance.'

'In what way?'

'When Mad Max was killed we got word that Callaghan was behind it. We were extremely worried there would be an all-out war between the gangs, but thankfully it didn't happen. Ray's slicing up of Dirty Harry was very badly timed. We were on the point of pulling Callaghan in for questioning and we were sure we'd get a shed-load of information, even if we couldn't pin Max's murder on him, but Ray jumped the gun and got there first.'

'Inconvenient, to say the least,' Nash agreed. 'But given what I've read about Callaghan, what made you so certain you'd get info from him? He didn't seem the type to cough easily.'

'He wasn't, but we'd got something on him. Not criminal, this was personal. We thought it was something Ray Perry didn't know. Obviously we were wrong.'

'What was it, can you remember?'

Wellings smiled. 'Oh yes, I can remember well enough. It was a woman,' the retired officer kept a straight face. 'They cause a lot of trouble, attractive women.'

'You don't need to tell Mike that,' Mironova interjected.

'Ray had a girlfriend, a nightclub singer called Frankie Da Silva. She was an absolute stunner. She'd a good singing voice too. Not top class, but good enough to earn a decent living, and to be honest, when she was on stage, very few men noticed her voice. What she saw in Ray Perry, I've no idea. She could have had her pick of men. But then, women seem to fall for the most disreputable types.'

'You don't need to tell Mike that, either,' Clara added again.

Wellings grinned. 'Max Perry's wife, Corinna, was another case in point. She was a really good-hearted woman; do anything to help anybody. Mind you, that was probably due to her training. She was a nurse before she married Max,' he explained. 'Corinna did a lot of fund-raising for local charities, that sort of thing. She was a bit younger than Max, which was another reason I couldn't understand the match. Pretty, too, although nowhere near as lovely as Frankie.

'Anyway, just before Tony Callaghan was killed, we got word that he had been seeing Frankie when Ray wasn't about. Our snout told us Callaghan had been seen going to Frankie's flat – a lot. After Max's murder, we were told that it was Frankie lured Max to the place where he was killed; an empty lock-up under the arches near one of the big railway stations. Apparently, the plan was for her to set Max up for the kill, before which they'd get him to tell her where he kept his stash. They'd grab that and scarper. Frankie agreed to do it, both for the money and for Callaghan. Hardly an original scheme, but apparently it worked, at least for Frankie. The only problem was, Ray must have found out what they were up to and got to Callaghan before they could fly off into the sunset.'

Wellings paused, frowning slightly. 'What is it?' Nash prompted. 'Something you remembered?'

'I sat in on a couple of the interviews when Ray Perry was being questioned. When the boss asked him about Callaghan and Frankie, he didn't pull any punches.'

Wellings glanced apologetically at Clara before continuing, 'He suggested Callaghan was screwing Frankie left, right and centre and word was she couldn't get enough of Dirty Harry's dick. He went on and on about it, trying to goad Perry.'

'And did he get a reaction?'

'He did, but it certainly wasn't the one he was hoping for. Ray burst out laughing. For some reason, the idea of Frankie and Callaghan tickled him, in spite of the mess he was in.'

'And you've no idea why?'

'None at all.'

'What happened to Frankie, do you know?'

'She was never seen again. We were told at the time that she'd decided to go solo.'

'Where did you pick up all your information?'

'Our DCI had a contact. No idea who, although I suspect it might have been a member of Max's organization, or someone on the fringes of it. Whoever he was, he was bloody reliable. He'd passed us a load of stuff before all this blew up, all of it top class, so we'd no reason to doubt this was genuine.'

Nash slid a photo from the folder he'd brought with him, 'Do you recognize this woman?'

A nostalgic smile spread across Wellings' face. 'That's Frankie.

Frankie Da Silva. One of the most beautiful women I've ever laid eyes on.'

'Did anything strike you about the way Max Perry was killed? The pictures and description of his injuries in the file are fairly graphic.'

Wellings grimaced. 'Not half as bad as being at the crime scene, believe me. I actually felt sorry for Max. I know he was a villain, but God knows what agonies he must have suffered before he died. They tortured the poor bastard, trying to find his stash, we thought. To do that they burned his balls with cigarettes. He must have been bloody stubborn, that's what we reckoned, because they also yanked his teeth out with pliers.

'Did you read how he died? The only way we could identify him was by the bloody great gold chain Corinna had given him. That and his signet ring. Later, we matched his prints with some we lifted from Max's flat. The place where he was killed was a blood-bath, if that's what you meant by anything striking.'

'Not precisely; I wondered if you'd got any clue as to the killer's identity from the MO?'

'No, it was a new one on us. Why do you ask?'

'What Mike's getting at, Mr Wellings,' Clara interrupted, 'is that we've got the body of a young man in our mortuary and as far as we can judge from the pathology, this young man's injuries are a carbon copy of those inflicted on Max Perry.'

Wellings looked stunned. 'I've no idea how that could have happened. As I told you, we'd no clues and only a rumour that suggested Frankie was involved, plus the opportune way she vanished.'

'You mentioned something about Max Perry's stash. There's no mention of it in here. What's the story behind that?'

'Again, a lot of it is rumour. We accumulated a fair amount of circumstantial evidence following Max's death. Surprising, the number of people who talked then, people who were too scared even to say good morning to us beforehand. That was the sort of fear Max and Ray inspired. The story was that Max had been collecting diamonds for years.'

'Any particular reason?'

'Max said he didn't trust banks; that they were too easy to rob. Well, if anyone should know, he'd be the one. Also, he didn't want his money tied up where he'd have difficulty getting to it in a hurry. With some of the things he'd done, he wanted his assets easily portable and able to be converted into readies at a moment's notice.'

'What sort of sums are we talking about, any idea?'

Wellings spread his arms. 'The rumours got wilder and wilder with every telling. But I think you'd be safe in starting with seven figures. And then maybe working up. If they're still out there the value would be astronomical. Better than a lottery jackpot, even with a rollover, I guess.'

'They might well be out there,' Nash said soberly. 'We may never know for sure. What we can say with some certainty is that there's a ruthless and sadistic killer who is still out there. One with no qualms about inflicting some of the most horrific injuries I've ever seen on anyone who gets in his way.'

'Is there anything else you need to ask?' Wellings glanced across at the clock on the mantelpiece. 'It's just that I help the missus prepare the guests' evening meals. This time of the year is our busiest.'

'I've just one more thing. Both files are fairly detailed but neither of them gives much clue as to what sort of criminal activity the Perry organization was involved with.'

'Pretty much anything that made a profit, I'd say. Their power base was built around the scrapyard and the chain of casinos, discos and nightclubs. That's where Ray met Frankie. Around that time there was a string of bank robberies and bullion hold-ups round the south of England. In those days bank branch security was archaic, making them easy pickings. We heard Max did all the planning, whilst Ray recruited and controlled the muscle. Nothing was ever proved, but it's surely not coincidence that the robberies stopped after Max was killed and Ray was put inside. Max was bloody clever. He was without doubt the brains behind the heists. We knew it, but he was so careful we could never prove anything. We didn't even have enough on him to pull him in for questioning. Meticulous, that was Mad Max; into everything from robbery to prostitution and protection.' Wellings paused and stressed his next point, 'Everything but drugs. That was one thing they never got involved in. I heard Ray wouldn't stand for it.'

Wellings paused, as if undecided whether to say what was on his mind. 'There is one more thing – the mention of diamonds made me think of it. Around that time, we were contacted by Dutch police, asking for help to trace two men reported missing by their wives. They were known to act as diamond couriers from time to time and their car had been logged boarding a ferry for the UK, and coming off at Harwich. We did the usual searches, but as far as I know, no trace of them or the car was ever found. It was a while later, long after Max was killed, that we heard another whisper. It concerned blood diamonds. Do you know what those are?'

Both Nash and Mironova nodded.

'Years ago, there was a big, highly illegal trade in them, which the authorities were keen to stamp out because of their connection to war crimes and genocide in places such as Sierra Leone.'

'And you think Max was involved in that trade?'

'That was what we heard, and it was also rumoured that the two men who vanished were carrying blood diamonds, which was why the theft of them couldn't be reported.' Wellings then added, 'There was also talk that Max's murder might have been a hit ordered in revenge for the diamond theft, but that's all it was, bar room gossip.'

'Are you hungry?' Nash asked.

'Too right, it must be the sea air.'

'Then I reckon we should get some fish and chips before we set off back. Sit on the prom and eat them.'

'What do you reckon about what we heard this morning?' Clara asked between mouthfuls.

Nash watched a small fishing boat chugging slowly out of the harbour. 'The first thing Wellings did was strengthen my doubt about Ray Perry's guilt.'

'I'd have thought it was the other way round. Surely, if Perry thought Callaghan had killed his uncle and was having an affair with his girl, and was about to run off with her, that would give him a strong motive for killing Callaghan?'

'There's only one flaw in that argument, a flaw that a lot of other people missed, too. Either missed or deliberately overlooked.'

'What are you thinking of, the anonymous tip-off?'

'Yes, somebody fed that information to the police. But they overdid it, gave too much detail.'

'I see what you mean. In order to know as much as he did, the caller had to be the killer. And Ray Perry wouldn't have shopped himself.'

'Exactly, and when you set out the motives just now, you prefaced your argument with the word "if". And that's the other weakness in your case. Everything seems to be based on supposition, hearsay and "information received". Let me put an alternative scenario to you. It's a case of "what if", but no more so than yours.'

'Go on, try me, this is fascinating.'

'Right, let's start with Max Perry's murder. Everyone seemed to take it for granted that Callaghan ordered it. Why? Because that was the rumour. Don't get me wrong. The way the system works in London, underworld rumour's more often right than wrong. But that doesn't mean it can't be manipulated. Max was tortured before he was killed, presumably to reveal where this alleged fortune in diamonds was stashed. I accept that could have been Callaghan. I also accept that Callaghan and Frankie Da Silva could have been lovers. What doesn't sound right is this supposed plan for Callaghan and Frankie to take off for a new life somewhere and walk into the sunset holding hands. Very Mills & Boon,' Nash added dryly.

'Why do you find that so hard to believe?'

'You've to understand the world occupied by characters like Callaghan and Perry – and having worked in the Met, I've met a few. Callaghan had a highly successful criminal organization working for him, probably earning as much in a year as Max Perry, and a much worse background than Ray Perry's. He wouldn't have walked away from that because a good-looking female fluttered her eyelids at him.

'What if someone else killed Max, making sure everybody "knew" that Callaghan ordered it. Then murdered Callaghan, making sure they framed Ray; the one person who had two reasons for wanting him dead. The only questions that leaves are: who was the target – was it Tony Callaghan, Max or Ray Perry – and who actually was the killer?'

Clara sat thinking this over for a while. 'That is some theory,' she said eventually, 'and I can see the sense of it. But proving it after all this time is going to be well nigh impossible.'

Nash picked up their empty fish and chip cartons and deposited them in the nearest litter bin, to the dismay of a pair of screeching, hopeful seagulls. He walked back to the bench and glanced across at the sea. 'If you don't fancy a paddle, we might as well set off back.'

Nash had just got into the car when his mobile rang. He glanced at the screen. 'Yes, Viv?'

'I thought you'd want to know that Raymond Perry recovered consciousness early this morning. It was only brief, barely a moment. Apparently he's now in a deeper coma than before. The surgeon in charge of the ICU wants to have a word with you. I'm not sure, but I wondered if they're considering switching the life-support machines off.'

'Did Perry say anything?'

'Yes, one word, apparently, but nothing anybody can make sense of. Lianne was on duty at the time, she told me about it.'

'OK, I'll talk to the surgeon tomorrow.'

'How did the meeting with Wellings go?'

'It was highly informative. More so than he realized, I reckon. I'll tell you all about it in the morning.'

Nash put his mobile back in his pocket and looked across to where Clara was watching him.

'What is it, something wrong?' she asked.

'Raymond Perry came round briefly; then relapsed. Viv thinks they want to switch the machines off. If they do that, it means we'll have lost our best potential source of information as to who might be behind this.'

'It's far too soon, surely; unless his condition is worse than we think.'

The following morning, Nash and Mironova listened as Pearce explained what had happened at the hospital. 'It was just after I'd dropped Lianne off to start her shift in the ICU. I thought whilst

I was there I ought to check with the uniformed man we have guarding Perry and the hospital reception, to see if Raymond's had any visitors, or anyone asking after him.'

Nash nodded approval and Viv continued, 'All I can tell you is what Lianne told me. Apparently, Perry woke up briefly. She went to his bedside immediately. He looked at her, muttered something and that was it. Before she could respond he was out like a light.'

'Did she catch what he said?'

'She wasn't sure; said it might have been a name. But she was too busy summoning the rest of the ICU team, checking his vital signs or whatever they do, to take too much notice. I saw all the flap going on and kept well out of the way.'

'I'll need to have a word with her. If Perry dies, she'll probably be the last one to have had any contact with him, so we'll need a formal statement. That might as well be done now. If you're right about the reason the head of the ICU wants to talk to me, and they have decided to switch the machines off, Perry will become a murder victim, and Lianne's evidence might be needed in court, if it ever comes to that. Particularly as he regained consciousness.'

'I think she's expecting that. I'll give her a call. Will later this afternoon be OK? She's on early shifts all this week.'

'No problem.'

Pearce hesitated. 'There's something else you should know. I'm not sure how significant this is, but Perry had a visitor, or at least someone asking about him. I'd left instructions that if anyone inquired about Perry someone should contact me immediately, or if I wasn't there, the uniformed man on duty. Just before I left, reception buzzed through to the ward to say there was someone asking for Perry. I went straight down, but he'd disappeared. I checked the CCTV, but the picture's so hazy you couldn't tell if it was a man or a woman. System's been like that for weeks, actually, but they can't get it repaired. That's how strapped for cash they are. I asked for a description, but to be honest it's not much use. It could fit millions of men. Medium height and build, grey hair and casually dressed.' Pearce paused. 'However, the receptionist did tell me the man spoke with a very distinct accent.'

'Don't tell me, let me guess. A cockney accent?'

'Wrong! Way wrong. She said his accent was from Belfast. I asked her how she could be sure. Apparently her husband's from there. She said Perry's visitor had an accent that was "pure Falls Road".'

Nash shook his head in bewilderment. How many more surprises was this case going to bring?

It was lunch time before Clara asked Nash, 'Did you ring Perry's surgeon?'

'I did, but he's in theatre all day. I'll try again later.'

Later that afternoon, Pearce ushered Lianne into Nash's office, which, with Clara and Viv in as well, was a little crowded.

'Thanks for coming in, Lianne,' Nash smiled, 'I won't keep you long, you must be keen to get home and put your feet up and let Viv cook your tea for you.'

'That'll be the day.' Lianne smiled and raised her eyebrows.

'So can you tell us exactly what happened this morning?'

'Mr Perry's monitors started showing increased activity, so I went over to his bedside. His eyes opened momentarily and he stared at me. Then he spoke, but his voice was so weak I hardly caught what he said. I thought it was someone's name, but I couldn't swear to it. Now I've had more time to think it over, I'm more than ever convinced that's what it was, but I don't seem to be able to recall it. Before I'd time to think about what he'd said, he was unconscious again. I got busy, and afterwards I seem to have blocked it out.'

She turned her head slightly, averting her gaze from Nash's. Obviously her failure to remember was irritating her.

Clara had a stroke of intuitive genius. 'Lianne,' she said softly, 'that name, how many syllables did it have?'

'One, I think; no, possibly two.' Lianne starred at some point in the distance, trying to recall.

'Did it sound like "Frank"?'

She stared at Clara. 'Yes, it could have sounded like Frank. Although that's not quite right.' She thought about it, repeating the word in a low mutter. 'Frank, Frank, no, Frankie, yes, I think that's it. Now you've said it, I'm sure that's what he said. How did you guess?'

'Something we found in his file,' Clara said ambiguously.

'Lianne,' Nash said, 'I need you to go with Viv and make a statement.' He turned to Pearce. 'Get Jack Binns to take it, given your personal involvement.'

He stood up and shook hands with Lianne. 'Thank you for coming in. Your information has been most helpful.'

'Well, at least we know what was on Ray Perry's mind,' Clara said when they were alone.

'Mmm, makes you wonder if that was the reason he came to Yorkshire, though, doesn't it? Looking for Frankie Da Silva, I mean. By the way, that was clever thinking on your part.'

Clara bowed. 'Thank you, kind sir.'

chapter eight

Nash's phone call with the doctor was brief and to the point. 'We've done everything we can for Mr Perry,' the medic told him. 'He needs specialist treatment, which we're not able to provide here.'

'What do you suggest?'

'The nearest centre capable of handling a case like this is the Freeman Hospital in Newcastle. I've spoken to my colleagues there and they're trying to organize the transfer for as soon as possible. Because of your involvement, I wanted to be sure that you were kept in the loop before we move him.'

Nash gave the doctor his mobile number. 'I'd like to be informed as soon as it's done. I'll need to get the local police to sort out protection. Have you any idea when he might be conscious and able to answer questions?'

'That's impossible to say. I'll phone you when the transfer has been done.'

Nash received the phone call before he set off to Netherdale headquarters next morning. 'Inspector,' the surgeon told him, 'Raymond Perry was moved in the early hours. I'll send you all the details through if you wish.'

'Please, if you would, and thank you for letting me know.'

Nash called Mironova into his office, and told her what had happened. 'Accepting the fact that the attack on Perry wasn't the random act of a psychopath, I think we should try to give whoever was responsible the impression that we don't realize it was done deliberately.'

'How do we do that? If we've no idea who did it we can hardly send them a message, can we?'

'Oh, yes we can.' Nash outlined his idea.

'Mike, has anyone ever mentioned that you have a very Machiavellian streak to your personality?'

'I believe something akin to that may have cropped up in conversation somewhere along the line.'

As he was speaking, his phone rang. Nash glanced at the caller display. 'The chief's back,' he told Clara before picking up the handset.

'Mike,' Chief Constable Gloria O'Donnell began, 'I've just been looking through the paperwork on my desk. What's been going on in Helmsdale? I go on a well-earned holiday, leaving everything peaceful and serene. When I get back, what do I find? Axe murderers and gangsters running amok.'

Nash grinned. 'Actually, we believe it was a sledgehammer, not an axe, but I take your point, ma'am. And I wish I knew.' He explained what little they knew about the two events.

'Any idea what's behind it?'

'A couple, thanks to an ex-DCI from London. But who might be responsible is another matter entirely.' He told her of his interview with Wellings. 'Fortunately, Netherdale's been relatively quiet, so I've been able to concentrate on what's been happening here. Now, if you'll excuse me, ma'am, I have to make an urgent phone call.'

'Anything interesting?'

'Yes, I'm going to ask the *Netherdale Gazette* to print an article for me.'

Phil Miller was reading the morning paper. The item he'd been looking for was on the front page. The article told him all he needed to know. He picked up his mobile. 'Here, listen to this. "Police are appealing for witnesses following the discovery of a seriously injured man on the Helmsdale to Kirk Bolton road, close to Drover's Halt. The man, described as being in his late forties, has since been identified as Raymond Perry, recently released from Durham Prison having served a life sentence for murder. Police are anxious to interview anyone who was travelling along that stretch of road last Thursday night, particularly if they saw the victim, who was wearing white trainers, blue jeans and a maroon sweatshirt, and was believed to be walking towards Drover's Halt. A police spokesperson commented that the injuries sustained by Perry are consistent with some form of collision, but until further tests have been carried out, they refused to speculate on the cause." That means they haven't a fucking clue. Dim set of bastards. So, Perry's on his way out. That will be one less problem. I was worried when he was headed this way, at the thought he might find out about you know what. I went to the hospital, did I tell you? I wanted to finish the job, but I was panicking over nothing, I guess. Now we can get on with the next bit. When do you think you can get away?'

He listened. 'Can't you make it sooner?' Had to accept the reality, 'No, I suppose not.'

He rang off and glanced around the cottage. His thoughts made him edgy. He hated this place. Couldn't understand how people could actually enjoy coming here on holiday. He'd hated it all those years ago. Remembered how glad he'd been at the thought that he'd never have to return. Now, here he was and hating it all the more. He was used to the hustle and bustle of the city. He hated the silence. Hated the people; their weird accents and way of talking. Hated the countryside. Couldn't sleep here. Too quiet. Just as he was getting used to it, some creature would screech or yelp, or whatever they did.

He wanted to be back on home ground. Even when Corinna had been here, he'd wanted to be away as fast as he could. He missed her, not simply because they were two of a kind, her and him: survivors. And they would survive again. Survive and prosper. But first, they'd got work to do. And mooning about wasn't going to get it done.

Shortly after lunch, Tom Pratt popped into Nash's office with a query regarding a case that he was getting ready to send to CPS. It was a question, Nash knew, none of the others would have thought to ask. As they were talking, Clara and Pearce joined them.

Clara cleared her throat. 'I was trying to work out how Ray Perry came to be in Yorkshire. It seems strange to me that Perry headed here immediately he was released; as if he knew where to come.'

There was a long silence before Nash spoke. 'You're right, Clara, we questioned it before and I should have spotted it. Do you want to sit here?' He pointed to his chair. 'So, what you're thinking is, who did Perry know here? Because that has to be the key to the whole mystery.'

'Perhaps he came here looking for his lover; the mysterious Frankie Da Silva,' Clara suggested.

Nash shook his head. 'We've no evidence connecting her with this area. Mind you, at the moment the same applies to Perry.'

Nash turned to Pearce. 'I've a job for you, Viv, on much the same lines as the one Clara's doing. I don't want you to feel left out. Contact all the theatrical and entertainment agencies you can find. Concentrate on those based in London, to begin with. See if anyone remembers a nightclub singer called Frankie Da Silva who was on the circuit during the eighties. She would have needed an agent. Without one, she wouldn't have got any bookings. If you manage to locate someone who still has her name on file, I need to know if she listed a next of kin, a contact address and especially, I want to know her real name, because I feel sure the agency will have that, as well as her stage name.'

'Changing the subject, Mike,' Clara added, 'I checked voters' rolls looking for relatives of Graham Nattrass and there are no families called Nattrass living in the area. I checked back via the *Gazette's* new online service and came up with an obituary for Mrs Grace Nattrass, widow of F. G. Nattrass. She died six years ago, but there was no mention of how long he'd been dead.'

'Six years,' Nash said. 'Isn't that about the time that Graham Nattrass moved into his flat?'

Clara nodded. 'I thought some of that furniture looked a bit old-fashioned for somebody of Nattrass's age. I bet he moved there after his mother died. That would explain the healthy bank balance, and the sports car. If he sold the family home, he'd have plenty of cash to spare. What's more, the initials of the husband mentioned in that obituary interest me. I checked with the registrar's office and the "G" stood for Graham.'

'Which puts Graham Nattrass's background to bed. All we have to work out now is why he was killed in the identical manner to Ray Perry's uncle twenty odd years ago.'

'That still leaves the unanswered questions of who attacked Ray Perry and what happened to Frankie Da Silva,' Pearce pointed out.

'True, and although we're no nearer working either of those out, I've an idea that the fate of Frankie is the key to the whole puzzle – don't ask me why.'

The meeting broke up without the team reaching any further conclusions about the way forward. Pratt remained seated when the others left. He appeared deep in thought. 'What's troubling you, Tom? You've obviously got something on your mind.'

'That obvious, is it? Not troubling me exactly, but I was just going over everything I heard about this missing woman, this Frankie Da Silva. Do you remember that trip we took out to Bishops Cross? To the site where that murder victim was found? I wondered if that was the same woman.'

'Remind me of the details again.'

'The post-mortem showed that the woman had been dead for a long time before the phone call that tipped us off. Bear in mind, I'm going from memory. I seem to remember something about the pathologist testing the soil beneath the body, and concluding she'd been killed elsewhere. The body had been attacked by a wide variety of predators, so there wasn't as much for us to work with. Given the way the science was in those days, the pathologist did the best he could, but nowhere near what Mexican Pete can achieve nowadays.'

'Yes, I remember, and didn't you say the body had been exhumed, and a DNA sample taken? As part of a cold case review, as I remember it? In which case, Mexican Pete should be able to trace that result. It may lead nowhere, but it might answer a whole load of questions. Unfortunately, it might also raise a whole lot more.'

Nash repeated their conversation to Clara.

'You don't subscribe to the notion that she cashed in the diamonds and is now sitting on a sun-kissed beach drinking cocktails, then?' she asked.

'I'm not sure I ever did. However, this one seems about as far-fetched from what little we know at present.'

In the holiday cottage the chirping of Phil Miller's mobile surprised him. Not that he should get a call, but that there was any signal in this outlandish place. Tension was immediate, but the caller ID on his screen relaxed him.

'How's it going?'

'I'm still here, aren't I?' he sighed heavily.

'You mean you haven't got it?'

'Oh yeah, like, I'd choose this spot for a bloody holiday, wouldn't I?'

'No progress?'

'Only the wrong sort.'

'So, what's our next option?'

'I've got to try and backtrack from the boy's adoption. We know the mother didn't give him up. She wasn't available. So it had to be the relative named on the papers. The only problem is I can't find any trace of her. She was at the Harrogate house, though.'

'Did you get all the papers? You're sure you didn't miss anything?'

'You saw them.'

'What are you planning to do next?'

'Try and trace this elusive relative.'

'Do you want me to come back up? Everything's running OK down here.'

'Tempting, but there doesn't seem any point, yet, apart from keeping me company. One of us having to suffer this place is bad enough. When we're in a position to go after the stuff; that's when I'll need you to be here.'

'Just be careful.'

'Don't worry about me. I can take care of myself.'

Although the club was in London, it wasn't one of the more salubrious West End nightclubs, where the rich and famous gather in the full glare of the paparazzi. It was, to be honest, a dive. The ground floor comprised a large bar, alongside which a gathering of presumably tone-deaf punters gyrated to an uninspiring selection of music.

Upstairs, some of the rooms were given over to gambling, despite the fact that the premises weren't licensed. In yet more private rooms, men were entertained by specialist club employees. Here, the gambling was with the clients' health, betting against contracting any number of sexually transmitted diseases. The premises certainly weren't licensed for this type of activity. In fact, the rumour was that the only reason the police didn't oppose renewal of the club's licence was that with the place open, they found it easy to locate members of the clientele who were wanted for a variety of offences.

The owner of this, and a dozen other similar clubs, by the name of Trevor Thornton, was seated on a bar stool at one end of the counter, watching the Friday night throng. Thornton, known to his close associates as Mr T, bore no physical resemblance to his famous namesake. In fact this short, balding and tubby middle-aged man was about as far away from the other Mr T as could be imagined. They did share one common trait, however, the ability to strike fear into those who had crossed them. In Thornton's case it was via several bouncers who doubled as enforcers and bodyguards.

A small, nervous, thin-faced man sidled up to Thornton, who inspected him, aware that the man had something to say. 'What do you want, Freddie?'

The tone was brusque, but the newcomer was used to that. Freddie 'The Ferret' Perkins was a betting shop clerk who made a precarious added income by peddling information. This sideline involved the collection and distribution of news items that didn't make it onto TV, radio, the press or the internet, although in many cases the subject matter ended up in all of them.

'I got a bit of a puzzle, Mr T, and I thought, my friend Mr T's just the man to solve it for me.'

If Thornton was offended by Freddie's claim of friendship, he didn't show it. Freddie often chose an obscure method to introduce the news item he had to impart and he guessed this was another example of just such an oblique approach. 'Ask away, Freddie, you know I'll answer you if I can.'

'Well, the thing is, I heard on the grapevine that an old friend had suffered an accident. More of an acquaintance than a friend, really. Someone who hasn't been seen around these parts for a long time' – Freddie gave a sly, sidelong smile – 'hasn't been seen anywhere, truth to tell. And the thing is, I was quite surprised when I heard that one of his nearest and dearest had gone dashing off to the place where this happened. Obviously, they'd gone to visit the sick, I thought. Except that I then found out that they'd rushed off there before the accident happened. Well beforehand, in fact. And I found that really curious, as if they knew it was going to happen, if you understand me.'

'Presumably, if the person you're referring to had been ill, they might have been summoned to his bedside,' Thornton pointed out. 'I don't see anything unusual in that.'

The Ferret nodded in agreement. 'That's exactly what I thought, Mr T, except that the information I was given was that the illness was a sudden one, an extremely sudden illness. A hit-and-run accident that remains a mystery, as I understand it.'

'I agree, that certainly sounds odd. Can you tell me anything more? Like the names of the people we're talking about? Then I'll be able to judge if there's any interest for me in this story.'

'I think I can assure you of that,' Freddie told him, making a gesture with his thumb and forefinger indicative of the passing of money.

He was right, of course. He always was. One of the reasons Freddie had survived so long was his ability to judge how much a story was worth, and who to sell it to – or who not to sell it to. Mr T pulled out his wallet and placed ten twenty-pound notes on the bar. Freddie smiled. Thornton's eyes opened wide. 'This has to be really good,' he warned Freddie, adding yet more notes. 'For five hundred, this has to be really, really good.'

Freddie, who had been something of an amateur magician in his younger days, made the notes disappear into his pocket in the blink of an eye. 'The injured party has been a guest of Her Majesty for many years, a quarter of a century or so. This was the result of an unfortunate encounter with an old friend of yours, someone who was in the motor trade. Shortly before that, as I recall, the man's uncle had passed to the other side, and many people believe the two events weren't tragic coincidences.'

'Ray Perry? You're talking about Ray Perry? What makes you think this is worth five hundred quid? It would be if the bastard was dead.'

'Yes, that was what I thought at first. I thought, that's interesting, but no more than that. Maybe some folk would place more significance on it than me, but no, not really valuable. Then, when I knew that my revered employer was dashing off up north with the man who is now making her eyes sparkle, long before Raymond's accident, I got to wondering why. And at the same time, I wondered why Ray had opted to go to such an out of the way place. Why would someone like Ray Perry want to go there, unless there was something in that place that attracted him? And what could that be, I wondered?'

Freddie paused, but Thornton didn't interrupt. He knew there would be more to come. Freddie always saved the best until last. 'And then I remembered something I heard a long, long time ago,' Freddie continued, 'and I started to wonder if perhaps they'd all gone looking for something. Something they thought might be there, in this out of the way spot. Like on a sort of treasure hunt, perhaps.'

If Freddie had any doubts about Thornton's interest, the final couple of sentences resolved them. 'Treasure?' Thornton asked. 'What sort of treasure?'

'Well, it could be all sorts of things, but I do recall hearing of something that was said to have gone missing at around the same time as Ray Perry went into solitary confinement. A large collection of diamonds, that were worth a lot of money, even in those days. What they would be worth today is anyone's guess.'

'Where is this place that seems to have attracted so much attention all of a sudden?'

'It's a small town in Yorkshire, I believe.'

'How did you get to know all this?'

Perkins explained. 'The thing is, a few weeks ago I was right outside the office at the time and just happened to overhear a phone call. Then, a bit later on, when I went into the office, I saw an address written down on a pad. Then after I heard the news about Raymond I got to thinking, I bet all this would interest my friend Mr T, so I came to tell you.'

'You don't happen to remember that address, by any chance?'

'I can do better than that, Mr T' – Freddie passed Thornton a slip of paper – 'I copied it down, see, so I didn't forget. Even got you the postcode.'

'I think you're right, Freddie. That story was worth the money after all.'

There was one other piece of information that Freddie could have passed on, but he thought it better to keep it to himself, for the time being, at least. In a few days he would have the documentary evidence and when he had that, the money he'd just got from Thornton would be chickenfeed compared to what he could earn from the other news.

It is a curious, though well known fact that when people foregather at a bar, they often forget the existence of the person who has just served them drinks. Many professional and personal secrets are leaked out within the hearing of members of the bar staff. Some scandals reach the general public this way, which is probably why journalists are so fond of barmaids. Or at least, that's one of the reasons.

Candy, the barmaid at the club owned by Thornton, had listened to his conversation with Freddie without understanding much of what they were discussing. The names were unfamiliar, the events they referred to had happened before she was born. Nevertheless, she stored them in her memory. One word had stood out, a word that interested Candy greatly. The word was diamonds. Not only that, a fortune in diamonds. Now that was sure to be of interest, Candy thought. Because Candy had her own secret, a boyfriend she adored, much more so than his ex-wife had done. Sadly, even without matrimonial duties standing in his way any longer, Candy could only see him occasionally. The frequency of their meetings was curtailed by the antisocial hours she worked, and also by his duties as a detective in the Metropolitan Police.

Half an hour later, Thornton walked into the upstairs room, where a game of blackjack was in progress. The croupier in charge of the roulette wheel was spinning the ball idly, watching it bounce around the various numbers before settling. There were no punters around the table. Thornton wandered over. 'How do you fancy a holiday?'

The croupier eyed his boss with interest. When Thornton

mentioned a holiday, it usually meant a trip to Spain. He wasn't averse to that – if someone else was paying. And when Thornton went on holiday, he always took the croupier along, not for his expertise with the roulette wheel, but for his other talents. In addition to relieving gamblers of their hard-earned, he also acted as Thornton's minder. It was this talent that led to his nickname.

'Where to?'

'Yorkshire, I've just heard a very interesting story. Apparently there might be a small fortune in diamonds up there, and we might be able to get our hands on them.'

'Whereabouts is it we're going?'

'Some place called Bishops Cross, near Helmsdale.'

'Never heard of it.'

'Neither had I until half an hour ago. Let's just hope the satnav can find it. I want to make an early start in the morning. I'm off now to sort out somewhere to stay and book rooms. Be at my place first thing.'

Thornton stopped at his office where his second in command was watching the CCTV monitors. 'I'm going away for a few days.'

'OK, Mr T. Anything special you want sorting?'

'Better ask someone to fill in on the roulette wheel for a few nights. I'm taking Mr Muscle with me.'

chapter nine

It was late when Candy awoke, as often happened when she'd been at work. Thornton's club stayed open until the last punter had been relieved of his cash in any of the various ways Thornton had devised, either by the exorbitant drinks prices at the bar, the less than favourable odds in the casino or by the services offered by the hostesses in the 'entertainment suite', as Thornton described the private rooms.

Candy wondered about getting up, when her mobile rang. She fumbled on her bedside table for it and grunted something that might have been, 'Hello.'

'Did I wake you?'

'No, but I didn't get home until gone five, so I'm still in bed. What do you want?'

'Apart from you, nothing.'

'That's not fair, saying things like that when I'm here in bed alone and you're miles away.'

'No I'm not.'

'You're not what?'

'Miles away, I'm sitting in my car outside your front door. I was going to ask about coming in, but if you're in need of more sleep, I'll go away.'

'Don't you dare! Hang on a minute while I let you in. If you want coffee, though, you'll have to make your own.'

'I can assure you, coffee was the last thing on my mind.'

'Oh, good.'

Several hours later, Candy woke again. She looked at Detective Sergeant Brian Shaw, who was asleep alongside her. She snuggled up to him, wanting him to wake up. Wanting him. Without opening his eyes, he reached across and pulled her closely and began to nuzzle her neck.

Later, they talked. 'How was work?' he asked.

She knew why he asked what was a fairly mundane question. Thornton had tried to enlist her as one of the hostesses and got quite nasty when she refused. That had been dealt with very smartly, courtesy of the sight of a Metropolitan Police warrant card and the threat of closure of the club.

'Fairly boring,' Candy told him. 'The place is going downhill, I reckon.'

'I thought it was already at rock bottom.'

Candy smiled. 'Maybe, but it doesn't help with Thornton buggering off up north somewhere.'

'What's he done that for? I thought he'd get lost north of the river?'

'It's got something to do with diamonds, although exactly what I can't be sure. I only heard part of the conversation. Bloody customers needed serving.'

'What on earth has Thornton got to do with diamonds?'

'It was something a character called Freddie told him. Thornton must have thought the info was good because he paid Freddie a monkey without whingeing, which is out of character.'

'Five hundred? That's steep. It must have been really good news. Who is this Freddie bloke? Do I know him? Is he one of your regulars?'

'No, I don't think so. I've only seen him in the club a couple of times. Thin-faced little runt, sly manner. He has a nickname, some kind of animal. Weasel? No, that's not it.'

'Freddie the Ferret? He's selling info to Thornton? Wow, what's he got? A death wish?'

'I don't get you. Why is it a death wish?'

'Because Freddie works for Thornton's biggest competitor. And Freddie's bosses won't like it one little bit if they find out. And knowing what I do about the firm Freddie works for, I wouldn't like to be his life insurance company if they do get to hear about it. What exactly did the Ferret say?'

'I only heard bits between serving punters. It was something to do with his boss going to see a bloke somewhere up north, someone who had an accident. Freddie mentions this, and Thornton's mega unimpressed, but then Freddie says something else I didn't catch and then they're talking about diamonds and I could see Thornton was getting a real hard on by the news. Next thing I know he's gone, clutching an address and taking Mr Muscle along for protection.'

'Did you catch the name of the man they were talking about?'

'Berry, I think. Raymond Berry.'

'Not Berry, Perry. Ray Perry?'

Candy nodded.

'That's a real blast from the past and I can see why it would interest Thornton – and Freddie the Ferret's employer. It might also interest my old mate DI Mike Nash.'

'I've had some success,' Clara began. 'Remember, you asked me to try and find out what had happened to Ray Perry's mother? I made some enquiries around the area where the Perry family was based – the local council, Social Services, local charities and even the local branch of Alcoholics Anonymous. They wouldn't tell me anything about their members, naturally, but they put me in touch with a retired pastor who's been very active in helping down-and-outs and homeless people over the years. I spoke with him and he remembered Mrs Perry very well; regarded her as one of his success stories. Contrary to what we suspected, Mrs Perry didn't die of alcoholism. In fact, at around the time of her brother-in-law's murder she went in for a prolonged course of rehabilitation. Once she'd dried out, she spent a long time helping the pastor deal with women in a similar situation, or who had become homeless, or were escaping from an abusive relationship.

'The pastor told me he all but lost contact with her after she joined what he referred to as a "quasi-religious sect". I say all but, because he still receives a Christmas card from her every year. The last one showed a picture of the headquarters of the sect, which, as he remembered it, was based in an old country mansion somewhere in the Scottish borders.

'I rang various local authorities and got lucky. The sect is based in the Kelso area and is known as The Children of the One True Light. I rang them' – Clara grinned – 'and after I'd waited for them to announce their title, I spoke to someone who referred to herself as their almoner. She was quite open, said they didn't believe in hiding anything and that Sister Evangeline, as Mrs Perry is now known, is one of their most respected elders. I asked if it would be possible to speak to her, but was told she was instructing some novices in the ways of the brotherhood and would be tied up for most of the day. I also asked about the possibility of a visit, and was told that was quite permissible. I said I'd ring back after I'd spoken with you.'

'That's extremely good work, Clara, and I've been doing a bit of thinking.' Nash smiled as he heard Mironova groan. 'Let's face it, we're making little or no progress as things stand, with either end of the case, so here's what I suggest. We believe that the same person killed Graham Nattrass and Max Perry, even though there is a quarter of a century gap between the two murders and half the length of the country. At about the time that Nattrass was being killed, Max Perry's nephew Raymond was also being attacked only a few miles away. Conclusion?'

'That all three events were linked, even though we're not sure what the link is.'

'OK. Any ideas?'

'It could be the missing woman, Frankie Da Silva, although I'm not sure in what way she could be connected to Nattrass. Similarly, it could be this talk of diamonds.'

'I don't see how Nattrass could be connected to the diamonds, Clara. He wasn't born at the time, besides which the diamond story is just a rumour.'

'Which leaves the woman.'

'Possibly, but without more fact, more background, we're snookered.'

'That was what Wellings told us, barroom gossip I think he called it, all those years ago.'

'I think we have to try and force things to happen.'

'How?'

'Let's start with background on the people concerned. Begin with Ray and Max Perry. I think we should visit the Children of the

Whatever-Their-Name-Is and interview Sister Angelica, or whatever Ray Perry's mother calls herself these days. If anyone can shed any light on their activities, she can. Besides which, she needs to know what's happened to Ray.'

'Her name's Evangeline. OK, I'll phone for that appointment, shall I?'

'Please, and when Viv gets in ask him to concentrate on Graham Nattrass, find out more about his parents and upbringing. He can make a start on that. It will make a change from his trawl through theatrical agencies, although I'm still hoping that will yield something about the mysterious Frankie Da Silva.'

'And what will you be doing whilst we're busy with that? Nothing, same as usual, or sitting here pretending to think?'

'No, I'm going to go through these files again and then phone my friend Brian in the Met. He might be able to tell us more about what happened to Max Perry's organization after he was murdered. He might also be able to shed some light on what became of the one person involved in all this that we haven't given much thought to.'

'And who might that be?'

'Max Perry's widow, Corinna. It might be interesting to find out where she is and what she's doing these days.'

'You haven't forgotten it's my long weekend and I'm off tomorrow have you? I'm going to visit David; he's got a weekend pass.'

'Of course I haven't forgotten.'

'DS Shaw, please?' Nash identified himself and waited.

After a couple of minutes, he heard, 'Morning, Guv'nor. I was just about to phone you.'

Nash laughed. 'It's a while since anyone called me that.'

'What can I do for you this time?'

'I need some background information, if you can help.'

'Would this have something to do with the Perrys?'

'Yes, I'm trying to piece together the past and present.'

'The odd thing is, I was going to ring you with something that might be relevant. This girl I'm seeing, Candy, she works behind the bar in a club run by a slimeball, name of Thornton. Going back before our time, he used to be apprentice to Dirty Harry Callaghan, took over after Callaghan was killed. Anyway, Candy overheard a conversation during which Perry's name was mentioned. By what she told me, Thornton was being fed a load of info and then he called in one of his hired goons and they shot off up north somewhere. At a guess, I'd say you'll now have the pleasure of their company.'

'Did your girl hear any more? Was there anything mentioned about diamonds?'

This time it was Shaw's turn to be astonished. 'How did you know?'

Nash explained, adding, 'Which leads me to think there might be more than a grain of truth in this old diamond rumour. What I really wanted to know was what had happened to Max Perry's set-up after he was murdered, and where his wife Corinna is nowadays.'

'That's easy. She's shacked up with the guy who's now running Max's old firm.'

'Really? Who is it? Do I know him?'

'I doubt it. He's a fairly unpleasant character; goes by the name of Phil Miller. Nobody knows too much about him, and nobody likes to ask. The odd thing is, Thornton was told Miller and Corinna had headed north before he decided to do the same.'

'Strange how everything points towards these alleged diamonds,' Nash said. 'There's another link with the present day, though, apart from Ray and the supposed diamonds.' Nash explained about the identical MO. 'We wouldn't have made the connection but for the attack on Ray, which caused us to request Max's file as well.'

'Yes, but I thought it was Ray Perry you were interested in? Max was before my time. Ray was, too, come to think about it. I reckon when his Uncle Max was murdered, I'd have still been in kindergarten but I can ask one or two blokes who have been in this division a lot longer than I have. I'll find out what I can and get back to you.'

'Thanks, Brian, that's great.'

'One thing I do know. The guy who was feeding Thornton with

information is braver than he looks. He works in a betting shop run by Phil Miller. If Miller gets to hear he's been passing the news, he'll be very unhappy. And when Phil Miller gets unhappy, somebody usually finishes up getting hurt. Oh, and one other thing, watch out for Thornton's hired hand. Goes by the name of Mr Muscle, but he's more of a deterrent than a detergent.'

Next morning, Nash's Range Rover was already in the car park when Viv arrived. He made two coffees and took them to the office where Nash greeted him, 'Morning, Viv, how did you go on in Netherdale yesterday?'

'It was bloody frustrating, to put it mildly. I went to the register office to get Nattrass's birth certificate, which I thought was going to be quite straightforward. No such luck. As far as they're concerned, Graham Nattrass doesn't exist, and never did.'

'You mean they've no record of his birth?'

'No, and I made sure I'd got my facts right. I took his date of birth from the form he filled in when he applied for the job at the garage, because I thought that's one thing you're never going to get wrong, or forget, and the register office has no record of anyone by the name of Graham Nattrass born on that day.'

'Perhaps he was born elsewhere, in a district covered by another office.'

'No, they checked the records nationwide. Even then there was nothing to show for it.'

'He could have been born abroad, I suppose.'

'That was one thought I had,' Pearce agreed, 'but if I had to guess, I'd rather go for him being adopted.'

Nash stared at him in surprise. 'It's a possibility, but why put that at the top of your list?'

'After I left the register office, I went for a coffee to think it over, and that's when I had the idea. If he was adopted, that would explain the change of name, and also why we couldn't locate him on the births register. So, as I was next door to the council offices, I thought it might be worth asking them to check their adoption records for that and the next couple of years. I thought that would be enough to start with, and then if we didn't get any result from that, we could extend it, because he could have been adopted at any age.'

'Good thinking. Did it pay off? Did you find anything?'

'Absolutely nothing.'

'So, unless he was adopted later, that's another dead end.'

'No, I don't think it is, actually.'

Nash frowned, his expression puzzled. 'Why do you say that?'

'Because when I said I found nothing, I meant there was nothing in their files to find. In fact there were no files to look through.'

'Sorry, Viv, you've lost me. Completely.'

'The files for that period are missing.'

'How do you mean, missing?'

'Missing, as in vanished, disappeared, lost or stolen. Except that I think stolen is the most likely case.'

'What on earth happened?'

'That's what is exercising the so-called brains of the department at the moment. All they were able to tell me is that every adoption file from the year Nattrass was born and the three years afterwards has gone. They reckon there is no way they could have been accidentally lost, or mislaid, so they feel sure they must have been taken deliberately.'

'Have they any evidence? Any sign of a break in?'

'None whatsoever. The only thing they could think of that might have some relevance was a false alarm they had about three weeks ago. Somebody phoned the fire brigade to report a fire in the council offices. The whole building was evacuated whilst the fire brigade checked it out, and it was over an hour before they were allowed back in. The chief reason they remember it,' Viv's tone was sarcastic, 'is that it was pouring down that day and they were all soaked through by the time they got back inside. Actually, I remembered the incident once they mentioned it, because the fire department turned out a couple of appliances and a raft of men, for what turned out to be a hoax. Some of the men were furious.'

'And you reckon the phoney alarm call was designed to give the thief time to remove those files whilst he was sure to be undisturbed? How would he get in, though, if everyone was being kept outside?'

'He could have stayed hidden in the building or gone in dressed as a fireman. And if that was the case, who would challenge him?'

'That sounds feasible,' Nash agreed after a moment's thought. 'But it does mean we're at a dead end as far as Nattrass is concerned, at least for the time being. It might change if we are able to find out what his original name was, but at the moment I can't see how we could do that. Better go back to trawling through the theatrical agencies and see if you have any more luck tracing the mysterious Frankie Da Silva.'

It wasn't until late that afternoon that Nash's sense of frustration lifted, and then only marginally. Pearce came into his office bearing a mug of coffee and news that Nash hoped signalled the beginning of a change in their fortune. 'I've managed to locate Frankie Da Silva's agent,' Viv told him. 'Luckily, the receptionist at the agency has been there over thirty years, and remembers not only all their clients, but which particular agent handled them. The bloke who handled Frankie has retired now. He lives in Chichester, and when I rang him he was really helpful' – Pearce grinned – 'once I could get him off the subject of gardening.'

'Did he come up with anything useful?'

'Yes, he remembers Frankie well. He reckoned she had potential for a big showbiz career and it was one of the biggest disappointments of his time as an agent when Frankie told him she'd decided to quit.'

'So she didn't simply vanish without informing him, then?'

'Not according to him. He said she went in to see him, he wasn't able to recall the date, but said she told him that she had decided to retire because her circumstances had changed.'

'What did he think she meant by that?'

'He said she didn't exactly spell it out, but he got the impression it had something to do with Ray Perry. I got the feeling he didn't like Perry much, possibly because he thought Ray was taking away a rich future source of income. He told me Frankie had been working at one of those dinner-cum-cabaret spots. She was on a rolling engagement there and apparently the management were quite peeved when she decided to leave.'

'I don't suppose the agent kept her file, by any chance? We

couldn't be that lucky.' Nash's despondent tone reflected their lack of progress.

'He didn't need to.' Pearce smiled and tapped his temple. 'It's all in there. He recited everything he knew, even down to her last address. I know it's correct because I checked Ray Perry's charge sheet, and he'd got it, spot on.'

'Did he tell you her real name, or was that asking too much?'

'No, he remembered that too, pretty much. Like us, he thought her name was too exotic to be real; invented for her stage career. But apparently, when he challenged her about it, she proved it. The agency insists that all their prospective clients fill in a biography, with next of kin and so forth, and when he told Frankie he didn't believe her, she produced some document, passport, driving licence, he wasn't sure which, that proved it to be correct.'

'That should make her easy to trace; there can't be that many people called Da Silva around.'

'It was her Christian name he had a problem with. He said Frankie wasn't exactly correct. Everyone called her that, but her proper name was longer. Like Mike and Michael, I suppose.'

'I get you. So her real name could be something like Francine, or Françoise?'

'That sort of thing, certainly, although I tried both of them on him and he said they weren't right.'

'Nevertheless, the fact that he was able to confirm her surname is a start. Did he know where she came from? Before she moved to London, I mean? Although I suppose she could have been from London all along.'

'No, the only information he had was a London address, even before she and Ray Perry moved in together. Where she came from originally, he'd no idea.'

chapter ten

With the intervening weekend, it was Monday before Mironova returned to work. 'Do you want to bring me up to date with what's happened whilst I've been away?' she asked Nash.

'That won't take long,' he muttered. He related the curious tale of the missing adoption papers, and then gave her details of Pearce's success with the agent. When he'd finished, Clara sat for a few moments in silence.

'What are you thinking about?' Nash asked.

'I'm not sure. I was trying to look at what Viv was told, viewing it from a woman's perspective, and it doesn't seem right.'

'What doesn't seem right?'

'We were told that Frankie was allegedly going to run off with Callaghan, but if that was true, the last thing she'd do is tell her agent and the management of the place where she was working that she was quitting. That would be inviting all sorts of trouble if word got back to Ray Perry.'

'Perhaps she did, and Ray actually did murder Callaghan.'

Clara shook her head. 'No, that's wrong. A woman wouldn't think or act like that, especially if she was cheating on her partner, given that he had a reputation for violence. There had to be some other reason.'

'Any idea what that might be?'

'I can think of two possibilities. Either because she had decided to get married, or—'

Nash caught on quickly. 'Or because she was pregnant?'

'Exactly, and of the two, I'd go for the latter as being the more likely explanation. Women don't stop working simply because they've got married, but they do when they're going to have a baby.'

'If your theory is accurate, that means all our previous ideas about Frankie, and all we were told about her, are wrong. Is that what you think?'

Clara nodded. 'No way would she consider eloping, unless the child wasn't Ray's. All her thoughts would be about protecting her baby.'

'Maybe that's what happened. Maybe she got pregnant by Callaghan, and that gave them reason to run off, to get out of Perry's reach. But Ray got to him first.'

'I still don't buy it. If Ray wasn't the father, she'd certainly not have told her agent or the place where she was working. That would be close to suicidal.'

'That story of the diamonds is also less credible now. For much the same reason. If she was intending to nick a fortune in precious gems, she wouldn't want to give anyone a clue beforehand. Which puts us back to square one. I think when we do visit Sister Evangeline to tell her about Ray we should try to get some information from her.'

'She might be too upset to be of any real help.'

'I don't think so. Women are surprisingly resilient, even when faced with the worst possible news.'

The caller display on Margaret Fawcett's phone simply read INTL. Margaret knew only one person who would be ringing her from abroad.

'Hi, Mom, how ya doin'?'

The accent was passable American, but Margaret knew better. 'Hi, Tina, darling. How are things in the land of the free?'

'Pretty busy at the moment,' Christina abandoned her transatlantic twang. She'd been called Tina since her first day at pre-school nursery, and in the end even her mother had adopted the shortened version.

'The good news is that we've made really good headway towards finishing the contract,' Tina continued. 'In fact, if the next few days' work and the testing go OK, we should be finished and I could be back home in a week.'

'You mean home, as in home for good?'

'Yep, apart from an annual visit to install more systems and a bit of maintenance, that's it.'

'That's terrific. Oh, damn.'

'What's wrong, Mum?'

'I've booked a continental coach tour starting next week. I'll have to cancel it.'

'Don't be daft; you'll do no such thing. It's been nearly two years; a few more days won't matter. I'll be fine at home on my own. I can take care of myself, you know.'

Margaret did know. Tina always had been self-sufficient, independent; at times wayward. She listened, and although it took some time to persuade her, eventually Margaret agreed to continue with her planned excursion. Tina's deciding argument was that the money Margaret had paid would probably be lost if she cancelled now.

'How will you go on for transport? Getting food and things? You can't go using taxis, and there's only one bus a week into Helmsdale. My car will be here in the garage.'

'That's all right, Mum. I'm not covered to drive yours anyway. The firm will pay for a rental car. It'll be waiting for me to collect at the airport.'

'That sounds very extravagant.'

'Mum, that's the way it works. Since I've been out here, all my hotel bills, food and transport have all been on expenses. The only things I've paid for are clothing and having my hair done. Right now I'm ringing on my cell phone, but the company is picking up the tab.'

'I'll leave a set of keys next door, shall I? That way you'll be able to get in whenever you arrive. He never goes anywhere. Not during daylight hours, anyway.'

Margaret smiled as she put the phone down. Tina had said 'rental car' and 'cell phone', very American. It was time she returned home.

Nash had gone through to Netherdale when Ramirez phoned Helmsdale. Mironova took the call. 'What can I do for you,

Professor?' As soon as she asked the question, she realized that she had laid herself open to the sort of innuendo Mexican Pete thought amusing, but it appeared he was in business mode. 'I've been going through that file again, the one Nash asked me to look at,' he told her.

'Was that the Max Perry murder case?'

'That's right, and I believe I have something that might be significant. It's to do with the place where Perry's body was found. It was an old railway arch that he had rented and used as a lock-up. At some time in its history, the place had been whitewashed. Over time, with the vibration from the trains constantly passing overhead, some of that dried whitewash would have flaked off, and dropped from the roof. Bear in mind we're talking really small fragments here. When the pathologist conducted the post-mortem, they found minute traces of the whitewash on the body.'

'OK, I follow that,' Clara wondered where this was leading.

'What they didn't pick up on at the time, and I confess it escaped me when I first read the file, was that a substantial amount of the whitewash they recovered had found its way into Perry's wounds.'

'How is that significant?'

'I'm not saying it is, only that it might be. What it suggests is that Perry was held captive there for some time before he was killed, probably before he was tortured, even.'

'I see, thanks, Professor. I'll be sure to let Mike know.'

After lunch when Nash returned, and entered his office, his phone was ringing. The caller was Brian Shaw. 'I had a word with my boss. He's been here since charge sheets were written in Latin, so he knows all there is to know about some of our more distinguished citizens.'

Nash smiled at Shaw's sarcasm, and listened with interest to what he had to report.

'Here's what my governor says about Phil Miller. This is more or less word for word, right? "He's a slimy character, good with numbers. Miller's been suspected of being behind a lot of computer-based crime. You know the sort of thing, spoof letters in imperfect English from Nigeria purporting to be from someone with millions to dispose of. Just give us your bank details and we'll empty your account. Phil Miller's a pure money-making machine. All business, highly successful and totally devoid of scruples. He appeared some time after Max Perry was killed, took over his business empire having moved into Corinna Perry's bed. If ever a man shagged his way to the top, it was Phil Miller. He wasn't even on the radar beforehand."'

'Did your boss say where Miller appeared from?'

'I asked him if anyone knows anything about his background, and he said, "Miller goes out of his way to discourage anyone from getting too close or asking indiscreet questions. He emerged from the shadows and very quickly took control of Max Perry's organization. It was after that he moved in and tried to annex part of Callaghan's old operation."'

'What happened, then, did he say?'

'He told me Miller came up against Callaghan's replacement. Apparently, Callaghan had been grooming him to succeed when he retired. That's the man I told you about, Trevor Thornton. My boss agreed with my opinion of Thornton; as nasty a piece of work as you could come across. The clubs Thornton runs are a one-stop shopping experience for every kind of vice you can think of. Gambling, nightclubs, drugs, booze, prostitutes, both his and hers, you name it, Trevor supplies it. At a cost, of course. Anyway, rumour was he and Miller cut a deal so the big turf war everyone was anticipating never took place.

'One thing you should be aware of, if only to show how things have changed. Although Max Perry was never involved in the drugs trade, Phil Miller goes in for it in a big way. We've never had sufficient on him to put him away; witnesses tend to get amnesia. You know how it works. It's a bloody shame, because if we could put him out of circulation I reckon we could roll up a good percentage of the drugs trade in the area. He lives part of the time in Spain. Got a ruddy great palace of a house near Marbella.'

'Anything else I should know?'

'Only a word of advice. If you're planning on going near him – don't! But if you have to, watch your back and those of everyone around you. He doesn't deal kindly with anyone who crosses him. There are one or two women down here who are still wondering if they're widows or not because their husbands upset Phil Miller.'

'If it comes to it, I'm really looking forward to meeting him.'

Nash could almost see Shaw's grin as the DI replied, 'I didn't think that would faze you much. All I'm saying is be extremely careful.'

'Thanks, Brian, that's been very useful.'

After Shaw rang off, Nash told Mironova what he'd learned. 'Which more or less confirms what Wellings told us,' she responded after he finished. 'This Miller character sounds really unpleasant, and the other guy, Thornton, doesn't sound much better. By the way, I'd a call from Mexican Pete whilst you were out.'

She reported what the pathologist had told her. 'What do you make of that?' Nash asked.

'I had a look at the file. I wondered if they tortured Max to get the combination of a safe or something from him. If that was the case, they'd be desperate to keep him alive until they'd got it.'

'If they succeeded and got hold of the diamonds, that wouldn't explain why people are running around frantically looking for them now,' Nash pointed out.

'Oh, no, I hadn't thought of that. Why now?'

'Sorry?'

'Why have those diamonds suddenly become so important, if that truly is the reason for these crimes? According to what your pal in the Met told you, Miller doesn't need the money, hasn't needed it for years by the sound of things. Admittedly, all criminals of his sort are greedy, but that sort of greed wouldn't wait a quarter of a century, either.'

'I don't honestly know. Perhaps it was to do with Ray Perry being released from prison.'

'But if he's been locked away all this time, he wouldn't know where they are. Unless he hid them, in which case why try to murder him? You'd be more likely to want to capture him and torture him for the information. Besides which, I can't remember the exact dates, but wasn't Ray Perry arrested soon after his Uncle Max was killed? He'd hardly have had time to stash the diamonds away somewhere that would remain safe for twenty-five years.'

'All very valid points, Clara. And they illustrate the difficulty of looking into events that occurred such a long time ago. Scratch Ray Perry as the catalyst then, but speaking of him, have you had any success raising Sister Evangeline?'

'No, she was giving a lecture this morning. I've to call back later this afternoon.'

'What on, water divining as a source of prayer?'

'I don't think you're treating the pious community with the reverence you should,' Clara told him.

Shortly before he left for the day, she reported progress. 'We can visit Sister Evangeline the day after tomorrow, if that's convenient.'

'Good, that will give me time to prepare myself. I'll take you along, to ensure I'm on my best behaviour. Do me a favour beforehand, will you? Get me a couple of phone numbers. One for Northumbria Police, and one for the Freeman Hospital in Newcastle.'

Margaret glanced at the clock for the fifth, or was it the sixth time in as many minutes. She checked her handbag again, making sure her passport was inside, and that she hadn't forgotten the euros and traveller's cheques she'd collected from the bank. It was the fourth time she'd done that. Then she walked through to the kitchen, and read through the various post-it notes she'd left for Christina on the work surfaces, the fridge-freezer and the larder cupboard door. She made certain she'd written the milkman and newsagent's phone numbers down correctly, together with those for the greengrocer and butcher, who each had vans that delivered in the village.

She walked back into the lounge and her gaze went automatically to the photo on the mantelpiece. It had been taken several years ago when Christina had graduated from university. In the photo, Margaret and Christina had been standing together outside the imposing edifice of Durham Cathedral. Those few people, neighbours or tradesmen who had seen the photo on her fireplace commented on the likeness between them, but Margaret knew she had never been as lovely as Christina. Margaret was by no means an ugly sister, but she was nowhere near as stunning, as head-turning as Christina, or for that matter. . . . She shook her head at a distant memory.

Her suitcase was positioned ready, close to the front door. She fiddled with the labels, making sure they were firmly attached.

She ran through everything she'd packed, making sure she hadn't missed anything. She'd checked everything off against her list as she'd put it in the case, but in her mounting excitement, that fact had slipped her mind.

Although she was looking forward to the trip, Margaret still had reservations about leaving Christina alone at the cottage. She dismissed these altogether. All the neighbours knew Christina would be there, and what possible harm could befall her in this village, of all places, a village where nothing ever happened? After all, Christina had just spent over two years in America without coming to any harm, and that was a far more dangerous, violent place.

A car had pulled up opposite her cottage. Not her taxi. She frowned then saw the driver struggling with a map. She smiled fleetingly; tourists were forever getting lost round here. Part of that was down to the youths of the village, whose favourite sport was turning the arms of the signposts round. Any other time, she'd have gone out and offered assistance, but she'd more important things on her mind.

A taxi drew to a halt right outside her front gate. This was it, then, the start of her big adventure. The front door led straight from her lounge onto the front path, via a small wooden porch. She waved to the taxi driver and lifted her case over the threshold then returned to collect her handbag, casting a final look round. She'd locked the back door already. There was only the front door to lock; then she was off. There was absolutely nothing to worry about.

Her driver had already loaded her case into the boot of the taxi and was holding the back door open for her. In the periphery of her vision she noticed the driver of the other car still struggling with his map reading. She felt a brief pang of sympathy, then as she climbed into the back seat of her taxi she forgot all about him.

Phil Miller, the man classified by Margaret as a tourist, was far from being lost. He watched her departure out of the corner of his eye as he pretended to study the road map. The suitcase interested him. If the woman was going to be away, and by the look of the case it seemed her trip might be a prolonged one, well that suited him just fine.

He followed the taxi at a discreet distance. When they reached Helmsdale he watched Margaret transfer into the waiting coach emblazoned with the legend, British and Continental Tours. As soon as the vehicle pulled off the cobbled market square he got out of his car and walked across to the coach company's office.

'I wanted to have a word with a friend of mine. I think she's leaving on one of your coach trips this afternoon. Can you help me, or have I missed her?'

The receptionist adopted a sympathetic expression. Silly sod, she thought, leaving it to the last minute. Aloud, she told him, 'I'm sorry, I'm afraid it's just left. I can contact the vehicle and speak to the tour guide if it's extremely urgent.'

'No, it's not vital. Nothing that won't keep. How long is she going to be away for, can you tell me?'

'It's our regular fifteen-day tour of the capital cities of Europe.' The receptionist indicated the large poster on the wall behind her desk. 'Are you sure you don't want me to ring the coach? I can have a message passed to your friend.'

'No, not to worry. I'll see her when she gets back.'

He drove slowly back to the cottage he'd rented. The woman's holiday meant he could change his plans. With her away for over two weeks there was no reason to rush the job. He picked up his mobile.

'How did it go?' Corinna asked.

He smiled triumphantly. 'Found her! And she's just gone away. She'll be gone a couple of weeks. We can get into her house dead easy and search it together. With two of us looking, the job will be much easier.'

'Are you sure this is the right one?'

'Yeah, has to be. There's only a couple in that dead-and-alive hole fit the age group, and one of them is a carrot top. This one's just right. Apart from anything else, she even looks a bit like the other one. Or how she might look these days.'

'And there's no one else at her place?'

'No, I told you. Besides, I saw the way she locked up before she left. No way you'd do that if there was someone else inside.'

chapter eleven

The first leg of the journey to Kelso was conducted for the most part in silence. Clara's brief, once they were clear of more familiar territory, was simply to give directions. 'Why don't you get satnav?' she asked, as she stared at the road atlas.

Nash shrugged. 'Never got round to it. About the only distance I travel these days is to Harrogate, ferrying Daniel to and fro, or to France to the cottage there and I know those routes off by heart.'

With little else to do but stare at the passing countryside, Clara speculated as to what their interviewee would be like. It was uncertain how badly the long-term alcohol dependency had affected her, and there was the risk that they would have undertaken a long journey for nothing. Nash, whilst concentrating on driving, was also mulling over the way the case had gone, the forthcoming meeting and the questions he wanted to ask Mrs Perry, or Sister Evangeline as she was now known. He wondered briefly what the sect she'd joined was like. From Clara's telephone conversations with them, it seemed they were more open than he'd expected, even being receptive to a visit to their community.

Once they'd cleared the industrial sprawl of Newcastle and were heading towards the Scottish border, Nash asked Clara to keep her eyes open for somewhere to stop for lunch. 'After we've eaten, you can drive for the rest of the way.'

It was almost twenty minutes later that Clara told him to pull in at a roadside café. Once they'd parked up, Nash asked why she'd picked this particular establishment. 'You let me drive past three similar places in the last twenty miles. What was wrong with them?'

Clara pointed towards the line of heavy goods vehicles in the lorry park. 'All the other cafés had no wagons outside. Truckers always know where to go for the best food and value for money.'

'Smart thinking.'

Her theory was proved correct. They emerged half an hour later, well content, and with Nash's wallet escaping relatively unscathed. 'I reckon we've only about another hour's driving ahead of us,' Clara told him as they rejoined the carriageway.

It wasn't far from her estimate when they slowed outside the grounds of the sect's headquarters. The building was old, but time had enhanced its beauty rather than diminished it. Once, Nash thought, this would have been a substantial residence for a family of considerable affluence. He wondered briefly what they would have made of the current occupants. Built on four storeys, the Georgian façade of the house sat astride the end of a long, arrow-straight drive. The double wrought-iron gates were wide open. Clara edged slowly onto the drive. No one emerged from the lodge to challenge them, so she accelerated gently between the lines of tall, graceful poplar trees that stood like sentinels on either side of the drive. Interspersed between the trees were huge banks of hydrangeas that provided a riotous, colourful display of blooms.

At the end of the drive they stopped near to the massive studded-oak front door. Emerging a trifle stiffly from the car, Nash heard a voice behind them. 'Good afternoon, brother and sister.'

They turned, to see a venerable figure in a long smock leaning on a Dutch hoe close to one of the flower beds. The man was tall, unbent despite his age, his plentiful white hair paling into insignificance against his long, flowing beard. Clara, who enjoyed Tolkien's epic trilogy, was reminded of Gandalf, or Saruman.

'I'm Brother Gabriel, the principal elder of this establishment. I believe you must be the visitors Sister Evangeline is expecting. Forgive me for not joining you, but as you can see, I have a considerable task tending these gardens. Please go on inside. Sister Evangeline will be waiting.'

The door opened onto a large hall with a wide staircase to one side rising towards the upper floors. A woman walked down the hall towards him. 'Sister Evangeline' – Nash thrust out his hand – 'I'm Detective Inspector Nash, Mike Nash. And this is my colleague, who you spoke to on the phone, Detective Sergeant Mironova.'

The woman smiled. 'I rather assumed so,' she replied dryly.

Nash assessed Raymond Perry's mother and was secretly amused to notice that the older woman was doing the same to him. Her face was lined with either sadness or age; her colour, however, was good, and her eyes, dark pools so deep a brown as to appear almost black, reflected as much joy as unhappiness. Her handshake was firm, her voice strong and clear. Sister Evangeline gestured to one of the multi-seat sofas that lined one wall. 'Shall we sit down? I've arranged for refreshments to be brought to us after your journey.'

Nash asked if she'd mind answering some questions.

'Oh, I think I should.' She smiled. 'It would be an awful waste, coming all this way to sit in silence drinking tea, don't you agree?'

'All right,' he admitted, 'it was a stupid thing to say. No more platitudes.' He glanced at Clara, for support. 'But first,' Nash continued, 'I want you to prepare yourself for a shock. I'm afraid I've some distressing news for you.'

Nash went on to explain what had happened to Ray. Sister Evangeline sat clutching a handkerchief, tears coursing down her cheeks. Clara comforted the older woman as Nash sat quietly waiting for the initial shock to subside and refilled her cup. Evangeline accepted it with trembling hands. 'I can't believe it,' she sighed. 'You're sure he's going to be all right? He will survive?'

'I spoke to the specialist yesterday, and he assures me he is out of danger. What they're less sure of is whether there will be any brain damage, and they won't know for certain until he comes out of the coma.' Nash waited for Evangeline to recover her composure before continuing. 'I'd like to take you back to what happened before Raymond went to prison.'

'You may want to take me,' she retorted, 'but there's no saying I want to go with you. What has this got to do with things that happened a quarter of a century ago?'

'We believe current events may be connected to what went on back then,' he insisted, 'even though we're still not certain exactly how. Any information you can supply will be extremely helpful.'

The woman nodded. 'Very well, but that was during what I call my dark period. My disease was at its worst then. I have little memory of that time. But ask your questions anyway. I will do my best.'

'When did you last see Raymond? Can you remember that?'

She paused for only a second before answering. 'It was after my brother-in-law was murdered. Not long after, I think, because Raymond was arrested soon after that. I remember he was very upset about something. Upset and,' she paused, 'excited, I think. No, not excited, that's the wrong word. Agitated, yes, he was very agitated.'

'Do you know what about? His uncle's death, perhaps?'

A shadow passed over Evangeline's face. 'No!' Nash was surprised by the sharpness of her tone. 'It was something else, but I can't remember whether he told me or not. He might have said something.' Her voice sank to a barely audible murmur as she strug-gled with her memory. 'Yes' – her voice rose again with the triumph of her memory search – 'he definitely started to say something, but then he stopped. Almost as soon as he began. I can picture him now. He held my hands' – she glanced down at her lap – 'he said he couldn't tell me. That it wouldn't be fair. And something else . . ..'

She raised her eyes to the ceiling, as if seeking guidance. 'He said,' she spoke slowly now, 'that although there was a lot he wanted to tell me, he couldn't bring himself to do it. That's right; he couldn't bring himself to do it, because if he told me he'd be putting me in great danger.'

'Can you guess what it was he wanted to tell you?'

'After he'd been arrested, I assumed he had intended to tell me what he was about to do.' She shrugged; a gesture of helplessness for what had passed. 'But I could have been wrong. Like I said, I wasn't capable of much in the way of rational thought in those days.' She looked at Nash, her gaze piercing. 'Are you suggesting it was something else?'

'I'm not sure,' Nash hedged, but knew he hadn't lied; he wasn't sure. 'Can you remember his exact words? Before he changed his mind, I mean. Before he stopped and said it was too dangerous.'

'He started to say something about Frankie.' Nash saw her face change, saw the smile cross her features. 'Yes, that was it. He was going to tell me something about Frankie. Do you know something, Mr Nash? I've never thought about that conversation in all these years. But now you've prompted me I can remember it like it was yesterday. He said, "Mum, I want you to know that Frankie—" that was when he stopped. And I still don't know what he was going to tell me.'

'I think I do,' Nash told her, 'but we'll get to that shortly. You liked Frankie, didn't you?'

'Oh yes, she was a lovely girl. Not only her looks, which were quite spectacular. But she cared for people. Genuinely cared for them, I mean. And she was good for Raymond. Frankie was just what he needed. She was starting to undo all the harm that had been done to him after—' she stopped suddenly. 'After his father died.' A single tear ran down her cheek.

'She ran away,' Evangeline's voice changed again, and it was as if she was repeating something she'd learned off by heart. 'She ran away. That's what they told me. "Frankie's run away". Every time I asked, they told me that. Time after time, the same answer.'

She stopped speaking and stared straight ahead of her, lost in her own world, in the past, in the depths of her alcoholism.

'Tell me about Max.' Nash's demand broke the spell. He almost recoiled at the change in Evangeline's expression; the benevolence replaced with venom.

'Max,' she spoke slowly, every word enunciated with hatred, 'was an evil, conniving, scheming bastard. God forgive me for saying such a thing, but he is the one man who really deserves that title. Max was responsible for everything bad that Raymond became; every crime he committed. Max, and me, I'm ashamed to admit. If Jimmy hadn't been killed it would all have turned out different. It is a dreadful thing to lose your husband and your son at the same time, Mr Nash, but that's what happened to me.'

'Jimmy was your husband, Raymond's father?'

She nodded. 'Jimmy was Max's older brother. He felt he ought to look after him. So every time Max got into trouble, he turned to Jimmy for help. That was often, I can tell you. I used to argue with

Jimmy about it, but it did no good. Then, when Jimmy died, I lost it completely. Went to pieces, in a massive way. That was when Max took over. He took Raymond from me. Gave me money instead. That was what I wanted, what I needed. Not a small boy. How could I care for a small boy when I was no longer capable of looking after myself? So Max took Raymond and I got the money to spend on alcohol to make myself worse. Money to keep me drunk and keep me away from my son. That way he could get on with corrupting Raymond, teaching the boy his own wicked ways. Max Perry was about as evil a man as I've ever met. We were all right until Max came along and Jimmy fell soft; fell for his hard-luck story and took him into partnership in the scrapyard. Before I knew what was happening, I'd lost everything. My husband, my son, my house, our business. Max took the lot.'

'How did your husband die?'

'It was an accident; so they said. Some accident, I don't think! It was at the yard. They used to stack cars one on top of the other waiting for the crane to put them in the crusher. A stack of cars slipped and came down on top of Jimmy. That's the official version. Those that wanted to believed it. As if Jimmy would be that careless.'

'You said Jimmy took Max into partnership? I take it Max wasn't involved in the business from the start, then?'

'No way, Jimmy built that business up from scratch. Started with a handcart and worked up from there. Max was still harbouring dreams of becoming a great entertainer. The only thing he was good for on the stage was sweeping it.'

'Max was on stage? Doing what?'

'He was an impersonator. Toured the country, but the variety clubs were dying and by the sound of it he wasn't anything special. Good, but not that good. Gradually the bookings dropped off, and that was when Jimmy offered him a way out.'

'So' – Nash switched tack – 'you've no idea what happened to Frankie? No idea what it was that Raymond was going to tell you before he changed his mind?'

Evangeline shook her head.

'Could it have been,' Nash continued, 'that he was about to tell

112

you that Frankie was pregnant?'

Her eyes had been lowered, but at Nash's question she raised them and stared at him in surprise. 'Pregnant?' She thought for a moment. 'I suppose he might have been going to tell me that. But what makes you ask that? And why would that be dangerous for me to hear?'

'I'm not sure that was the dangerous part. Did he say anything else, anything at all?'

'There was something.' A long silence followed whilst Sister Evangeline struggled to remember. Eventually, she raised her head, memory triumphing. 'He said that whatever happened, I hadn't to try and contact him until it was all over. No visits, no phone calls, nothing. At the time, I assumed he meant at the flat, then after he was arrested, I thought he meant in prison.'

'When he said "until it was all over" what do you think he meant by that?'

'I'd no idea, so I asked him. I said, "What do you mean, Ray? What's going on? Until what's all over"? At that point, I'm not sure if I'd even heard of Max's murder.'

'And can you remember his reply?'

'He said it was better that I shouldn't know, then I couldn't be coerced into saying anything. He said, "It's all about the blood. . . ." Those were his words, but he was going to add something else, I'm sure. At the time, once I heard of that man Callaghan's death and that Ray had been arrested for it, I thought he must have meant the blood feud that had been caused by Callaghan murdering Max.'

'There was another rumour going around at the time, apparently,' Clara said, her first contribution to the interview. 'It was about Frankie and Callaghan. Apparently, from what we were told, there was a lot of gossip that they might have been having an affair. Could that be why Frankie ran away? Might she have been carrying Callaghan's baby, not Ray's?'

To the astonishment of both detectives, Evangeline began to laugh, a rich, earthy chuckle.

'Sorry, did I say something funny?' Clara asked.

'Yes, you certainly did, but you weren't to know any better.' Sister Evangeline paused for a moment. 'And I can see how that rumour might have got about, or at least originated.' She saw Nash and Mironova exchange puzzled glances and explained. 'The block of flats where Frankie lived was owned by her agent, and let for the most part to his own clients. I visited Frankie there several times, and on one occasion, I saw Callaghan, who I knew slightly, going into the building. I asked Frankie what he was doing there and she told me. Callaghan was having an affair, but not with Frankie. He was having the affair with a dancer who lived in the flat opposite hers.'

'Can you remember what she was called? The dancer, I mean,' Nash asked.

'I think the name was Charles, but I may be wrong.' Sister Evangeline's tone was dry.

'Charles? You mean Callaghan was. . .?'

'Musical, I think the theatrical expression was. Gay, is what I believe is now the more acceptable term.'

'Good heavens! Why didn't that ever come to light?' Clara asked.

'Reputation,' Evangeline told her laconically. 'With a reputation as a hard man to maintain, that was hardly the sort of thing Callaghan would want his enemies to find out. Admittedly, he wouldn't have been the first gangland figure to have such tastes, but the others generated such fear nobody dared mock them for it.'

'You're talking about the notorious twins, I assume?' Nash stated.

'That's right, however, one thing I can tell you for certain, if Ray did kill Callaghan, then jealousy over Frankie certainly wasn't the motive. Now, I've answered a lot of questions about things that happened a long time ago. I think it's time you answered some of mine, about things that are going on now.'

It was over an hour later when Nash's car pulled away from the grounds of the religious order, but instead of returning the way they had come, Nash followed Clara's directions, setting them on course for Newcastle.

Trevor Thornton leaned across the driver and peered down the lane towards the holiday cottage. 'That's it, down that track. Stop the car here. That place is a bit of a comedown for Lady High and Mighty

Corinna,' he muttered. 'There's one of the cars parked outside. Drive round that bend and see if there's a place to stop where we can't be seen from the house.'

Mr Muscle drove slowly for the fifty yards that took them behind a small copse. Thornton pointed to a small gravel area to one side of the road. 'Perfect, pull in there.' His henchman swung the Mercedes off the tarmac, the vehicle bumping over the uneven surface before coming to a halt, shielded from view by the trees' summer foliage. 'Stay there,' Thornton instructed him. 'I'm going to take a dekko.'

Mr Muscle watched with some amusement as Thornton struggled to climb over the post and rail fence that surrounded the small strip of woodland. His small, rotund frame and short, plump legs were hardly suited for such athletic activity.

Not without difficulty, Thornton made it and paused, panting slightly from the unaccustomed exertion. Now he was faced with another, even trickier obstacle. From a distance, the trees had looked to be easy to walk through. It was only when Thornton inspected the terrain close to that he found his way barred by a dense patch of briar and bramble that had grown over the years to almost head height, especially for someone as vertically challenged as Mr T.

After some minutes, Thornton spotted a gap in the undergrowth, or rather a small area where the vegetation wasn't quite as thick. He forced his way through this, at the cost of several scratches on his hands, his neck and his cheek, and was rewarded when he reached the edge of the wood with an uninterrupted view. Across the field, in which were a surprisingly large number of sheep, Thornton could see directly into the cottage windows, but although he watched for some considerable time, spotted no sign of life. From this distance, it was impossible for him to gauge how easy it would be to enter the property. Going closer was not an option, not until they were ready to act. What he needed was to take another look. But in order to do that, he would need a pair of binoculars. And possibly a pair of gloves.

chapter twelve

'Shaw!'

The DS looked up. 'Yes, Guv'nor?'

'My office, now.'

Shaw followed his superior into the glass-walled cubicle in the corner of the main CID room. There was already one occupant, a young man of little more than twenty years of age, or so Shaw guessed.

'Last week, when you were asking for all that info about Max and Ray Perry and their organization, what prompted it?' Shaw's boss asked.

'It wasn't for me. I had a phone call from DI Nash in North Yorkshire. He wanted as much background as we had.'

'Mike Nash? Why is he interested in them? Is he doing a degree in modern history or something?'

Shaw smiled. He glanced across at the third occupant before replying. The meaning of the look wasn't lost on Shaw's superior. He apologized and introduced the young man, adding, 'I'd better explain.'

After he told Shaw of the reason for the young man's presence, he continued, 'After we spoke last week I was talking to our commander and happened to mention that you and I had been discussing Max Perry. I only said it because I knew he was marginally involved in investigating some of the crimes being committed by the various gangs around that time. He told me that this gentleman' – he indicated the young man – 'had been to see him about six months ago, but they were unable to act on the information he gave back then. However, he thought it worthwhile asking him to come and visit us, so that we can hear his tale, although even now I'm not sure whether there is much we can do about what he has to say.' The DCI nodded to the young man, 'Please tell DS Shaw what you told me.'

Shaw listened carefully and went on to explain what he had been told about Thornton's sudden departure to Yorkshire in search of diamonds.

'It seems as if things have kicked off again,' the DCI said, summing up, 'although why that has happened now is as much of a mystery as what happened back then. I think for the time being the best thing to do is for you to let Nash know about all this. It may be of some help to him, even if at the present moment I can't for the life of me think how.'

Shaw rang the Helmsdale number, only to be told that Nash was out with his DS and wasn't expected back until the following day. Shaw left a message for Nash to ring him back. The news he had for him was over a quarter of a century old. Another twenty-four hours wasn't going to make any difference.

Next morning, Sergeant Binns handed Nash a note. 'This came in yesterday whilst you and Clara were sightseeing in the borders,' Binns told him.

'It was hardly sightseeing; we were interviewing a witness,' Nash told him severely. 'In CID we're kept far too busy to waste time sightseeing, or doing sudoku puzzles,' he added, staring pointedly at the open paper half-hidden by a folder on Binns' desk.

As Nash walked away he was joined by Mironova. She studied the note he passed her. 'What do you reckon this is about?' she asked. 'It's only a few days since you spoke to Shaw, isn't it? I wonder what's happened since then?'

'We'll soon found out.' Nash dialled the number and switched on the speaker so Mironova could hear both sides of the conversation. 'Brian, it's Mike Nash. I've DS Mironova with me. Sorry we were out yesterday.'

'First off, Mike, my governor has been doing a bit of digging around and talked to one or two people here who know more about the Perry family, and he's come up with a lot more background. You may know a lot of this already, but some of it could be new, and there could be bits of it that are particularly relevant in the light of what happened yesterday.

'Going back to the time just before Max Perry was murdered, from what we could gather he was already losing a lot of power and influence. The competition was fierce, especially from Callaghan's mob and the triads, who were just beginning to flex their muscles. Both lots were better financed, because they were dealing in things Perry wouldn't touch. Matters didn't begin to improve until a while after Max's death, and it was Phil Miller who started to turn the gang's fortunes around. He disposed of the competition and began dealing in more lucrative products. He virtually took over the drugs trade in certain areas, as well as becoming heavily involved in the protection racket and providing a stable of high-class call girls. The cash flow from these operations and the influence that could be exerted by many of the call girls' clients made him immune from prosecution.'

'What does that mean?' Clara asked.

'It means that Miller was able to buy or obtain the best legal advice,' Shaw replied. 'I'm referring to the best solicitors, barristers and judges that money could buy – or persuade to offer their services by other means. Blackmail is the word that springs to mind. Again, much of this is rumour or hearsay, but I think it's fairly informed gossip. Sadly,' he added with a heavy sigh, 'that also extends to include some police officers. Apparently, there was a lot of loose talk at the time about officers taking backhanders but nobody was ever brought to court – although there were a few suspiciously early retirements. Let's face it, this sort of thing is by no means new, in fact from what I heard and read the big gangs that were operating in the sixties used to brag openly about the people they had on their payroll, from politicians to policemen.'

'Where's all this leading?' Nash asked.

'Be patient, I'm getting there. By the time Miller had the old Perry organization firing on all cylinders it had become the biggest, most powerful set-up in the capital, and that continued to be the case until recently, despite the new threats from the likes of the Eastern Europeans.'

'When you said until recently, I take it something has happened to change that?'

'Again, it's more rumour than hard fact, I'm afraid, but there's a lot of evidence to back it up. The story is that Miller lost a shed load of money when an investment of his went sour, big time. I haven't got the details, but the info comes from one of the guys in the Serious Fraud Office, so I think you can take it as genuine. From what they told my governor, Miller sank several million, more than even he could afford, into a company controlled by that American financier, the one who made off with all his clients' money.'

'That would certainly explain why Miller is so keen to get his hands on those diamonds all of a sudden.'

'What prompted all the interest at your end, Brian?' Clara asked.

'It was after I mentioned your interest in Max Perry to my governor. He repeated the conversation to our commander, who remembered a visitor he'd interviewed a few months back, a young man who told him a most interesting story. The young man's grandfather had died shortly before then, but before he died, he spoke to his grandson at great length, and told him a very strange tale, one which was in effect a death-bed confession. The old man was a diamond dealer who from time to time bought and sold diamonds on behalf of Max Perry. Apparently, Perry chose him because the old man was often able to purchase diamonds at a more favourable price than other dealers. Reading between the lines, I think that might have been because he didn't enquire too closely into their source. This was certainly the case with the last transaction Perry asked him to undertake; a large consignment of blood diamonds. The order was placed and the couriers set off from the continent, bringing the stones which they would exchange for cash at a pre-arranged meeting point.'

'What happened?' Clara asked.

'The stones never arrived. They vanished, along with the couriers and their car. As the old man told it, the supplier got a phone call shortly before the men set off, purporting to be from the London dealer, changing the venue for the exchange. The old man swore, and continued to maintain, even when he was dying, that he never placed that call. Soon after that Max Perry was murdered, presumably because the owner of the diamonds was convinced it was Max who had double-crossed him. The old man told his grandson that he had been visited by a couple of heavies who roughed him up a bit, until he was able to prove that he had nothing to do with the heist.'

'That can't have been it, surely? They must have made more of an effort to recover the diamonds,' Clara suggested.

'I asked that same question,' Shaw told them, 'and he said that the owner and his grandfather hired a man to look for them. The man was a specialist, who had been very successful in tracing stones on behalf of mine owners in Africa, where diamond theft was rife.'

'What happened, did he find anything out?'

Shaw's reply stunned both Nash and Mironova into silence. 'Nobody knows; he set off for England and was never seen or heard from again. He vanished as completely as the couriers had.'

'The interest shown in those diamonds by Miller now would tend to suggest that Max Perry did have a hand in the theft,' Nash said.

'Yes, but that still doesn't explain what happened to the stones,' Clara pointed out, 'unless someone else stole them from Max.'

'Or unless the couriers did take them and are living it up in some tropical paradise,' Nash suggested.

'Both of which are really interesting theories,' Shaw agreed. 'But unfortunately, neither of them has a shred of evidence to back them up.'

Nash thanked Shaw for the information and promised to keep in touch as soon as they had anything to report. After he rang off, he looked across at Mironova. 'I think I phrased that wrong,' he told her, 'I should have said if we ever have anything to report.'

Before she could reply, Nash's phone rang. 'Good morning, Professor,' he said, 'how can I help?'

He listened and Clara wondered what the pathologist had for them. It was obviously something of interest – she could tell by Nash's frown of concentration. Eventually, he muttered his thanks and replaced the receiver. He stared at Mironova for several seconds, but Clara realized his thoughts were elsewhere.

After a while he said, 'The professor's received the DNA test results on Graham Nattrass. The first thing he did was compare the profile to that of Ray Perry.'

'Let me guess, Nattrass is Ray Perry's son.'

'Wrong! That was exactly what I thought, but apparently Graham Nattrass and Ray Perry aren't related in any way, at least not blood relatives.'

'Was that all Mexican Pete had to say?' Clara tried hard to hide her disappointment at what seemed like yet another dead end.

'No, there was far more. And what he did tell me was far stranger than our guess. He did find a close familial match to Graham Nattrass in the DNA database.'

'Who might that be?'

'That's an exceedingly good question, and the answer is, we don't know. Not by name, at least. However, Mexican Pete is one hundred per cent certain that Graham Nattrass is a close blood relative of the woman whose remains were found in the woods near Bishops Cross almost twenty-five years ago.'

Following the shock revelations of the link between the DNA from Graham Nattrass and the unidentified woman, the Helmsdale team met early the next morning. Nash phoned Netherdale and asked Tom Pratt to join them, given his involvement in what was now a reopened investigation.

Mironova began by updating Pearce and Pratt on the news supplied by Brian Shaw and Mexican Pete. Following which, Nash asked them for their thoughts and ideas. 'I don't care how wild or irrelevant they might seem,' he told them, 'in fact, the way things are, the wilder the better.'

If anything could have been guaranteed to cause silence, it was this request. For some time it seemed that none of them would come up with anything constructive, until eventually, and with a great deal of hesitation, Pearce suggested, 'What about this woman, Corinna Perry? She seems to be the one constant in all this other than Ray Perry. She is the only link I can see between what happened then and events now. Do we know anything about her? Her background and character, I mean?'

Nash thought this over for a moment. 'Not a great deal,' he

admitted. 'Wellings, the retired Met officer, told us she was involved in a lot of charity work, fund-raising and the like. He seemed to think she was a fairly decent sort of woman. I think he also said Corinna was a nurse or something, didn't he?'

Clara nodded confirmation.

'I reckon we ought to have another word with Sister Evangeline and see what she can tell us about Corinna Perry.'

'Now that I think about it,' Clara commented, 'I got the impression Wellings might have been blinded by the fact that Corinna was an attractive woman.'

'What makes you say that?'

'He seems that type. He positively drooled over that photo of Frankie Da Silva, and it was all he could do to keep his eyes off my legs.'

'That wasn't exactly what I meant,' Nash said dryly. 'Why do you think he might be wrong?'

'Because, if Corinna is such a saint, how come she keeps taking up with really dodgy characters? Max Perry was an evil, violent gangster, and by what we've heard, this Phil Miller sounds a whole lot worse.'

'On the birds of a feather theory? I guess that makes sense. Give Sister Evangeline a call and see if she can come up with any info on Corinna. If we can find out where she hailed from or where she worked, we might be able to talk to someone who knew her then and get some idea as to what makes her tick.'

Their plans had to be put into abeyance, for Clara reported to Nash, 'Sister Evangeline has gone into Newcastle. She isn't due back until this evening.'

'In that case, leave me the number and I'll call her, no doubt you'll be on the phone all evening to your beloved.'

Nash's intention that evening was thwarted for some time by a conversation with his son, regaling him with his continued success with the cricket bat. Once Daniel had rung off, Nash dialled Sister Evangeline's number. 'How are things?' he asked, when she came to the phone.

He was encouraged by her response. She had, it seemed, been

coping very well. 'I've been busy,' she told Nash. 'It's far more complicated than I imagined it would be, although he has come out of the coma now and he does know me, Inspector. The doctors say that is very encouraging, especially after all these years. Fortunately, everyone has been very understanding, which has helped enormously. Was that why you rang?'

'Partly,' Nash replied, 'but I also wanted to see if you can help me with some information. We were discussing the case this morning and we realized we know next to nothing about Corinna, Max's wife, and we didn't know who else to ask.'

There was a hard edge to her voice as she replied, 'Oh, yes, the lovely Corinna. Soft and smooth as silk on the outside, and inside: granite. She cultivated such a good-hearted, caring image. Charity work, champion of the needy, sitting on committees. But underneath she was as hard as nails; in fact, Inspector Nash, she was a bitch. She and Max were well suited.'

'That's interesting, because that's not the impression I was given.'

'Well, she worked hard at it, no question of that.'

'I know she was a nurse, but can you remember anything else about her?'

'Not very much, to be honest. I didn't take to her from the word go, which doesn't help. Her maiden name was Smart, that I do remember, from the wedding service.'

'Where did she and Max meet? Was it in London?'

'No, Corinna wasn't from London. It was whilst Max was on tour when he was still an entertainer. Somewhere in the Midlands, I think. Where the cathedral got bombed.'

'Coventry?'

'That's right,' Sister Evangeline chuckled. 'I remember it now, because Jimmy, my husband, made a rude joke about it at the reception. Something to the effect that it would be Max who was riding bareback that night.'

Nash laughed.

'Yes, I thought you'd appreciate that,' Evangeline commented.

'Is that all? About Corinna, I mean.'

'There was something else, but I can't for the minute think what it was. I'll phone your office if I remember, shall I?'

Nash thanked her, and was about to ring off, when she exclaimed, 'Captain Cook!'

'What?'

'Where Corinna worked before she was married. The name, I think it had something to do with Captain Cook.'

'But Captain Cook was from round this way. As far as I know he had no connection with the Midlands. Are you sure you have that right?'

Sister Evangeline sighed. 'I'm not certain of anything these days, Mr Nash, and I'm sorry I can't be of more help.'

'What are you doing, Mike?'

Pearce looked over Nash's shoulder at the computer screen. He had been sitting at the terminal when he arrived in the CID suite the following morning.

'Trying to find some information about someone. Tell me, what do you remember about Captain Cook?'

Viv blinked. 'Why are you researching him? Not as a suspect, I hope, because I've got news for you. Arresting him won't be easy.'

Nash chuckled, and explained. 'I've tried Newfoundland, St Lawrence, Whitby, Great Ayton, Middlesbrough, Australia, Botany Bay, Sydney, Hawaii, all sorts of things, but no joy.'

'You missed the most obvious one of all.'

'What was that?'

Pearce told him, and seconds after Nash typed the name into the search bar, they stared at the result, transfixed by what they were reading. The news item was old, but the topic was red hot, literally. 'Is this to do with our case?' Pearce asked.

'I can't tell you for certain, because I don't know. But there is a connection, of that I'm sure.' He pressed print and handed Viv the papers. 'I'd like you to research that place, Viv. Find out everything you can. What sort of cases they handled, for one thing. I'm particularly interested in anyone who worked there, apart from these unfortunate people.' He pointed to the paper.

Pearce stared at the article. Under the headline 'Three Dead in Blaze at Endeavour Clinic', the news item described a fire that had destroyed a wing of a private treatment centre on the outskirts of

Coventry. 'I still don't see the connection,' Viv said.

'Neither do I at the moment. All I do know is that Sister Evangeline told me that Corinna Perry worked there prior to her marriage. Of course, the fire could have been pure coincidence, but—'

'You don't believe in coincidence.'

Tina's flight had been delayed. Her sense of annoyance was compounded by helplessness, which did not sit easily with one who was used to being in control. As she had already completed the security procedure, she was unable to return to the main body of the airport, and had to remain for several hours in the restricted zone. Apart from the highly expensive bars and cafés, there was little for her to do to pass the time but browse the duty-free shops.

As a way of killing several hours it had little to recommend it, even for a far more confirmed shopaholic than Tina. During her several passes through the various stores only one item caught her fancy. The garment looked elegant, even when draped around the lifeless mannequin in the shop's window display. When Tina tried it on and turned to study her reflection in the full-length mirror, she already knew that she was going to buy it. Ignoring the price tag, which seemed designed to make the eyes water, she examined the cloak, feeling the way it clung to her slender figure, certain in her own mind that it had been woven for her and no one else.

As she walked out of the shop, the carrier bag in one hand and her cabin luggage in the other, Tina heard the announcement summoning her to the departure gate. This signalled the end of her delay, and if she needed further proof that the purchase was meant to be, this was surely it.

The delay had thrown her schedule into disarray, and she knew that it would be late afternoon before they touched down in the UK. Fortunately, Tina had the ability to sleep wherever she was, and ignoring the airline food and the complimentary drinks on offer to recompense passengers for their inconvenience, she managed several hours' rest over the Atlantic.

When she emerged from the baggage reclaim and collected her hire car, she glanced at the clock and realized that if she set off on her trans-Pennine journey at that point, she would get snarled up in the very worst of the early evening rush-hour traffic. After almost two years since she had driven on the left, this was not a prospect she relished, nor was the alternative – a night in a hotel close to the airport – one she was prepared to consider.

She opted for compromise, and with the aid of the relevant software on her smartphone, selected a restaurant only a few miles from the airport. She made her way there and ordered a leisurely meal. Once she was happy that she had managed to avoid the worst of the traffic, Tina set off on the final leg of her journey.

When she finally arrived at the village, it took her some time to retrieve her keys from the next door neighbour, who was keen to hear of her experiences in America. After a quarter of an hour, by the end of which Tina was beginning to shiver from cold, the neighbour relented, and Tina was able to house the car in the double garage, collect her luggage and let herself into the house.

Tina was aware that her body clock was several hours wrong, that by rights she should be weary to the point of exhaustion, but the transatlantic nap had revived her, and coupled with the change in time zones made sleep impossible, for the time being, at least.

Her automatic reaction on entering the cottage was to reach for the light switch, but as she glanced across towards the bay window of the lounge, she caught sight of the sunset. The staggering splendour of the evening sky, lit by the setting sun in every imaginable hue of pink, was breathtaking, far too beautiful to be marred by artificial light, so Tina settled for the far less powerful competition provided by the small table lamp in the far corner of the room.

Tina had spent far too long in cities, far too many nights in hotel rooms with minimal views, if any, and the stunning scenery of the Yorkshire countryside was compelling and not to be missed on any account.

Even in the height of summer, England, particularly the north, seemed cold to one who had more recently been accustomed to the warmer climate of the southern states of the USA. Tina shivered, but was certainly not prepared to go to the trouble of unpacking one of her cases simply to retrieve a sweater. She thought of raiding her mother's wardrobe, before she remembered her recent purchase.

She reached into the duty-free carrier bag and drew out the light-weight cloak, a combination of cape and snood, in an attractive gunmetal grey. It was ideal for her immediate needs. Even her ears were cold, the result of her prolonged stay outside, so she pulled the hood over her head and stood for several minutes, watching the colours of the sky change as the sun sank further below the horizon.

At around the time when Tina was unlocking the door to go into her mother's house, a few miles away, Phil and Corinna were leaving the rented cottage. As they pulled out of the lane, their departure was watched by Thornton and Mr Muscle. 'They've gone; time for us to move. Drive down their lane and pull round the back. We can hide the car behind the hedge in the field where that straw or whatever it is has been wrapped in those round bales.'

Mr Muscle obeyed Thornton's instructions. Thornton's knowledge of agriculture might have been close to non-existent, but his choice of a hiding place for their vehicle was ideal. Even close inspection from within the cottage would not give them away. And if they needed to leave in a hurry, their position gave them the perfect route.

'Bring the tools, and we'll go in by the back door.'

Thornton took the jemmy from Mr Muscle and attempted to force the tool into the narrow slit between the door and jamb. After several fruitless efforts, he passed it back. 'You have a go,' he wheezed.

The contest was an unequal one and the door yielded with a loud splintering sound that echoed in the still night air.

'Good, now let's see what Miller and Corinna are up to.'

On their way through the small lobby, they failed to notice the sledgehammer leaning against the side wall. They passed through the kitchen with barely a sideways glance, before moving into the lounge.

Their search of the cottage took less than an hour, but by the end of it, they had found no trace of the diamonds. Thornton spent a good deal of the time examining a set of folders, which contained records of adoptions from a quarter of a century earlier. They aroused his curiosity, but although he felt sure they must have some bearing on Miller's hunt for the stones, Thornton was unable to work out the relevance.

'What now, boss?'

'We keep following Miller. Sooner or later he's going to lead us to the diamonds.'

'What do we do about the door? They're going to know some-one's been inside.'

'In that case, we prove it beyond doubt. We mess the place up, take that computer and printer, and the cash we found upstairs in the bedroom. That way they'll assume it was a burglary.' Thornton smiled. 'The money will pay for that dump of a hotel we're staying in.'

chapter thirteen

The road leading to Margaret Fawcett's cottage curved from the outskirts of the village in a long, shallow bend. As Tina watched the light show in the evening sky, a car passed, heading towards the village green. Tina went through to the kitchen and opened the fridge door. She looked inside, smiling at her mother's thoughtfulness. She had left a carton of long life milk for her. Tina switched the kettle on and brewed herself a mug of coffee, which she carried back into the lounge, in time to see that the reds and pinks of the sunset had given way to an equally impressive array of purple and blue shades. As she watched, her attention was caught by a most evocative sound, a sound that truly signalled her return home. It was the rusty croak of a cock pheasant. Saying goodnight to the ladies of his harem, Tina thought. She turned her head slightly towards the source of the sound, and as she did so, the gentle illumination from the table lamp fell on her face.

A little way past the cottage, Corinna pulled to a halt. She turned and looked back at the house, before transferring her gaze to her companion. 'I thought you said the woman had gone away and the house would be empty. How come there's a light on, if that's the case?'

'Relax, that's what people do. They leave a light attached to one of those timers, so it comes on at the same time every night to fool burglars into thinking someone's home. I'm willing to bet that's what she's done. It'll be a table lamp or something like that, you'll see. But just to be on the safe side I'll go take a dekko and if it's all clear, I'll come back for you.'

From behind a bank of bushes inside the front gate, Phil Miller saw the apparition at the window. As her face came into sharp focus, he felt the short hairs on the nape of his neck stand on end; his jaw dropped open and his eyes bulged. He remained transfixed, wanting to be away from this place, from that sight, yet unable to move. Then, even as he stared at it, the figure vanished leaving him uncertain as to whether she had been there at all.

He blinked, shock coursing through his whole body. As the spell was broken, strength returned to his limbs and he turned, vaulting the wall and bolted; arms and legs pumping like an Olympic athlete, lungs bursting from the unaccustomed effort until he reached the safe haven of the car.

He flung himself into the passenger seat and gasped, 'Get moving. Get out of here. Now!'

Corinna stared at him. 'What on earth's the matter? You look as if you've seen a ghost.' As she spoke she started the ignition, and as the car pulled away, Miller cast a final, fearful glance through the rear window, as if expecting to see something or someone following them.

'That's it,' he gulped in reply to her question. 'That's exactly what happened. I have seen a ghost.'

She drew the car to a halt. 'Don't be ridiculous.' Her cold hard logic was the catalyst that caused his common sense to return. 'It was probably nothing more than a trick of the light, added to the reason for you being here. The combination probably caused the suggestion to enter your mind.'

'In other words you think I was seeing things?'

'One thing's for certain, you weren't seeing what you thought was there. That I do know – and so do you. The only way to make sure the house is empty is to go back and watch.'

He agreed, reluctantly. As they drove back past the cottage, they could see the light still glowing in the downstairs window. 'That doesn't prove anything, one way or the other,' she told him. 'It could mean there's someone inside or it might be a lamp on a timer, as you suggested originally.'

They parked where they were able to get a good view of the front of the house. It was almost forty minutes later before the light went out and they stared at the darkened facade of the building. They waited several minutes longer just to be on the safe side, before he said, 'You were right, it was a timer after all. The rest must have been my imagination, just like you said. Come on, let's get it over with.'

They made their way cautiously to the front boundary of the property, where they paused alongside the gate. 'We're better going over the wall,' he told her, 'that won't squeak. The gate probably will – and we don't want to alert the neighbours.'

Miller climbed over and turned, stretching out to help Corinna cross the obstacle. She had just grasped his hand when he noticed a change in the light value. He looked at Corinna who was staring over his head, her expression one of shock. He turned and followed her gaze. For a brief second, backlit by the illumination from the ceiling light, they caught a fleeting glimpse of a figure in front of the upstairs window. It was only momentary, then the figure vanished and the curtains were drawn.

Although the figure was unrecognizable in the deep shadow, the watchers could tell beyond doubt that it was a female. Enough was enough. He re-scaled the wall and they hurried back to their car. This time there was no reconsideration, no second thoughts. As they drove rapidly out of the village, neither of them had the slightest intention of returning that night. Although, as Corinna pointed out later, 'That clears up your ghost theory; ghosts don't open and shut curtains. At least, I've never heard of one doing it. That means the house isn't unoccupied. So we'll have to rethink our plans.'

A further shock awaited them on their return to their cottage. As soon as they entered the building, they knew there had been an intruder. Papers from the adoption files were strewn across the lounge carpets. The laptop and printer that had been on the table were gone, and when they checked upstairs, they discovered that over three hundred pounds in cash had vanished from the dressing table.

'Do you think this is to do with why we're here?' Corinna asked.

'How can it be? Nobody knows where we are. For all they know we could be in Spain. I told you before, I hate this place. Now you can see why. Burglars, ghosts, hour after hour of bloody silence during the daytime, and then the minute you try to get to sleep, a load of weird noises that might have come off the sound track of a horror film. Give me a city any day.'

Although Corinna had mocked his dislike of the countryside, for once she had to agree with him. 'The sooner we get this sorted, the better. Then we can go back home and put our retirement plan into action.'

'We are not alone.' Phil Miller was standing gazing out of the cottage window.

'What? Has what happened last night affected you? Next you'll be saying you believe in aliens, flying saucers and beings from other planets.'

He grinned, a little shamefaced at this reminder of his belief that he had seen a ghost. 'No, I mean there is someone watching the house.'

'How do you know that? Are you sure, or has last night's burglary made you paranoid?'

'I saw something in those trees. A few minutes ago. Just briefly.'

'Something? What sort of something? Was it a woman in a long grey dress walking through solid objects? Or a troop of soldiers dressed like beefeaters? A headless horseman, perhaps? Or a phantom stagecoach flying through the air?'

'No, nothing like that.' Corinna's sarcasm was beginning to irritate him. 'I saw the sunlight reflecting on glass. I think it might have been binoculars.'

She looked out of the window but could see nothing untoward. 'It was probably a birdwatcher. Twitchers, I think they're called. Quite apt, I suppose, because this place is making me twitchy, and it's definitely doing it to you. In case you hadn't noticed there are a lot of birds around here. Very noisy birds, that wake me up at some ungodly hour singing their bloody heads off. So what you thought you saw was nothing more sinister than some peasant with nothing better to do than gawp at a lesser-spotted something or other. You can't blame them. Christ knows, there's bugger all else to do around here.'

She paused and looked outside again. 'Either that, or somebody dumped their old TV in the woods and the sun's reflecting off it.

Pull yourself together, Phil, we've been through all this once before. Nobody knows we're here, or anywhere near here. Therefore, nobody can possibly be watching us, right?'

'I suppose so.' Her cold, logical argument made him realize how irrational his reaction had been. 'Yes, of course, you're dead right, Corinna. Like you said, it was probably all down to what happened last night. What do you suggest we do about that, by the way?'

'I think our best bet would be to go out there during the hours of daylight and have a good look around, see if we can spot the woman we thought we saw last night.'

'What time do you want to go?'

She drained her mug of coffee. 'I'm going for a shower. Then we'll have a late breakfast and set off after that.'

Tina hadn't slept at all well the previous night; the residue of her jet lag, she assumed, coupled with the unfamiliarity of the bed. She was up and about early, showered, dressed and drinking her first coffee of the morning by the time the eight o'clock news bulletin came on the radio.

She decided her first task should be to go into Helmsdale and do some shopping. Although Margaret had left her freezer well stocked, her ideas of food and Tina's were quite different. Added to that, Tina was of an age that had become addicted to one-stop supermarket shopping. Even the thought of Good Buy's home delivery service didn't occur to her.

By ten o'clock she was on the road, determined to reach Helmsdale and complete her shopping before the tills got busier around lunchtime. Having spent so long in America, Tina's idea of a decent cup of coffee was radically different from Margaret's instant brand, so she added a cafetière to her shopping list. Once she had completed her purchases, she decided she would pop into Helm Café for a sandwich before returning to complete her unpacking. The text she received from her boss whilst entering the supermarket changed all that. 'Give me chance to touch down, for goodness' sake,' she muttered as she read it.

Nevertheless, she changed plans and decided to drive through to Leeds. Better to get the work side of things out of the way, she thought, then she could have a decent break. She had left her laptop at the cottage, but fortunately everything she might need for the meeting was on the flash drive in her handbag.

At around the time Tina was reading the text, a car pulled up outside Margaret's cottage. In daylight, the house looked empty, deserted. 'The curtains at that window are open,' Corinna pointed out. 'Somebody must be living there, and yet you said you were sure there was nobody else in the house when she went away, didn't you?'

'I'm absolutely certain of it. The way she locked up, you could tell she was leaving the house empty for longer than a couple of hours or so. She tried the front door twice after locking it, which is what convinced me.'

'Maybe last night was a burglar. There seems to be a lot of that going on around here.'

He smiled. 'I hadn't thought of that.'

'Alternatively, she could have employed one of those house-sitters. You know, they come and look after houses whilst you're away on holiday.'

'That's probably far more likely. If that's the case, they don't look to be in residence at the moment. Shame we can't do it now, but it's far too risky.' He pointed down the road towards the village green, where several of the residents could be seen. Two of the older inhabitants were making their way towards the pub, which also housed the village shop, whilst a young mother was watching her two small children clambering over the play equipment on the green itself.

'So, when do we come back?'

'Late tonight.'

'What about the house-sitter, if there is one?'

'It's not going to be the best job they've ever had. We go ahead with it anyway, and if they get in the way, tough. By what I've seen of this place, it'll be days before anyone realizes anything's wrong. Even the stink won't be noticeable amongst all the others around. Talk about fresh air! All I can smell is shit, most of the time.'

'I suppose the only advantage of operating in a place like this is there is absolutely no danger. Not like at home. Nobody's likely to stick a gun in your face here.'

They were confident in their ability to enter the house, over-power the occupant and find and remove what they needed without fear of detection or reprisals. But then, neither of them knew the remotest thing about the rural scene, and how life in the country-side works.

On the crown of the bend, some two hundred yards away from where they had parked, Thornton was watching them through his binoculars. 'What are they doing, boss?' Mr Muscle asked.

'By the look of it, they're gawping at those houses. Why, I've no idea. I can't see either of them wanting to buy a place here. Even as a retirement home it wouldn't be their style.'

'What do you think they're looking for?'

'I've no idea, except that I think it must have some bearing on why we're here. Hang on, they're moving again. Keep behind them, and don't get too close, but don't lose them either.'

'Can you see that Mercedes behind us? It's about half a mile back.' Corinna asked.

Miller looked in the rear-view mirror, and after a few seconds, caught sight of the car. 'A silver one? Is that the one you mean? What of it?'

'I can't be sure, but I think that car was behind us when we left the cottage this morning.'

'Now who's being paranoid?'

'There can't be many cars like that around here. All I've seen is Volvos and bloody Land Rovers. Say what you like, I think that car is following us. And no, I'm not being paranoid. There's a world of a difference between paranoia and taking sensible precautions.'

'In that case, try losing them. You know how to, and that should tell us one way or the other.'

'How do you want me to play it?'

Miller knew how capable Corinna was. She'd done this before, more than once. 'Head for town,' he told her. 'You'll be able to lose them on that long straight bit just before the built-up area. When you get to the first turning, pull off and we can watch them, see who they are, maybe.'

'Them?'

'Them, him, her, whoever's driving that car.'

Even before she had finished rounding the final bend, Corinna had hit the accelerator, and they both felt the pull as the powerful sports car rocketed forward. When they reached the houses, the Mercedes wasn't even in sight, but disaster looked imminent as Corinna went to turn right at a speed that would have caused most cars to overturn. Miller was relaxed; Corinna was an expert and the roadholding of the car was legendary.

By the time the car they suspected of following them passed the road end, Corinna had parked the Porsche neatly behind the only vehicle on that street. 'There they go; whoever they are, we've lost them,' she said.

'Yes, it's a shame we had to hide behind that van, though. It would have been good to get a clear view of them and see if it was anyone we know, but the Porsche is too recognizable to take the chance.'

The owner of the outdoor leisure shop in Helmsdale was happy to take their money. It had been a quiet week and the sale of a second pair of expensive, high-powered binoculars was more than welcome. When, almost as an afterthought, the man bought a pair of walking boots, the owner was unable to disguise his pleasure. Even when the shop doorbell ceased ringing after their departure, he was able to look at the amount showing on the cash register display and prolong his elation.

'What's the idea of the boots?'

'If we were being tailed, I've a plan to sort them out, that's all. Drive back to the cottage and we'll take it from there. When you get within a mile or so, slow down. I want to check out the lie of the land.'

As they approached the cottage, Corinna did as he instructed, giving Miller ample opportunity to inspect the terrain. 'Perfect,' he muttered.

'What is? What were you looking for?'

'I wanted to see if it was possible to leave the cottage and get to those trees on foot without being seen.'

'And?'

'It can be done by leaving via the back door and going across the yard to the far side of that hedge, then walking along it to where that field meets up with the one that comes back towards the road. After that, it's difficult to be sure, it depends on the slope and how tall the hedge is.'

'All this is highly fascinating,' Corinna said as she pulled the car to a halt in front of the cottage, 'but why would you want to do all that? You don't even like walking.'

'To deal with the nosey bastards who have been watching us.'

'Are you sure about that?'

'Not yet, but like I said, this is just in case, a sort of insurance, if you like. The binoculars should tell us, one way or the other.'

chapter fourteen

There had been angry words between Thornton and his henchman before they reached Helmsdale. Thornton accused him of carelessness. 'You've lost them, you stupid pillock. I told you we should have kept closer behind them. They could be anywhere by now. For all we know they could have collected the diamonds and be heading for the M1 and back to London already.'

'If you think you can do better, you drive. How do you suggest I could have stayed closer on that long straight without drawing attention to this car? Do you think they're so thick they wouldn't have worked out whose car this is? That personal registration is a dead giveaway. I might just as well have hung a sign out of the window telling them we were following them.'

The argument continued until they reached the centre of the town where they drove around for a while. Eventually, Mr Muscle pointed to the sleek lines of the Porsche that was parked prominently in the market place. He reversed the Mercedes into a vacant bay on the opposite side of the road and switched the engine off, glad of the silence, not from the noise of the car, but from Thornton's whining.

They waited over twenty minutes before Thornton saw the couple returning to their car. Both were carrying shopping bags. 'Here they are,' he pointed, unnecessarily, for his driver was already firing the ignition. 'This time, don't lose them. You got lucky once, the next time you might not.'

Mr Muscle pulled the Mercedes into the stream of traffic several cars back from the Porsche, muttering something under his breath as he did so. Fortunately, his comment on Thornton's parentage was too quiet for the older man to hear. Thornton watched the Porsche in front, wondering idly what they had been buying. Helmsdale shops weren't exactly Oxford Street, which was where Corinna liked to do her shopping.

During their journey they managed to keep the Porsche within range; helped by the fact that the couple in front seemed in no hurry. It didn't occur to either of the men in the Mercedes to wonder why the Porsche had been pushed to the limit on the way into town, and was now being driven at a pace best described as a dawdle. When they eventually saw the brake lights come on, Mr Muscle, obeying Thornton, brought the Mercedes to a halt near their previous vantage point.

They waited, to give their quarry chance to go to earth, and as they did so, Thornton's minder asked his employer the question that had been at the back of his mind ever since they had set out for Yorkshire. 'What's the special reason for wanting to get hold of these diamonds? I mean, apart from the fact that I know they're probably worth a small fortune, but I get the idea there's more to it than that, something more personal.'

Thornton didn't say anything for a long time, and the driver was just beginning to think he'd overstepped the mark when his boss spoke. 'First off, those diamonds aren't worth a small fortune; they're worth quite a large fortune. Second, and just as important, when they went missing, my boss got the blame for it. At that time I worked for Callaghan. Dirty Harry Callaghan. I guess you've heard of him?'

'Yes, I have, didn't one of the Perry gang stick him?'

'Maybe, maybe not. I knew Callaghan hadn't stolen the diamonds, but that was what everyone was saying. Before it could be proved one way or the other he was found stabbed to death. Ray Perry was standing over him with a ruddy great knife in his hand. I'm not sure to this day if Perry did stab Callaghan, or if he was simply in the wrong place at the wrong time. My own opinion was that the original owner of the diamonds was taking revenge on the people he thought might have done the dirty on him. Max Perry had also been killed, and the other story doing the rounds was that Callaghan had done it, but I knew for a fact that wasn't true.

Whatever did happen, if I can get hold of the diamonds it won't bring either of them back but at least it'll be a bit of poetic justice.'

'What about the bloke who supplied them? I'd have thought if he was angry enough to do all that back then, he'd still be prepared to resort to the same tactics to get them back, even now. He's fairly sure to hear about them being found if he's in the trade.'

Thornton smiled mirthlessly. 'The only way he's going to get to hear about them is if someone uses a Ouija board. He was found dead in a canal in Amsterdam four months after the stones vanished. He didn't sink, despite having a considerable number of knife-sized holes in him.'

'There seem to have been a lot of deaths connected to those diamonds. Doesn't that worry you?'

Thornton shrugged. 'It does, a bit, even though a lot of the people who are most interested in the stones are no longer with us. To be on the safe side, I took out some insurance.' Thornton opened the glove compartment, to reveal an automatic pistol inside. 'One thing the Boy Scouts got right is that motto of theirs. "Be prepared" works for me every time.'

He closed the glove compartment and reached over to the back seat to retrieve the binoculars. 'I'm going to take a look and see if they've bedded down for the night, or if they're going cavorting off on another moonlight ride like they did last night. I'm still trying to work out what that was all about, and what the attraction of that cottage is.'

Corinna was in the kitchen preparing a meal. She glanced through into the lounge, in time to see Miller standing in front of the window, fiddling with the binoculars. Several minutes later, she looked up again, to find him standing in the kitchen doorway. She was surprised to see he was wearing the walking boots he had bought that afternoon. 'What are you doing, going for a walk?'

He looked down. 'Well, I'm not going swimming, that's for sure. Will that meal wait?'

'Yes, why?'

'When I've been gone ten minutes or so, I want you to take stuff out to the car. It doesn't matter what, exactly. A couple of coats, a bag, whatever you can find. Make it look as if we're going to set off like we did last night.'

'Whatever for? What will you be doing?'

'I'm going to have words with the bloke who's watching the house.'

'Who is he? Someone we know?'

'I can't tell. Even with the glasses, he's too far away for me to make him out clearly behind those bloody trees. But I want to know what the hell he's playing at. You haven't been cavorting about in front of the bedroom window naked, have you?'

Corinna grinned. 'I haven't been, but if that's what he's waiting for, I'll gladly oblige.'

'No you bloody well won't. That floor show is for me alone, baby.'

'What about going back to the cottage like we planned?'

'That's going to have to wait. I want to deal with this first. It's making me feel uncomfortable.'

'Be careful, Phil. If it's some deranged local, they could be dangerous.'

Phil Miller was a planner by nature, always had been. Planning, he found, was the only way to avoid the unexpected. In his world, unexpected happenings were usually unpleasant in nature. Some unforeseen events couldn't be planned for, but he tried to keep these to an absolute minimum. As he closed the back door behind him, Phil was already planning his strategy for approaching the watcher. As he passed through the lobby, he had collected the sledgehammer from its resting place against the wall. By the time he reached the woods, he felt sure his arms would be aching from the weight of the tool, but having the weapon along would be worth it.

Getting through a gap in the hedge was easy, and Phil was confident of being able to reach the next field without being seen. After that, much depended on the height of the hedge, and the density of the foliage. Phil hoped it would be tall enough; he didn't fancy creeping several hundred yards in a crouching position. Either way, that was probably going to be the most risky part of the venture, and he knew he would have to be extremely cautious.

He reached the junction of the fields, slipping easily through the space between the gate and the hedge. He was tempted for a moment to use the gate, but rejected the idea. It looked to be on the point of collapse, and Phil was convinced that if he did try to open it, the gate would protest – loudly.

Fortunately, the hedge was both tall enough and thick enough to give him excellent cover. Not only that, but the slope he had been concerned about was far gentler than it had appeared to be when viewed from the cottage window. The field had been harvested and the stubble was dry underfoot. Phil was able to make excellent progress towards the road.

His only moment of panic came when he was halfway up the slope, almost level with the edge of the trees that were his objective. The cause of his alarm was a pair of blackbirds that rocketed out of the hedge only a few feet in front of him; their screeches sounding like wailing sirens breaking the quiet of the still evening air. Miller froze, and remained motionless for several minutes after the birds had vanished into the gathering dusk.

He muttered several savage curses under his breath, all targeted towards the avian population thereabouts and blackbirds in particular. The notion that their noisy exit from the hedge that was their dormitory might have been the result of his approach didn't occur to him. Once peace and quiet had been restored and his heart rate had slowed to something close to normal, Miller continued, more cautiously now, bypassing the woodland as he headed for the gate in the top corner of the field.

It had never been Phil's intention to seek out the watcher when the man was within the confines of the wood; that, he knew, might be a recipe for disaster. Far better to locate his vehicle and surprise him as he returned to it. There were other advantages to this plan. He would be able to check if the watcher was alone, and if not, deal with the danger posed by being outnumbered. He could also, if need be, disable the watcher's motor, thereby preventing his escape. Finally, he felt sure that when the watcher's stint in the woods had ended the man would be off guard and therefore easier to overcome.

When he reached the edge of the field and looked cautiously to his left, Phil knew that his plan had been the right one. No more than thirty yards away, a man was leaning on the side of a

Mercedes, the car Phil guessed had been following them all day. The man was smoking a cigarette, and as he watched, Miller both saw and smelled the smoke drifting towards him. That meant that what slight breeze there was would be in his favour, for both scent and sound would be carried away from his quarry.

Not that he had to worry too much about sound, for the car window was open and the man was listening to the radio. He had the volume turned up high enough to mask the sound of anyone approaching. As Miller watched, the man shifted position slightly, and Phil's eyes narrowed as the man's head turned sufficiently for him to be recognized. Miller's gaze switched to the registration plate of the car, and as he noted the lettering, he knew beyond doubt the identity of the watcher within the woods.

At the same time he realized there was only one course of action available to him. If the watcher had been some private eye, or a low-level punk hoping to make a name for himself, that might have been different, but this represented too potent a threat to be dealt with in any other but the harshest way.

Assessing the terrain, Phil noted a large bush two thirds of the way between him and his target. If he could reach that without being seen, the man by the car would be almost within range of the sledgehammer. Two quick strides and one swing should do the trick. Miller climbed over the sturdy metal gate, thankful that it neither creaked nor groaned under his weight. Once on the other side, seven quick strides brought him to the cover he had marked out.

Five minutes later, Phil Miller leaned against the boot of the Mercedes, gasping slightly for breath. The exertion of putting Mr Muscle in the boot had almost been beyond him. All he had to do now was confront Thornton. Then he could phone Corinna to come and help; Thornton was far too overweight for him to manage alone. Besides, they would need her car to get back once they had disposed of the bodies. Miller had remembered to bring his mobile along and to put it on silent mode. He only hoped he'd be able to get a signal.

'What do you propose to do with them? Hiding two bodies and a car isn't going to be easy.'

Phil smiled at Corinna. 'Why not? We've done it before, and what worked then should work now.'

'That's all very well, but when we did it before we had it all sorted beforehand. We had a dump site.'

'Yes, but when I had to pass the time alone in there' – he jerked a thumb towards the holiday cottage – 'I was so bored I read a load of the junk they leave for the guidance of holidaymakers. One was a book on local history that describes a big disused quarry, well hidden from the road, ten miles or so from here. That should suit our needs, and by the time anyone finds them, we'll be thousands of miles away – with the diamonds, or the sale proceeds.'

'What about the car? Won't they be able to trace the owner? It's a personal number plate.'

'Why do you think I asked you to bring the screwdriver?'

'Are we going to torch it?'

'Yes, I checked the tank and it's almost full. The old soaked rag should do the trick.'

Two hours later, they were back in the cottage, and had eaten their meal. 'One advantage of the open air is it gives you a good appetite,' Corinna said as she inspected his empty plate.

'There are other advantages,' Phil replied. 'It will be weeks, possibly months before anyone sees that car.'

'Any other advantages?'

'Yes, this cottage has a huge bath. Easily big enough for two. At least I think so. Do you fancy testing it to see if I'm right?'

chapter fifteen

Nash was about to tell Clara the results of his phone call to Sister Evangeline and Pearce was waiting to add his findings, but they were interrupted by a phone call from Jack Binns, who asked Nash to come down to the reception area.

The young couple waiting by Jack's desk looked nervous. 'They're here to make a statement,' Jack said by way of introduction. 'They found a car ablaze in that disused quarry near Drover's Halt last night. It was burning fiercely when they got there. Apparently, the fire brigade couldn't check it out until this morning because the heat was too intense.' He turned to the young man. 'Tell Inspector Nash what you told me.'

'At first, we thought the car was an old banger somebody had dumped, but I went to check there was nobody inside. I don't think there was, but it was too hot to get close enough to be certain. What I could tell was that it was no banger. It was a fairly new Mercedes, the latest body shape, which means it must be worth quite a lot of money. Not now' – he smiled slightly – 'I mean before the fire. I thought it might have been stolen, joy riders, maybe.'

'That was very observant,' Nash said.

As he spoke the phone rang. Binns answered it. 'Yes, he's here.' He passed the receiver to Nash. 'Chief Fire Officer Curran for you,' he explained.

'Morning, Doug, how's things?'

The three people in reception saw Nash's expression alter, become instantly far grimmer. 'OK,' he said after a moment, 'we'll be out there as soon as we can get. Yes, I'll see to that.'

He put the phone down and turned to the couple. 'That

statement of yours has suddenly become very important, but I'm afraid I'm going to have to ask you to give it to Sergeant Binns here.'

He turned to Binns. 'I have to collect Clara and Viv and get out to the quarry. Before that I need to raise Mexican Pete and SOCO.'

The car had been a saloon, but so fierce had been the heat towards the back of the vehicle that the roof had all but collapsed, giving it the appearance of a coupe. Little remained of the paintwork, and what there was had blistered and peeled; such as hadn't been melted had lost its original metallic silver lustre, now appearing as a dull gunmetal grey.

'They took the plates off before they torched it,' Pearce pointed to the front of the car. 'Why do that?'

'Good question.' Nash stared at the vehicle, 'It could have been done to conceal where the vehicle came from, or who the owner was. Perhaps it was a personal number plate. It's that type of car. My guess would be they wanted to conceal the identity of the victims.'

'Always assuming one of the victims was the car owner,' Mironova pointed out.

'Whoever they were, the killer wanted time before we identified either car or victims.'

'They must surely have known that we'd be able to trace the car from the Vehicle Identification Number on the chassis. They can't have removed that. The engine number would also be enough to give us the car owner.'

'I assume they would know that, Viv, so maybe all they wanted was enough time to make a getaway. I'm going to talk to Doug Curran, and find out if he knows how they torched the car.'

Pearce and Mironova watched as Nash walked over to where the firemen were awaiting the arrival of the pathologist. He was whistling quietly and seemed unconcerned by the grim scene around him. 'Mike seems far more relaxed these days,' Viv commented. 'I know he's always been fairly easygoing, but nothing seems to faze him now. Is that Daniel's calming influence, do you think?'

'It could be, although I'd suggest that being a single parent is more stressful than relaxing.'

'Whatever it is, if Mike were any more laid back he'd fall over.'

'Morning, Doug,' Nash greeted the fire chief. 'What do you know? Any idea how the barbecue started?'

'And I thought some of my team have a sick sense of humour! It was the oldest trick in the book. Take a piece of rag, soak it in petrol and stuff it into the filler nozzle. Light it, and that ignites the vapour from the tank. You do know that it's the vapour that's inflammable, not the liquid, I assume?'

Nash nodded. 'Very unpleasant. And the victims?'

'We didn't find them until the vehicle had cooled off sufficiently to prise the boot open. We only did that because one of our guys smelled burnt flesh; said it reminded him of his mother-in-law's cooking.'

'More like meals on wheels, if you ask me.'

Before Curran could reply they saw a small procession of vehicles arrive at the quarry entrance. 'That'll be Mexican Pete and the body-snatchers,' Curran observed.

'You make them sound like an unsuccessful sixties pop group. It'll be interesting to see what the cause of death turns out to be. I hope they were shot, stabbed, poisoned, strangled or beaten to death.'

Curran stared at the detective. 'Why on earth do you hope that?'

'Because that would mean they were dead before they were put into that boot.'

Curran took in the implicit horror of Nash's statement. He swallowed. 'You actually believe that someone could be cruel enough to put these people into the car whilst they're still alive and let them burn to death?'

'I honestly don't know.'

The pathologist approached Nash and Curran. 'I think we can rule out natural causes and suicide. No cause of death until after my examination. I was hoping to do the post-mortem tomorrow morning, but I want the vehicle and contents taken back to the lab. There, perhaps we can remove the bodies more easily. Fused,' he said abruptly, as if by way of explanation.

'He's in a chatty mood today,' Curran said.

'I think someone told him that if he used too many words he'd have to pay a fine and he still believes it,' Nash said. 'I'm going to talk to our forensic officers. I don't see there's much more we can do here, apart from retrieving the car's VIN. I'll try and talk SOCO into doing an area search.'

'Good luck with that. Send Viv across and we'll sort the VIN out for him. I'll see if we can get the engine number, too.'

Nash was talking to the SOCO team leader when one of his fellow officers called the man over. Nash followed, and they reached the remains of the passenger door. 'I've managed to get the glove compartment open,' the officer told them. 'I thought you'd like to see what was inside.'

He reached out with a gloved hand and proffered a badly damaged automatic pistol. 'I had a quick look at it,' the officer continued. 'It must have been loaded and the ammunition has exploded by the looks of it. No way of knowing if it's been fired. Well, not in the normal way, that is.'

Nash smiled slightly. 'That's interesting.' He signalled Mironova and Pearce to join them and pointed to the gun. 'How many law-abiding citizens carry a loaded pistol in their car?' he asked.

'If they're carrying a pistol, they're not law-abiding anyway,' Clara pointed out.

'True, carrying one is an offence, but I was thinking more in the wider sense. Unless they were in fear of their life, only hardened criminals carry guns. So which is it, fear, criminality, or both?'

By the time Pearce had retrieved the numbers, the police low loader was reversing up to the burnt-out wreckage to remove it to their garage for further analysis.

'Right, I think we're done here. SOCO are going to search the area for possible clues, so we'll only be in their way. Let's go back to the station – I'm suffering from caffeine withdrawal.'

Once they were back in the CID suite, Nash explained about the information he'd picked up as a result of his conversation with Sister Evangeline, and Pearce added the details he had unearthed.

'The fire at the Endeavour Clinic remains a mystery,' Viv began. 'I spoke to a DS in Coventry, who remembered the case. He told me the file is still open, but inactive without new evidence. I asked him about the clinic and he told me that as far as he is aware, its main function had been as a sort of post-operative convalescent home operating in the private sector, not as part of the NHS. At the time of the fire, the clinic was undergoing major refurbishment; otherwise the death toll could have been far higher. There was some talk at the time that perhaps the material being used for the renovation might have contributed to the intensity of the blaze. He mentioned several gallons of paint that had been left close to a radiator, which doesn't sound a very sensible thing to do.'

'Far from it. Did he think that was what started the fire?' Clara asked.

'No, but it made it worse. He said the fire started in a basement storeroom, where there were a lot of chemicals, cleaning fluids, etcetera. The clinic was fully equipped with an operating theatre, but as far as he was aware no procedures were carried out there.' Pearce turned to another sheet of paper. 'I also found a press article that appeared in one of the local papers at the time. It was an interview with a doctor who had worked at the clinic in the past, and who, for some reason, didn't want to be named. He'd attended patients at the clinic up until a few weeks before the fire, when he left to go work abroad. He was asked to comment on the deaths and said all the usual things: terrible tragedy, sad loss to the medical profession and so on and so forth. To be honest, there didn't seem to be that much point to the interview, more a local reporter trying for a different angle on a story everyone was covering. The only interesting bit I could see was that the interviewee had left to go work in California, and wished to remain anonymous.'

'Why was that, I wonder?' Clara asked.

'No idea,' Nash said, 'but it does sound rather mysterious. Viv, see if you can get hold of that reporter, if he's still around, and ask him if he can remember the guy's name.'

It was half an hour later before Pearce reported back. 'The reporter was a bit reluctant to part with the details, but eventually he came up with a name and the hospital he worked at in California. I checked them out on the internet and it turns out our man is now on their board.'

He passed a sheet of paper across to Nash. 'The phone number is on there, as well as the email address.'

'Before I do anything, what time is it in California?'

'They're eight hours behind us,' Viv told him.

'I'll leave it until later.'

It was almost four o'clock when Nash emerged from his office. To find Clara looking like the cat with the cream. 'What's going on?' he asked.

'Nothing much' – she grinned even more – 'David's home! He sent me a text to warn me not to be alarmed if I find a strange man in my bed when I get home. Apparently, he's tired after the journey.'

Nash refrained from making an inappropriate comment and instead said, 'That's great news.'

'Thanks, Mike. How did you go on with the doctor?'

'I got hold of him and he told me that before he emigrated he took several jobs at the clinic to help pay his removal expenses. The reason for him wanting to remain anonymous was not as sinister as we thought. The work he did at the clinic was cash in hand, so he was anxious to avoid the Inland Revenue getting wind of it.'

'What sort of work was it?'

'That's where it gets really interesting. Apparently, one thing Viv's contact at Coventry CID got wrong was that the clinic *did* conduct operations and our man in California occasionally acted as anaesthetist. He couldn't remember the exact number, but he thinks there were around half a dozen, for which he was paid two thousand a time, which explains his reluctance to part with a lump of it to the tax authorities.'

Clara whistled. 'If the anaesthetist got paid that much, I wonder what the surgeon's fee amounted to?'

'I've no idea, but given the type of procedure involved, I would guess it would have been pretty steep.'

'What sort of procedures were they?'

Nash told them, adding, 'I'm not sure whether it has any bearing on our inquiry, but I've got a feeling it could be important. Just don't ask me why, because at this precise moment I have absolutely no idea.'

Pearce's phone rang. He listened, making several notes before thanking the caller. As he replaced the receiver in its cradle, he told them, 'That was the DVLA. They've given me the name of the Mercedes' owner they traced via the VIN. The car is registered to a company in London.'

Nash gestured to Pearce's computer. 'Look them up; see who their directors are and get me their phone number if you can.'

Several minutes later Pearce printed off a couple of sheets of paper which he handed to Nash. Having looked at the details, Nash said, 'I'm going to ring Brian Shaw. I'll do it from in here on speaker so I don't have to repeat myself.'

Fortunately, Shaw was at his desk and answered the call immediately. 'Hells Bells, Mike, have you nothing to do up there? If things are that quiet, maybe I should ask for a transfer. What is it this time?'

'I wouldn't start filling that form in yet if I were you. Remember that conversation your girlfriend repeated to you? The one where she told you all about her boss heading up this way, searching for some lost diamonds.'

'Yes, what of it? Has Thornton got himself into hot water up there?'

'You're closer to the mark than you think, I reckon. Certainly hot, if not water. I reckon you should advise your Candy to start looking for another job.'

Nash explained, adding, 'I think we're going to need to use DNA to confirm identities. One of us will get back to you on that. In the meantime, I'd like a favour from you. Assuming that the bodies were those of Thornton and his henchman, I'd like you to try and find that informant who gave the address to Thornton; presumably he'll remember it. We need to know where Phil Miller and Corinna Perry are staying, and we need to know urgently. They have to be prime suspects for these murders.'

Nash had a stray thought, one not directly connected to the subject of the conversation. He scribbled a single word on the notepad in front of him. By craning her neck to one side, Clara was able to read the word: 'timeline'. She was still puzzling over this when Nash ended the call by asking Shaw, 'When you do pick up that bloke, be sure to ask him about the dates Phil and Corinna travelled up here and exactly when he gave Thornton the information. Candy might also confirm the last bit.'

*

Corinna had begun to run water for the bath when Miller appeared in the doorway. 'Don't bother with that, take the plug out. We've work to do,' he told her.

'What sort of work?'

'You know the expression, one job creates another? Well, I think what we've just done has led to another little task.'

'How do you mean?'

'I got to wondering how Thornton knew where we were staying. There is only one way. When I made the booking, I was in the shop, and I wrote the details down. The Ferret must have seen them. Remember, I was talking to you on the phone about the diamonds and I reckon Freddie must have overheard. In which case, the Ferret has become both dangerous and expendable. If he passed the news to Thornton, he's just as capable of passing information to others.'

'What do you suggest?'

'I think we should silence him.'

'Good, I never liked that man.'

'It'll mean a long drive there and back. Are you up for it, or do you want me to go alone?'

'No problem, I'll manage.'

It was late afternoon by the time they returned, and by mutual consent, both headed straight for the bedroom. Two days and nights with next to no sleep had left them drained, exhausted. 'If the stones are in that cottage, they'll have to wait another twenty-four hours,' Miller muttered. 'They've waited long enough; another day won't hurt.'

'You don't think there's a curse on them, do you? It seems to me that every time we get close to them, something happens to set us back.'

Miller stared at her in surprise. 'It's unlike you to believe in superstition.'

'Yes, maybe you're right. Perhaps I'm just tired. But think about it. We believed Ray would lead us to the stones. He didn't. We thought the bastard boy must know. He didn't. Then we found out the place where the diamonds might be hidden, and we couldn't get in because of a ghost – or a house-sitter. Last night we were all set to go back and we had to deal with Thornton instead. Today, we should have definitely been going there, but we're both too knackered from the long drive to sort out the Ferret. Everything that's happened delays us finding the stones, and I haven't even mentioned the cause of the biggest delay of all. If she hadn't snuffed it before she could tell us where she'd hidden the stones, none of this would have been necessary.'

'I don't think there's a curse on them. People were dying because of those diamonds long before they came anywhere near us. Forget it; put it down to weariness. You'll be thinking straight in the morning.'

'We'll have to do something about them soon, though. For one thing, the woman from the cottage is due back.'

'No, it's a few days yet.'

'Even more important, our deadline's getting close. We can't afford to miss that.'

'If we have to, we have to.'

'The point is, we don't have to. This is everything we worked for, remember?'

'Mike? Brian Shaw here.'

Nash put the phone on speaker for Clara's benefit. 'Don't tell me you've picked up Freddie the Ferret already?'

'I haven't.' Shaw's tone was grim. 'Others have, though.'

'Problems?'

'You could say that. Freddie caught the underground this morning.' Shaw paused before adding, 'Unfortunately for Freddie, he caught it head on.'

'Oh, nasty! It sounds to me like someone is trying to cover their tracks.'

'According to the report I read, Freddie covered several tracks.'

'You two are really sick, do you know that?' Clara told them.

'Without Freddie's information,' Nash said, 'we can't find out where Phil and Corinna are staying. Unless we can do that, we'd struggle to prove they were here at all, and certainly find it difficult to pin any of the murders on them. Freddie's untimely close encounter of the Tube kind might just have set our whole inquiry back to square one.'

chapter sixteen

Nash was about to go out of his front door when the phone rang. He returned to the lounge. One glance at the caller display on the handset turned his thoughts into work mode. 'Good morning, ma'am,' he greeted the chief constable.

'Good morning, Mike, I understand there have been two more deaths? What exactly happened?'

Nash described the circumstances.

'When will you know more?'

'The post-mortems are this morning. In fact, you've only just caught me, I was about to set off when you called.'

'In that case, I won't detain you. Come and see me when you've finished at the mortuary. With Superintendent Fleming away, I need you to keep me in the loop.'

'I was hoping to do that anyway and I've got all the case files with me, just in case.'

When Nash arrived at Netherdale General, Ramirez was waiting in his office alongside the cold, cheerless morgue. The pathologist was kitted out for the procedure he was about to conduct. He wasted no time in greeting Nash, merely pointing to the viewing area. 'Let's get on with it. I have lectures this afternoon.'

Nash walked through into the glass-fronted area alongside the procedure room where he perched on the hard wooden bench that ran along the front of the gallery. The seat wasn't designed for comfort, but it was better than standing throughout what he knew was going to be a long, drawn-out complex operation. Two operations, to be exact, but at least the two bodies were now separated and laid on adjacent tables.

Via the intercom, Nash asked, 'How did you get them out of the car, Professor?'

'We didn't. We took the car from round them; less chance of damaging the corpses. Have you any idea as to their identities?'

'We're going to need DNA matches to be absolutely certain, but we have established who the car belongs to. We know the owner travelled up from London recently, together with another man. If your examinations can establish the approximate age of the victims, it will show us whether we're on the right lines or not. I assume both victims are male?'

Something that might have been a smile passed fleetingly across the pathologist's face. 'They are, even though that isn't immediately obvious. Certain body parts survive incineration far better than others.'

By the time Ramirez instructed his assistant to return the bodies to their drawers in the chilled cabinet they would occupy until they were claimed after the inquest, it was almost lunchtime. Not that Nash was in the least bit hungry. One post-mortem was a highly effective appetite suppressant. Two, banished all thoughts of food. He obeyed the pathologist's instruction to return to the office.

'Both men had been struck with some kind of blunt instrument,' Ramirez told him, 'what's referred to nowadays as blunt force trauma. However, that didn't kill them. I'm fairly certain they would both have been unconscious when they were placed in the boot of that car, but there is evidence of smoke inhalation in both sets of lungs. Which means,' he added grimly, 'that they were both alive when the fire was started and both suffocated. Whether they would have survived the initial assault had the car not been torched, I cannot say. Either way, both of them were murdered.' He allowed himself a faint smile. 'But of course you already knew that, so this is merely official confirmation.'

'What ages are they, or were they?'

'The shorter of the two would have been around sixty years old and far from fit. He was very overweight and his heart was in poor shape, which showed that he didn't take regular exercise. The younger man, the taller of the two, was just the opposite. He was in excellent condition, very much as you'd expect to see in an athlete, or someone who spent a lot of time working out. He was far younger, and I'd put his age as in the mid-to-late twenties – early thirties at the top side. Does that help point to their identity?'

'It certainly doesn't discount the two men we had in mind. By the sound of it, the older man was probably the car owner, a dodgy club and casino operator by the name of Trevor Thornton. All I can tell you of the younger man is that we suspect he was nicknamed Mr Muscle, and he was Thornton's minder.'

'He didn't do a very good job of it, I'm afraid. I'll check the dental records and let you know what I find.'

Nash left the mortuary and stood outside for a few minutes before getting into his car. There was a gentle breeze blowing, but any hopes he might have entertained that this would dispel the stench, even through the glass, he knew was unrealistic. It would take a long, hot shower and a complete change of clothing before the smell left him.

He drove the short distance across town to the police headquarters building, and after a few minutes spent talking to Tom Pratt, was ushered in to see the chief constable.

'Have you heard anything from Superintendent Fleming? Do you know when she'll be back?' Nash asked the chief as he sat down opposite her.

Gloria O'Donnell shook her head. 'I did manage to talk with her yesterday, but you know how these secondments can drag on. How are you managing without her?'

'We're coping fine. It's not staff we're short of but hard evidence. Certainly nowhere near enough to contemplate making arrests.'

Nash hesitated and smiled. 'Ironically, although we're low on facts, we do have a lot of suspicions and theories, some of them quite wild – and some of them even wilder still.'

'I've listened to your wild theories before,' O'Donnell pointed out, 'theories that later proved to be absolutely spot on, so how about trying a few more out on me?'

Nash took a sizeable stack of folders from his briefcase, which he passed across the desk. 'Those are in chronological order,' he told her, 'and I think it's best if we tackle them that way. There's a heck of a lot to go through, so this could take a long time.'

'That's OK. I'm not planning on dining early this evening because my husband's away on business and won't be back until late. In the meantime, I forewarned my secretary to bring coffee in at hourly intervals, so let's make a start.'

'I think we ought to begin with events that took place over twenty-five years ago, mostly in and around London, before Max Perry was murdered. We believe those events were the catalyst for everything that has happened since, including all the violence around here.'

Going through each of the files, searching for the most minute detail and fitting the pieces of the jigsaw together, was, as Nash had predicted, a long and tiring process. It wasn't until they had examined all the separate incidents and Nash had presented his conclusions that he dared mention his outlandish theory. 'I haven't even had chance to talk about this to Clara or Viv as yet,' he confessed. 'It only came to me last night.'

Nash outlined his idea, and they spent a further half hour re-examining the files. Despite this, neither of them could find anything to disprove the theory. 'The problem you have,' O'Donnell pointed out eventually, 'is proving any of it.'

'There is a way.' Nash explained how it could be resolved. 'That's only half the battle, though. Getting solid evidence to bring a case to court could be far more difficult, unless something else happens, or we get really lucky. At the moment I have absolutely no idea how.'

By the time Nash emerged from the meeting it was late. He phoned Helmsdale, and was lucky to catch Mironova. Clara, it seemed, had been hanging on in the hope of speaking to him. 'I'd like you to contact Shaw,' Nash told her. 'Tell him we're assuming the bodies are those of Thornton and his henchman, but we need to prove it beyond doubt for the inquest and to notify next of kin.'

'OK, Mike, I'll get on to him straightaway. Anything else?'

'Based on our assumption as to who the victims are, Mr Muscle's real identity would also be helpful. The only other thing we're going to need for tomorrow is a checklist of dates from the files, but we can go through that in the morning. Who's on call tonight? Is it you or Viv?'

'It's supposed to be me. That was why I was hanging on here, hoping to get a word with you. I asked Viv to swap, but he's got tickets to take Lianne to the theatre in York, so I was hoping you might agree to stand in for me. There's a programme about Afghanistan on TV tonight and David wants me to watch it with him. I know damned well that if I'm on call, I'll get a shout minutes before the programme starts, or halfway through, which will be even more annoying.'

'Don't worry, I'll cover for you, no problem. Just make sure you let the control room know about the change.'

Despite having gone through all the case files with the chief constable only hours earlier, Nash studied them once more as he ate his less than gourmet dinner, which comprised a quiche he'd bought at Good Buys supermarket on his way home, accompanied by a pre-mixed salad.

He ignored the bottle of wine on the dining table, conscious that the phone could ring at any time. As he concentrated on the Ray Perry file, he lifted the photo of Frankie Da Silva from the other paperwork.

He propped it against the half-empty bottle and stared at the image. When the shot had been taken, techniques such as air-brushing were all but unknown, except to top-class fashion photographers. If this photo hadn't been enhanced, Wellings' praise of the missing woman's beauty was no exaggeration.

Nash looked at the long, dark hair, the soft, lustrous brown eyes, the high cheekbones and the slightly olive cast to the woman's complexion, her face an almost perfect oval. If the name was genuine, and not one adopted for the stage, did that and the complexion argue a Mediterranean ancestry? Da Silva sounded Portuguese. Had her family hailed from Portugal? His admiration of her features was tinged with sadness. The more he heard about events from a quarter of a century ago, the more Nash was convinced that the key to them lay with what had happened to Frankie. Had she absconded with a fortune in diamonds?

Frankie would now be at least fifty years old. The passage of time would have done little to erode her looks. Hers was the type of beauty that withstood the ageing process well. On the other hand, if she hadn't run off to a life in the sun, taking the stones to fund her lifestyle, where was she?

Nash shook his head in sorrow. He thought he knew, and if his idea was right it would mean grief for at least one person. Like so many other facets to this case, Nash was unable to prove it one way or another. Nor would he be able to, unless. . . .

He returned to his quiche, which had been less than appetizing when warm, was completely unappealing now. He pushed the plate away, returned the folders to his briefcase and prepared for an early night. He might be able to get a good night's sleep, providing he could thrust the frustrations of this case from his mind.

Any thoughts Tina might have entertained of a break from work had been banished by her interview with the boss of the software company she worked for. Having been handed the new challenge, Tina presided over a succession of meetings and analytical sessions. She needed to assemble the best available talent to work on the lucrative contract the firm had recently secured.

It was almost midnight by the time she pulled up outside her mother's house. Once inside, she locked up and leaned against the door. A tide of weariness swept over her. She had been in Leeds by 6.30 that morning, and at seven o'clock was beginning the first interview. These had continued throughout the day, with only a twenty minute break for a sandwich and a soft drink. The early evening had been taken up with a meeting with her second in command, to discuss which operating systems they should be designing the new software for. After that, Tina had stopped at La Giaconda, the Italian restaurant in Helmsdale marketplace.

Now, Tina headed upstairs, force of habit taking her into her own room. She hoped tonight's sleep would be uninterrupted, now that she was beginning to get used to her old bed again.

Next door, as Tina tumbled into bed, one of her neighbours was preparing to go to work. Although far from a regular form of work and one that was all but unpaid, the task that faced him was one he would enjoy. It was a favour for his brother-in-law, who farmed the land surrounding the village.

'Bloody rabbits are playing havoc with my yields. I need them sorting out urgently. The trouble is the little buggers are breeding like – well, rabbits. Unless we get rid of them sharpish, the sods will bankrupt me. I tell you one thing, I'd welcome an attack of myxomatosis were it not for the awful way it afflicts them. If you could reduce their numbers a bit, that would be great.'

'I'll take my gun out and lamp them for a night or two. Do you want any for the freezer?'

The farmer shook his head. 'No, they'd stick in my throat. You keep what you need, and sell the others to pay for the ammo.'

He'd smiled at the farmer's optimism. The price he'd get from a game dealer wouldn't go far towards meeting the cost of ammunition. Nevertheless, he was willing to help out.

He checked the rifle and locked his gun cabinet. Before leaving the house, he was tempted to fill the magazine but decided against it on the grounds of safety. He had several stiles to climb and a loaded weapon in that situation could be extremely dangerous. Having tested his powerful, battery-operated spotlight, he placed it in his game bag alongside a couple of boxes of shells.

As he was balancing precariously on one leg and then the other in the act of putting his wellingtons on, a car drew up at the front of the end cottage. As soon as the headlights were switched off, the driver and passenger got out. The driver waited as her colleague removed a small holdall and a sledgehammer from the back seat.

'Ready?' she asked as he straightened up.

'Yes, we'll go round the back. Houses are always easier to enter from the back than the front.'

'How do you know?'

'It was on some insurance statistics I read. House-owners concentrate on making sure the front of their property is secure, but by and large they forget about the back.'

'Fascinating; you live and learn. Come on then, let's do it, and this time I hope we don't see any ghosts.'

They set off towards the track alongside the end house. Little more than a hundred yards away, the rabbit hunter locked his kitchen door and began walking down his back garden, before turning right on to the track that provided access to the back of the properties. Although he had only to pass one other house before reaching the farmland, he would walk several fields away before commencing operations. No point in upsetting the neighbours, one of whom was not the sort to approve and would welcome any chance to make a complaint.

He walked slowly, allowing his night vision to adjust. The moon was almost full and high in the sky. The light from it was so strong that with luck he might not need his torch. He had only gone a few steps when he stopped, his keen senses aware of movement off to his right.

He turned his head slowly, knowing that what he'd seen should not have been there, and not wanting to give his presence away by any sudden motion. He focused his attention on the end cottage, and the area directly behind it. He knew Margaret was away, but that her daughter was at home. The movement behind the house had nothing to do with the lovely Tina, though; that he did know. As he became aware of what he was looking at, he stared incredulously at the two figures half-crouched by Margaret's back door. A burglary? In Kirk Bolton? Such a thing had never happened before. Nevertheless, these two were definitely attempting to break into the house. He hesitated, wondering what he should do. One thing for sure, whatever he decided, it had to be quick. Within minutes, seconds perhaps, the intruders might have forced their way inside, and then Tina would be at risk. No way could he allow that to happen.

His choices were few, and stark. He could return home and call the police, but by the time they reached the remote village, the damage would be well and truly done. He had heard of cases, read about them in the press, where the police hadn't bothered to turn up until the following day to events such as this. Alternatively, he could call out in an attempt to scare them away, but if that failed, he would put himself in peril. For all he knew they could be armed. More and more burglars were going out to commit crimes 'tooled-up', as the papers referred to it.

Almost as a reflex action, he slipped the rifle sling off his shoulder and reached into the game bag for ammunition. He moved with great care, avoiding making the slightest sound that would alert the intruders. Once he had the shells in his hand he hesitated,

161

knowing that what he was about to do was highly illegal. He could think of no alternative, however, and the possible consequence of doing nothing was too terrible to consider. Whatever the outcome, he had to act, and act quickly.

He filled the magazine, something he had done so many times before that he didn't need light to work by. Once he had inserted the final round into the chamber, he looked up. In the short space of time he had been otherwise engaged, the intruders had managed to get the door open, only to be temporarily frustrated by the chain that Tina had wisely ensured was in position. The delay gave him all the time he needed.

The rear door of the cottage was half timber, with glass panes above. His object was to scare them away, and in order to achieve that, he would have to damage Margaret's property. As he lifted the rifle, the thought that he might hit one of the burglars by accident didn't occur to him. He was far too good a shot.

He settled the stock into his shoulder and lined up the target, took a deep breath and let it out again, before squeezing the trigger twice in rapid succession. The effect was dramatic, for the night air was filled with a cacophony of sounds that mingled into a horrendous din.

The reports echoed and re-echoed across the space between the shooter and the houses. These were augmented by the sound of breaking glass as the bullets demolished the top half of the door, before continuing unchecked into Margaret's kitchen. The range cooker opposite the door had a collection of heavy, cast-iron pans hanging above it, and the bullets hit two of these, sending them gyrating on the hooks they were suspended from, until one worked free and crashed heavily onto the tiled kitchen floor, smashing two of the tiles.

The bullets maintained their destructive path, ricocheting from the pans to destroy two glasses, a cola tin, and, in one final act of vandalism, smashing the glass door of the microwave.

'Somebody's shooting at us. Run for it!'

The instruction was hardly necessary. As the intruders made their escape, hampered by the tools they had brought, the gunman lined up one more shot. The end terrace had an outside light fixed to the corner of the building. It was about ten feet from the ground, with the lantern-shaped light suspended below.

As the intruders reached the corner, the gunman squeezed the trigger. The shot destroyed three panes of the lantern, showering the couple with glass fragments. The final shot hastened their departure even more and the neighbour watched with satisfaction as their car hurtled recklessly out of the village, close to being out of control.

He turned, and braced himself for the consequences of what he'd done. Already lights were going on in the terrace and the houses nearby. The sound of voices, angry voices, frightened voices, curious voices, reached him as he waited. Only when he saw a light appear at the rear bedroom window of the cottage occupied by Tina did her neighbour abandon his vigilante pose. He thumbed the safety catch of the rifle into the on position and walked slowly towards her back door, which remained ajar; witness to how close the intruders had come to gaining access.

Nash wasn't sure how long he'd been asleep, or how long the phone had been ringing before it roused him. He groped for the receiver, but only succeeded in knocking it off its cradle. He switched the bedside light on and rescued the instrument from the floor, in time to hear Jack Binns' voice. 'Mike, are you there? Mike, come on, wake up, you lazy sod.'

'Jack, what's wrong?'

'Ah, there you are. Sorry to disturb you, but there's been trouble at Kirk Bolton. Intruders tried to break into one of the cottages and a neighbour spotted them and started letting fly with a rifle. The reports are a bit garbled, but by what I can make out it sounds like the *Gunfight at the OK Corral.*'

'Anybody wounded?'

'I don't think so, but I can't be sure. I've sent a couple of cars to the village and I'm about to set off, but I thought you'd want to be involved.'

'I'll be on my way as soon as I'm dressed.'

'My apologies for waking you' – Binns paused, before adding slyly – 'and whoever else I may have disturbed.'

'Sorry, Jack, you couldn't be further from the mark.' Nash paused. 'Speaking of being off the mark, you'd better give me the address in Kirk Bolton.'

When Nash reached the village, he realized that the directions had been unnecessary. The flashing lights of three police cars were all the guidance he needed. The uniformed officer standing by the gate greeted him. 'Sheriff Binns is inside with Billy the Kid and the house-owner's daughter, a cracker of a girl called Tina.'

Nash walked down the front path, wondering how the officer managed to be so cheerful at this time of night, but then he hadn't been dragged out of bed. Binns was standing by the fireplace holding a rifle by the barrel and talking to a middle-aged man who had a game bag slung over one shoulder. Nash noted with approval that the sergeant was wearing gloves.

After Binns introduced the man, who he referred to as 'the neighbourhood gunslinger', Nash asked him to explain exactly what had happened.

The neighbour hesitated for a moment. 'I was going out to deal with a rabbit problem on my brother-in-law's farm and I saw two people trying to get into Margaret's, er, I mean Mrs Fawcett's house. They'd almost succeeded, but I fired a couple of warning shots to scare them away. It worked, too. I didn't know what else to do,' he added, explaining his dilemma.

'I understand the problem,' Nash told him, 'but discharging a firearm in a way that could have endangered life is a very serious offence and I'm afraid you will have to answer for it.'

Before he could elaborate and explain the precise nature of the trouble the neighbour was in, the door leading to the dining room opened, and a young woman came in, carrying two mugs of coffee.

Binns, who was looking at Nash as she entered, saw the detective's expression change. The colour drained from Nash's face as he stared at the newcomer in open-mouthed astonishment. The detective's mouth moved several times as if he was about to speak but no sound issued forth.

'Mike,' Binns introduced him, 'this is Tina. Her mother owns this house. This is Detective Inspector Nash.'

Tina handed the mugs to her neighbour and Binns before

turning to shake hands with Nash. The detective seemed to be in shock from the girl's appearance, but whether that was down to her undoubted beauty or some other cause, Binns couldn't be sure.

Nash shook Tina's hand but maintained his hold on it far longer than politeness decreed. As he continued to stare at her, Tina became uncomfortably aware of his gaze. She let go of his hand, before asking, a trifle awkwardly, 'I'm sorry, is something wrong?'

chapter seventeen

Despite their disturbed night, both Binns and Nash were in work early.

'What was up with you last night, Mike?' Binns asked. 'You looked absolutely gob-smacked when you saw Miss Fawcett. Was it another case of lust at first sight? That has happened before, as I remember.'

Nash explained. 'You've heard the expression, "You look as though you've seen a ghost"? Well that was pretty much it for me last night. I'd been looking at a photo of a woman who has been missing for years, and next thing I saw a young woman who could have been her twin.'

When Mironova arrived, Nash was waiting for her in the CID main office. 'Anything happen last night?' she asked as she hung her jacket up.

'It certainly did.' Nash told her about the Kirk Bolton shooting. 'Miss Fawcett and the Sundance Kid are due here any time now to give their statements. I want you to be here, especially when Tina Fawcett arrives.'

Clara groaned. 'Don't tell me, she's a gorgeous-looking girl and you fancy the pants off her?'

'Why does everyone around here automatically think the worst of me?' Nash grumbled.

'They call it previous experience, I believe.'

'She is certainly very beautiful, but it isn't her looks I want you here to witness. Well, it is and it isn't,' he added cryptically. He opened the Max Perry file and placed it in front of her.

At that moment the phone rang. 'Miss Fawcett and Wild Bill

Hickock are here,' Binns told Nash.

'OK, Jack, I'll come down for them.'

Minutes later, Clara looked up from her study of Frankie Da Silva's photograph, wondering why Nash had chosen to give her it at that precise moment, to see him re-enter the room. Her gaze switched to the young woman alongside him. Clara gasped aloud as she saw Tina. Or, as she thought, Frankie Da Silva.

Mironova shook her head in disbelief. This couldn't be Frankie. The girl was far too young. She looked at Nash, her expression an appeal for help. He nodded, as if in answer to a question. 'I know,' he told her, 'you can imagine what I thought last night.'

'Would someone mind telling me what's going on?' Tina demanded.

'I'm sorry. Clara, this is Tina Fawcett.' He reached for the photo.

Tina smiled. 'I'm afraid you are under a misconception, Inspector Nash, my name isn't Fawcett, it's Silver, Christina Silver.'

'That's your real name? So where does the Fawcett come from?' Nash asked.

'I don't know. I think it might have been my grandmother's maiden name, but to be honest I know so little of our family history I can't be sure.'

If Nash and Mironova had been shocked by the likeness of the photo, the effect on Tina when she looked at it was, if anything, even more dramatic. Only a very close scrutiny of the photograph revealed a couple of tiny variations, otherwise the two were identical.

'I don't understand. This is not me, yet it looks so like me. Who is this woman? Even I had to look twice, but I can assure you, that isn't me.'

'We know that,' Mironova reassured her. 'Even if we hadn't known who the woman in this photo was, after a while we'd have worked out it wasn't you.'

Clara looked across at Nash, who nodded. 'This photo was taken a long time ago,' Mironova continued. 'It's probably coincidence that your hairstyle is so similar, which strengthens the likeness even more.'

'I was going to have it cut today,' Tina remarked, 'I prefer it long, but my mother doesn't like it.'

'Any special reason for that?' Nash asked.

Tina shrugged. 'Not that I know of. She's got a lot of' – she hesitated – 'strange dislikes and prejudices. I put it down to another of my mother's whims. She never talks about the past, or our family. So tell me, who is this woman?'

'She was a nightclub singer who appeared on stage in London during the 1980s. Her name is Frankie Da Silva. She disappeared—'

'Did you say her name was also Silver?' Tina cut Nash short.

'No, not Silver, Da Silva.'

'Could Silver be the anglicized version? Could this woman be related to me?'

Nash avoided the subject. 'We're looking into all sorts of possibilities at the moment. I assumed Fawcett was your father's name. That your mother took it when she married.'

'My mother wasn't married – that much I do know. As for my father' – she shrugged – 'I have no idea who he is, or was, and from what little my mother told me, I don't want to know. My mother took the name Fawcett so that he couldn't trace her.'

'Did she tell you why?'

Tina hesitated. 'She certainly didn't go into much detail. All she said was that she was lucky to be alive, and if he ever found her, he would probably kill her, unless she managed to kill him first. I know she had a pathological fear of men, and for a long time she couldn't bear to be alone in a room with a man.' She smiled. 'I think she would have been far happier if I'd turned out to be a lesbian. She did her best to put me off relationships with men, told me they weren't to be trusted and all I'd get from them would be sorrow.' Tina seemed as if she was about to say more, but then changed her mind. Nash, who was watching her carefully, felt certain she was concealing something.

'That sounds to me like the consequence of an abusive relationship,' Mironova commented. 'Does your mother look like you, or like the woman in the photo?'

'A little bit, but the resemblance is nowhere near as strong.'

'Did your mother ever mention if she had a sister, or any other family?'

'No, like I said, she wasn't prepared to talk about family matters.' She frowned. 'But I believe there was some mystery, something that might happen at any time, although what it was, I've no idea.'

'That sounds strange,' Nash suggested. 'Do you know what she was hinting at?'

'No, all I know is she once told me, around the time I left school, that one day someone might knock on our door and ask for something. If they did, and she wasn't there, I had to ask them a question, which would act as a password. If they gave the correct answer, I had to contact her immediately, wherever she was.'

'Didn't that strike you as odd?' Mironova asked.

'Very odd, but then, I was used to her eccentricity by then.'

'Did she give you any idea what the mysterious object they would ask for was?'

'No, I did ask, but she said it was better if I didn't know. She said that the caller would be able to tell me, so long as they had the right answer to the passport question.'

'Passport question? Would you mind explaining?'

Tina looked at Nash and smiled. 'I had to ask them to tell me what my full name is.'

'Your full name?'

'Yes.'

'And that is?'

'Christina Evangeline Silver.'

Nash's biro clattered as it fell on the desk.

Although Tina pressed him, Nash refused to explain their reaction. 'We need to speak to your mother,' he said, 'does she have a mobile phone with her?'

'My mother doesn't own a mobile. She's a complete technophobe. She can't even work a video player. When DVDs came out, she was first in the queue, because she could just about manage one of them. Strange, really, that I should finish up working in computer software when my mother can't even switch one on. She'll be home in a couple of days, though. Won't it keep until then?'

'I think it would be better if we were able to speak to her before, if possible. Do you know which coach company she was travelling with?'

'I assume it would to be the local one. She certainly won't have booked online.'

'In that case, I feel sure the courier will be contactable. Either him or the driver. Failing which, the company will know their itinerary, and we could try the hotels they're stopping at en route.'

'Please don't take this the wrong way, but if you need to talk to my mother about anything personal, I think it would be better if Sergeant Mironova was the one to speak to her. She is still not comfortable around men, especially if the subject matter is delicate. I also think I'd prefer you to wait. If she gets the idea that I might have been in danger she'll be fretting all the time until she gets home. I don't want what happened last night to spoil her holiday. After all, I didn't come to any harm.'

Nash accepted Tina's advice. 'OK, we'll leave it for the time being. Sergeant Mironova will get hold of the contact details, but I promise we won't use them unless we have to. How's that sound?'

Tina smiled her appreciation.

'I'll go get the details now,' Clara said.

When they were alone, Nash said, 'I think it would be best if you were to move out of the cottage until this is cleared up, or at least until your mother returns. You could book into a hotel in Helmsdale and I'll make sure you're protected there. I really wouldn't be happy about you staying at the cottage, even with a police guard present.'

'I don't understand. Why would I need a guard?'

'Let's just say I don't think this was a burglary – it may be connected to something in your mother's past and I think we should take precautions for your safety.'

Tina studied him for a moment and realized he wasn't about to explain any further. 'That's all very well, but I have nothing with me. I'd have to go back to collect some clothing and other things I might need.'

'OK, if you'll agree to stay in town, we'll leave your car here and I'll drive you back to Kirk Bolton to get what you want after I've seen to your gun-toting neighbour.'

'Is he in trouble?'

'It's not my decision, but going by the strict letter of the law, he should be charged.'

'But that's so unfair. He only did it to protect me. Heaven knows what might have happened if he hadn't scared those horrid people away.'

She leaned forward, her expression pleading. 'Couldn't you use your influence on his behalf, Mr Nash? If he hadn't intervened, you could have been investigating my murder. Surely, you wouldn't have wanted that, would you?'

Nash looked into Tina's eyes. A mistake. Never the most resolute in the face of female charms, Nash was unable to deny Tina this request. He wondered fleetingly if Ray Perry had felt like this when he met Frankie Da Silva.

'Inspector Nash,' Tina's voice was little more than a whisper as she edged even closer to him. 'Please do it, for me. I would be ever so grateful.'

'OK, you win. I'll let him off with a caution.'

Nash wondered if the increase in his blood pressure was directly related to the radiance of Tina's smile.

Nash explained his plan to Mironova, and after collecting Tina's neighbour, set off with his passengers.

There was little conversation on the journey to Kirk Bolton apart from Tina once again thanking her neighbour for his intervention. 'And it's thanks to Inspector Nash that you didn't get into trouble for firing your gun,' she added.

'No, that was down to you,' Nash corrected her. 'I couldn't resist your pleading. Besides, I think justice would hardly have been served.'

Tina set off down the path and unlocked the front door, whilst Nash paused for a word with the constable on guard duty. The officer was standing alongside his car, which was parked close to the gate. His uniform jacket was lying on the back seat, and Nash guessed that prior to their arrival, his tie would have been loosened.

'Any suspicious characters around?' Nash asked.

The officer smiled. 'Not since Sergeant Binns left.'

'OK, but keep your guard up. Miss Silver won't be staying here tonight; we're not sure if she, or something else within the house, was the target, so they may be back for another go.'

When Nash entered the house, Tina was surveying the debris in the kitchen. 'I'll have to tidy this lot up. It shouldn't take long,' she said. 'If you want I'll make you a drink while you wait and I'm getting my stuff. Would you prefer tea or coffee?'

'Coffee for me, every time.'

Nash was staring at the wreckage of the microwave. Tina followed his gaze. 'I don't know how Mother's going to explain the damage to the insurance company if she wants to make a claim.'

'It would certainly make interesting reading,' Nash agreed.

She lifted the dustpan and brush from the cupboard alongside the range, which Nash saw with interest was actually a cellar head. 'Why don't I sweep up, and you can be making a start on your packing.'

'How do you like it?'

'Sorry?' Nash wasn't concentrating.

'Your coffee, how do you take it?'

The smile on Tina's lips showed she was well aware of the double entendre.

'Oh, white with one sugar, please. I've got the worst of the mess up now; where shall I tip it?'

She pointed to the cellar head. 'There's a swing bin behind the door. You've done a good job. I can see you're handy around the house. I expect your wife likes the help.'

'Oh, I'm not married.'

'No?'

'That comes of having to tidy up after an energetic eight-year-old boy.'

'You have a son? I thought you said you aren't married. Divorced then?'

Nash shook his head. 'Daniel's mother died three years ago.'

'I'm sorry, I didn't mean to pry.'

She turned away and headed for the stairs. If Nash had been able to see her face, it would have shown no trace of regret. Satisfaction, more like.

During their return journey, Nash asked Tina about her work. 'You said you'd been in America for a couple of years. What was it you were doing there? Something interesting?'

'The work was very interesting. The most frustrating part was that due to the nature of the job and identity of the clients, I wasn't allowed to talk about it; still can't, for that matter.'

'That must make it difficult at parties.'

Tina laughed. 'If I tell people I'm a computer software designer, I see their eyes glaze over and then they change the subject. I think that's because they don't wish to expose their ignorance.'

'Why, I wonder? I've watched pathologists and forensic scientists at work many times and I'm not afraid to admit that I understand very little of what they do. Actually,' Nash added, 'on reflection, I don't want to know much about what pathologists get up to. Attending post-mortems is bad enough. However, I also use computers both at home and at work, but I still don't know very much about them. If I ask the right questions or press the right keys I get the answer I want; that's all I need.'

'That puts you on a par with almost all other computer users.'

'Is your return to England temporary? Are you on holiday, or will you be staying here for a while?'

'The project I was working on in America is complete. All that's needed from here on in are some regular updates. I'm hoping that those can be done remotely, although our clients aren't too keen on that for security reasons. Some of their systems got hacked before we came onboard and it's left them feeling very touchy. Anyway, my transatlantic voyages are over for the time being. I was hoping for a nice break when I got back but my boss had other ideas. The company has gained another contract, even bigger than the one I was working on in America, and my boss put me in charge of a team to design a program for a big banking group. When I say he put me in charge, I mean that he told me to pick out the team members I wanted and start recruiting. As soon as they're onboard we can start work. Or rather, they can. I've already started. No rest for the wicked, isn't that the expression? Well, I must be really, really wicked.'

As she spoke, Tina crossed her legs, causing the hem of her skirt to ride up. Nash was concentrating on the road, but the movement in his peripheral vision didn't go unnoticed. Nor did the sight of her long, shapely legs go unappreciated.

When Nash returned to the CID suite Mironova and Pearce were waiting. 'I asked Viv to do some research,' Clara explained as soon as Nash entered the room. 'I think you'll find the result very interesting.

Pearce handed him a sheet of paper. 'Clara asked me to find out all I could about this Phil Miller bloke. But I came across this piece. It stood out because of the mention of diamonds.'

Nash read the item, which was taken from an entry in a South African newspaper. He looked across at Mironova. 'That tallies with your wild theory,' she pointed out, 'even the dates are right.'

'Yes, I agree. I think we ought to have another word with our Californian anaesthetist friend and see how good his memory is.'

Frustratingly, when they attempted to contact the anaesthetist, they were told that he was on leave, and wouldn't be available for another couple of days. Nash felt that the investigation had been put on hold. 'I almost want something to happen, simply to move things along,' he told Mironova. 'However, before you say anything, I am aware of the danger in wishing anything of the sort, because it usually results in far too much action for us to cope with.'

'We might be in with a chance of making progress once Margaret Fawcett returns,' Clara suggested, 'and it isn't as if that doctor's gone surfing or whatever they do in California for very long.'

Mironova had a wild theory of her own, and it was about the cause of Nash's unease. She'd known him long enough to be aware that being in the vicinity of a lovely young woman such as Tina Silver would often make him restless.

'I had a message from London; things are getting desperate.'

Corinna looked at Phil, then glanced down at his mobile. 'Go on, tell me the worst,' she said.

'We have until the end of the month. After that, it's curtains; they take the lot. Even the stuff we thought was safe. They've found out where we've stashed everything. Even some of the loans have been bought up.'

'Shit! How could you have landed us in this mess? All through your greed, and because you thought you were getting a better deal than others.'

'Hang on; I don't remember hearing you object when the money was rolling in. I don't recall any mention of greed, or the risk involved then.'

'No, but we should have known it was too good to be true, too good to last. And now we're stuck up here, next door to being skint, bailiffs about to hammer on the door and still no closer to finding the diamonds. What the hell are we going to do?'

'I've been doing some thinking and I've come up with a plan.'

'Another one! Go on then, tell me. Let's hope it works this time.'

'We're going back to that cottage tonight, and we're going to get inside. We're going to search the place from top to bottom, and nobody is going to stop us, nobody is going to get in our way.'

'Oh yes? And how do you intend to achieve that little miracle? Don't tell me, let me guess. We're going to disguise ourselves as Santa Claus, hire a team of flying reindeer and drop down the chimney; is that it?'

'No, not quite,' he said, calmly. 'I think we'll be able to achieve what we want without going to quite such extremes.' He explained what he had in mind.

Corinna thought the plan over for a few moments, before conceding, reluctantly, that it might work. 'That's all very well,' she pointed out, 'that'll get us inside the house, but how do we go about getting out again?'

'I've had an idea about that as well.'

chapter eighteen

For many people, working from a hotel bedroom would have been a struggle, but Tina was well used to it. Her main difficulty was the distraction caused by recent events. The upheaval of the previous night and the sparse information Mike Nash had felt able to give her that morning, were responsible for her lack of concentration.

She cleared her mind with a conscious effort that was almost physical, and began work on the project. Once she got started, Tina became so wrapped up in the task that she failed to notice the passage of time, and it was only when she reached the end of a long and particularly difficult piece of technical writing that she became aware of two matters requiring her urgent attention.

The first of these was hunger, and with it the realization that it had almost reached the time when the hotel dining room would close. Tina emailed the piece to her boss for him to look over and approve, then switched off her laptop. She stood up and stretched, remembering that one of the files she needed to continue her work had been left at the cottage.

As she went down the broad staircase to the ground floor and headed for the dining room, she smiled ruefully. Mike had assured her the cottage was being well protected, so it would be a simple matter for her to drive out to Kirk Bolton once she had eaten and collect the file without putting herself in the slightest danger. That settled, all she had to do was pick something palatable from the menu.

'Let me get this straight. Your idea is to start a fire at the village hall. Then you hope this will bring the coppers to investigate, or help, and whilst they're away, you'll nip into the cottage and begin searching for the diamonds or something that will show us where they are.'

'Right so far.'

'Meanwhile, I wait until you call me, and then start another diversion if the coppers have gone back to guarding the house, right?'

'Correct.'

'And in order to do that, you want me to make an attempt to break into the big house at the end of the village green, next door to the vicarage, thereby triggering the burglar alarm and getting the coppers away from the cottage again.'

'Correct. The coppers will have to go and investigate a burglar alarm going off. It's what we pay our taxes for. If by any chance they don't move immediately, start smashing a few windows. That'll fetch them running.'

'That's all very well, but what if the house-owner wakes up and comes outside blazing away with a shotgun? The locals seem very trigger-happy round here.'

'That's highly unlikely. Not unless he's got extremely good eyesight. The bloke who owns that house has gone to Italy to collect some sort of award or other at an international congress of genealogy.'

'I'm intrigued to know how you found that out.'

'I read it in the local rag. It was the name of the village that attracted my attention. I had nothing else to read at the time.'

'I suppose that's one of the benefits of total boredom.'

The village hall served as a focal point for activities, not only for the villagers of Kirk Bolton, but for the inhabitants of several other small villages, hamlets and farmsteads that clustered around the upper end of the dale. During the week, the hall was used on a daily basis by a pre-school playgroup, and in the evenings, activities as diverse as the WI, the local Scout troop, keep fit classes, Pilates and line dancing took place.

Except on rare occasions, the place had usually been vacated by ten o'clock at the latest, and before eleven it was deserted, in darkness. 'How do you plan to do this?' Corinna asked.

'Simple enough; I've a petrol can in the boot of the car. The building's made of timber, it'll go up dead easy, especially after the weather we've had. I'm going to start the fire round the back, away from sight of the village; that way it'll get a good hold before any busybodies come along and put it out.'

'What if no one notices?'

'Then you'll have to ring 999 from that phone box over there.' He pointed to an old red box along the street. 'Once the coppers hear the sirens they'll be bound to go take a look – they're nosey enough. Besides which, I guess they'll get a message about the fire. I think all those radios they wear are linked.'

Phil looked round, inspecting the houses that encircled the village green. Except for one or two, they were in darkness. 'You might have to do that anyway; it looks as if they all bugger off to bed as soon as it gets dark. Mind you,' he sniffed, 'there's nothing else to do round here.'

'That bloke with the cannon last night was still up.'

'I reckon he might have been a poacher. Anyway, with luck he'll not be around.'

It was a warm night, and the front of the vicarage had been in full sunlight all afternoon and evening until sunset. Before retiring for the evening, the vicar had asked his wife if it would be in order for him to open their bedroom window a little.

'Of course, dear. To be honest, I don't think I could sleep otherwise. Even with the summer-weight duvet, it's stifling in here.'

'It is rather,' he agreed. 'But I was concerned that the pollen would affect you. I don't want to spark a hay fever attack.'

'I don't think it will. It seems to have passed for this season, thank goodness.'

They had been asleep for less than an hour when her coughing woke him. At first, he thought she had been over-optimistic about her hay fever, but then he caught the faint smell of smoke. The thought that the vicarage might be on fire alarmed him enough to complete the waking process, and he thrust the duvet back. As he stood up, his altered position allowed him to see through the gap in the curtains he had left to allow cool air into the room. It was then that he saw the orange glow. The orange glow that should definitely not have been there. The orange glow that told him it was not the vicarage that was on fire. He moved swiftly to the window and peered out. One look was sufficient to confirm what he feared.

'Wake up, dear. The village hall is on fire!'

The vicarage didn't run to such luxuries as extensions for the phone, so he had to put his dressing gown and slippers on and was going out of the bedroom door before his wife was fully awake. She was still wondering whether she had been dreaming, or whether her husband had actually said something about a fire, until she sat up. Then she, too, saw the glow.

Phil and Corinna had driven to the far end of the village, well away from the fire, to await events. They could see the police car stationed outside the cottage. By driving slowly along the narrow lane that circled the village green, they had been able to approach without being observed. Having to drive without lights, even on so deserted a road, had been part of the reason they had taken it slowly. The other benefit was that as the car engine was little more than idling it could not be heard more than a few yards away.

By using their mirrors, they were able to see the glow as the fire became more intense. They had an anxious wait, as the minutes ticked by without any sign that their diversionary tactic had worked. Corinna placed her hand on Phil's arm. 'Listen.'

Through the open window, they could hear the sound of a distant siren. 'I hope that isn't an ambulance going to attend to a short-sighted farmer who's tried to milk a bull,' Corinna stated.

'I don't think they do milking this late at night.'

'If you've learned things like that, I reckon you've been in the countryside far too long.'

'Tell me about it. Hopefully it won't be for much longer.'

The sirens were much clearer now, signalling the approach of more than one emergency vehicle. 'I reckon things will start to happen soon. I can see blue lights behind us now,' Corinna told him, 'and look!' She pointed across the village pond to where the police car was parked. 'They're on the move.'

Tina was still seated in the dining room and was about to set off for the cottage when her mobile rang. She glanced at the screen, at first reluctant to answer the call, but it was from her boss, and she knew he wouldn't cease until she answered it. 'I don't believe you,' she told him. 'Go home and spend the evening with your wife and kids like any normal human being.'

'I am at home. I've been looking through that stuff you sent through and I've a couple of quick questions for you.'

The quick questions turned into an interrogation that lasted almost an hour, by which time the waiters had cleared Tina's table and switched off all but one of the lights. Eventually, even her boss ran out of things to ask, and Tina ended the call with a sigh of relief. It was gone eleven o'clock when she was finally ready to set off for Kirk Bolton.

Since her return, Tina hadn't yet enjoyed a decent night's sleep. Getting used to her own bed again hadn't been easy, and last night's disturbance at the cottage had ruined any chance of rest. These factors, combined with the jet lag involved in adjusting to life in a different time zone, converged suddenly to leave Tina feeling unutterably weary. Approaching Kirk Bolton, she found it increasingly difficult to keep her eyes open, let alone concentrate on the road ahead. More than once, as her eyelids drooped, the car wandered across the white line into forbidden territory.

She adjusted quickly and opened the windows to breathe in some fresh air. A mile or so from the village, the road diverged. Although both routes led to Kirk Bolton, the left fork took the driver on towards Bishops Cross. The right fork only went to one end of the village, before winding round past the duck pond and the village green, to rejoin its counterpart near the village hall.

The right fork was by far the more direct route to her mother's cottage, and Tina followed it out of habit. In so doing, she failed to see the dramatic events unfolding at the village hall.

She pulled up alongside the police car stationed by the front gate, got out and took several deep breaths, thankful that the journey had been completed without incident. She turned and hurried along the path. The sooner she could pick up the file, return to her hotel and get a good night's sleep, the better. In her tired, almost semi-conscious state, Tina failed to notice that the police car was empty, and that there was no sign of the driver.

Once inside, she headed for the kitchen. She was certain she had left the folder there, on a worktop, when she had been chatting to Mike Nash. In the short hallway, Tina noticed that the house felt cold, cooler than she would have expected. That was strange. It had been a hot day, and the temperature outside was still warm. On reaching the kitchen, Tina switched the light on and immediately discovered the reason for the house being colder than expected. The cellar door was wide open.

Tina made a mental note to chide Mike Nash for his carelessness. She would enjoy that, she thought with a smile. Obviously, when he had emptied the dustpan and replaced it after sweeping up for her, he had failed to ensure the door was closed properly. Tina walked across the kitchen to rectify the omission. As she neared the door, she felt rather than saw, a vague blur of movement to her left. Before she could react, before she even had chance to turn, she was pushed violently forward, the momentum propelling her down the cellar steps. As she fell, Tina flung out her arms to protect her. She collided with the wall at the bottom, feeling a sharp pain stab through her left arm; then her head hit something hard and she lost consciousness. Above her, the cellar door was slammed shut, and the key turned in the lock. A second later the kitchen light was switched off.

Breathing hard, Phil moved to the window and stared out over the back garden. There was no sign of movement there. He went through to the lounge and looked out of the window. All seemed quiet enough. He pressed speed dial on his mobile and waited for Corinna to answer. 'Yes, I've got it. Not the diamonds, but a way to get them. I was interrupted, though. I've dealt with it, but we need to get away from here – sharp. If the coppers are still tied up down the road, drive up to the front of the cottage and let's scarper.'

He exited via the kitchen, and using the key from the newly repaired door, locked it behind him. Phil stared at the envelope in his hand. Even in the faint light of the summer night, he could make out the single word written on the front: 'Frankie'.

Nash had been about to go to bed when the phone rang. 'Mike, it's Jack Binns. I know this is going to sound like *Groundhog Day*, but there's been trouble at Kirk Bolton. The village hall is on fire. Our guy went to help and when he returned to the cottage, Tina Silver's car was outside.' Binns took a breath. 'However, he says there's no sign of her, and the house is all locked up. What do you want to do?'

'What on earth is Tina doing there? I booked her into the Fleece and told her not to go near the cottage.'

'That's women for you. Do you want me to go?'

'No, I'll handle it, Jack. And give Tina a good telling-off into the bargain.'

If Binns noticed Nash's use of Tina's first name he didn't comment. But then he knew Nash well.

The journey from Bishops Cross to Kirk Bolton was achieved without Nash encountering another vehicle, which was probably as well, given the pace at which he was travelling. He negotiated his way round the fire engines parked in front of the village hall and sped down the main street. He had sufficient time to notice that the fire had been all but extinguished, but the damage caused by the blaze was considerable, probably beyond repair.

Even Nash failed to connect the fire with events at the cottage at that stage. He reached the house and pulled up behind Tina's car. The constable who was back on duty at the front of the house hurried forward to meet him and was in the middle of attempting an apology when Nash cut him short. 'Have you found her?'

'No, sir. I've tried banging on the front door and the kitchen door, calling out her name, but I can't raise her. I shone my torch through the lounge window and into the kitchen, but there's no sign of her anywhere.'

'Come with me. We'll have to break the glass in the kitchen door.' They ran round to the back of the building where Nash picked up a stone from the rockery and smashed the glass. He stepped inside and switched the light on. Everything seemed as it should be in the kitchen, and he was about to move further into the house when he noticed something over by the cellar door. He went across and picked up a car key ring; the fob bore the name and logo of the hire firm Tina had used. Nash tried the cellar door and was surprised to find that it was locked. He was certain he hadn't locked it, and knew that no one had been in the house since he and Tina had left that morning. 'Hang on a second. Come over here.'

He unlocked the door and felt for the light switch. 'She's here. And it looks as if she's been hurt. Call an ambulance.'

Nash hurried down the steps. His heart was pounding with fear for the girl's safety. She was laying face down, her body curled as if she was asleep. Nash felt her neck and located a pulse. He sighed with relief, his worry easing even more as he felt how strong it was. She moved slightly.

'Tina, can you hear me? It's Mike, Mike Nash. You've had a fall. Don't try to move.'

He looked up. The constable was waiting at the top of the steps. 'Is the ambulance on its way?'

'Yes, sir.'

'Right, go upstairs and find me a blanket or a quilt, something to keep her warm.'

He heard footsteps as the man moved to obey the command. Nash looked down at Tina. She'd moved slightly and he could see the side of her face. Blood was seeping from a cut on her forehead. He took a handkerchief from his pocket and carefully wiped the blood away. The cut didn't look too bad. Once he'd cleaned the area, Nash stroked her cheek gently. He wondered if she could feel the caress, and if she could, would it comfort her in any way. It was all he could do, except wait and hope for the best.

Tina's return to consciousness was accompanied by pain. She could feel a dull throbbing ache in her head and a sharper, stabbing sensation in her left arm. Added to these were a number of areas of her body and legs that felt as if they'd been hit with something hard. She tried to remember what had happened to her, but couldn't. She had been driving. Was that the answer? Had she crashed her car?

She opened her eyes, blinking in the bright light from what appeared to be a long tube above her. As her eyes focused she realized it was indeed a strip light. 'Where am I?'

She hadn't realized she'd asked the question aloud until she heard a voice from alongside where she was lying. 'You're in a cubicle in the A and E department at Netherdale General Hospital.'

The voice was that of a man and although Tina thought she should know who he was, for the moment, she couldn't identify him. She turned her head slightly to try and see who had spoken, but as she did so the pain intensified sharply. 'What happened? Did I have a car accident?'

'No, you weren't in your car at the time, but you did have some sort of an accident. I was rather hoping you could tell me.'

Her eyes were still not right, because she could see two people, both speaking at once, but as she blinked again they merged into one. Mike, that was his name, but how did she know him? Was he a friend, someone she worked with? 'How did I end up here?'

'I found you at the bottom of the cellar steps in your mother's house. Can you remember anything?'

'I must have fallen and banged my head,' Tina told him. 'I think I went there to get something.'

'Are you certain that was what happened? Because I don't think it was quite that straightforward.'

'Your name's Mike, isn't it?'

'That's right. Can't you remember anything more? It might be important.'

'I don't think so. I know your name's Mike, but I can't think who you are. I know this is going to sound silly, but are we. . . ?'

She saw his face change and wondered if she had upset him. 'No,' he told her gently, 'I was concerned about you because of something else that happened. Are you able to remember that? I'm a police officer, if that helps.'

It was really strange; one minute she could recall little or nothing about what had happened to her, the next, she remembered everything. 'I was staying at the hotel because of the break-in, and I realized I'd left an important file at Mother's house. I went back to get it. I went inside, and when I got to the kitchen the cellar door was open. I went across to close it.' Tina shivered. 'Then someone pushed me; pushed me right down the stairs. Then . . . nothing. Nothing, until I woke up a few minutes ago.'

'I knew it couldn't have been an accident because the cellar door was locked and you couldn't have done that.' Nash smiled. 'Not unless you limbo-danced under the door after locking it.'

'You think the same people came back again? The ones who tried to get in the night before?'

'I believe so.'

'Why did you come to the house? Did someone raise the alarm?'

'Yes and no. I got word that the village hall had been on fire and the officer detailed to guard the cottage went to see if he could help. He'll be in trouble for that. When he came back he found your car outside, but couldn't raise you, so I was called out and we broke the door down. That was when I found you.'

'I don't understand. If you had to break the door down, how did the burglars get in?'

'That wouldn't be a problem if they were professionals, believe me.'

'What were they looking for? My mother isn't wealthy; quite the opposite. There are no great treasures in the house, so what are they after?'

'I can't tell you that. Not at the moment, anyway.'

Tina looked down, and saw that her left forearm was encased in a pot. 'Is it broken?'

'Afraid so.'

'No wonder it hurts. My head's throbbing, too.'

'You've had a nasty bump on the head; that's what knocked you out. And you've got a gash on your temple. The doctors will be in to see you, now you're awake. They'll want to keep you in to make sure you haven't got concussion.'

'Oh,' Tina felt the plaster with her right hand. 'I must look dreadful.'

'Not from here, you don't.'

'How long will they keep me here for, do you think?'

'Another twenty-four hours at least, I reckon.'

'But what about my mother? She's due home this morning, and I promised to be at the market place to meet her. The coach arrives at six.'

Nash patted her hand. 'Don't worry; it's all taken care of. Sergeant Mironova is waiting there already. I've asked her to take your mother to Helmsdale police station. After we've had a word with her, I'm going to bring her here.'

'I'm sorry, I seem to be causing you a lot of trouble and extra work.'

'It doesn't matter. You're safe and you're going to be all right. That's what's important. Now, I have to go, but I'll see you later.'

Tina watched him leave. As he turned by the cubicle curtain he looked back and smiled reassuringly. Tina stretched, comforted by his concern for her. A hundred bruises protested.

chapter nineteen

As Clara introduced Margaret Fawcett, two things struck Nash immediately about the woman. The first was that, although there could be no mistaking the family likeness, her resemblance to Tina was nowhere near as strong as that of Frankie Da Silva to the younger woman.

The second of Nash's impressions, might, he thought, have contributed to lessening the likeness, for whereas the photo of Frankie Da Silva had shown her to be elegantly groomed and immaculately presented, the same could certainly not be said of Margaret. The kindest description of her, Nash felt, would be to say that she was dressed tidily.

Her hair was cut short and straight, more like a man's than a woman's. She wore no jewellery, not even studs in her ears, nor was there any other form of adornment about her person. She had no make-up on, and her clothes, although reasonably new, were of a style designed more with older women in mind, or certainly those who were making absolutely no effort to attract attention.

Her handshake was brief, little more than a slight, instant contact and release. As they took their places in the interview room, Nash deliberately placed his chair in the corner, well out of Margaret's direct line of sight, making a clear statement that he was primarily an observer in the proceedings, which would be under the care and control of DS Mironova.

He had not discussed how Clara should conduct the interview, or what line of questioning she should pursue, but if he thought her approach might be gentler, more tactful than his would have been, he soon realized that this was not to be the case.

Clara explained to Margaret why they wished to speak to her, told her about the two break-ins at the cottage, and, once she had reassured her that Tina's injuries were not serious, decided to tackle the woman head on. 'Why do you live under an alias? Tina informed us that the name you're using isn't your own, but we would have worked that out anyway.'

For a few moments Nash thought Margaret wasn't going to reply. After some hesitation, she began to speak, slowly at first but once she started there was no stopping her, even had the detectives wanted to. The story she told was one of almost unbelievable brutality.

'It has become a habit. And I suppose that although the main reason no longer exists, it could still cause . . . difficulties if certain people got to know my real name, or my whereabouts.'

'Can you explain?'

Margaret paused, little more than a slight hesitation. 'There are some people, friends of someone I was once involved with, who might wish to do me harm.' She faltered again. 'It all began when I went to work in Harrogate. I met a man there and fell in love with him. He seemed so nice, so devoted and attentive, but after we started living together, I found out that it had all been an act, designed to trap me.'

She smiled, but it was an expression of bitterness rather than pleasure. 'I have to admit it was a very convincing act, but then perhaps he was feeding on my desire to believe in him. We had only been together a few weeks when he announced that he was, as he put it, "going out with the lads that evening". I assume a lot of women hear that statement on a regular basis and think no more about it, but I soon learned to dread it.

'It was around three o'clock in the morning when he came home. He was drunk' – Margaret's eyes flicked momentarily towards Nash – 'and demanded sex. I wasn't exactly overjoyed at the prospect, but I didn't mind that much.' Her gaze once again went in the direction of the corner where Nash was seated, before dropping to study the table top. 'Because he'd drunk too much, he couldn't . . . well, do anything. And that infuriated him. He decided it was my fault and took his anger out on me, in the form of a verbal assault accompanied by a vicious beating. What I believe is known as giving me a good hiding. For someone with very little experience of men, and who only heard of such things happening to women in other countries, in other ways of life, the shock was almost as brutal as the attack. I had absolutely no idea how to cope with it. I soon realized there was nothing I could have done to prevent it, or to stop it recurring. It was the nature of the beast, I'm afraid.

'The same thing happened another three or four times, and I was still trying to work out how I might be able to get away from this dreadful situation I was in, when things got a whole lot worse.'

'Why didn't you leave him?' Clara asked.

'It wasn't because I wanted to stay, believe me. But I didn't know where to go, who to turn to for help, not then. As I said, I was young and inexperienced, and I didn't know very many people in and around Harrogate at that time. Certainly not people I could go to for help. As for the rest, my parents were dead, and other options were closed to me. We worked at the same place and a lot of people there knew we were together, and assumed we were happy. Above all else, in one of his more sober moments, he threatened that if I mentioned a word about what had happened, he would kill me, and make absolutely certain I suffered before I died.'

'And you believed that?'

Margaret shuddered. 'Of course I did. After his first attack I began reading articles about my situation. I soon found that many women who had endured what I was being subjected to commented that when their abuser sobered up he was apologetic, tearful, begged forgiveness. I regret to say, I experienced nothing of that nature.' Margaret's eyes dropped to her hands, clasped tightly on her lap.

'You said things became worse. I don't see how they could. What happened?' Clara asked, more gently than before.

'The drinking sessions became more and more frequent, and some weeks he was out four or five nights in a row. The only positive side to that was that often the knock-on effect of the continuous boozing made him fall asleep before he could beat me. However, his drinking was taking all our money. As soon as he'd gone through his own wage, he started on mine. I managed to pay the bills, but more often than not he'd blow the housekeeping money on drink and then complain because there was no food in the house. I told him once that the reason we had nothing to eat was because he'd spent the food money. That was a terrible mistake. I found out that the beating he could dish out sober was far more effective than what he could manage when he was drunk.'

Margaret paused for a long time and Clara was about to prompt her with another question, when she continued, avoiding eye contact with Nash. Her voice dropped to little more than a whisper as she described the next part of her ordeal. 'One Friday evening after he'd gone out, I decided to take a bath. I think it was as much to do with stress relief as anything. What I dared not do was lock the door in case he returned unexpectedly. That had happened once, and he'd accused me of having someone else in the house. That was nonsense, of course, because I would certainly not invite anyone there, but it served as a good enough excuse for another beating.

'I had just got out of the bath and gone into the bedroom. I was about to get dressed when I heard the front door open and close, and thought I'd done the right thing. I was sure he'd come back early, probably because he'd run out of money and wanted more. I actually called out his name, but there was no reply. The next minute, the bedroom door opened and I saw one of his drinking cronies standing there, a big brute of a man I'd disliked from the first time I saw him. One look at his face and I knew I was in trouble.'

Margaret stopped and took a deep breath. Nash could see that her hands were trembling and guessed she was close to tears as she described the harrowing details of her ordeal. 'He walked across and yanked the towel from around me. He stood looking at me for a long time, as I pleaded with him to go away, to leave me alone. I don't know ... I'm not sure ... I think my pleading simply made things worse. I think he wanted me to beg. He pushed me onto the bed, pinned me down and forced my legs apart. He started doing things, horrible things ... then he raped me. Not once, but several times. Even now, after all these years, I can still remember the obscenities he used as he was doing it, and the horrible smell of the cheap aftershave mixed with his body odour.'

In the silence that followed, Clara spoke, her tone a gentler one than Nash had ever heard her use. 'Did you report it, or tell your partner what the man had done to you?'

'How could I? In those days the attitude to rape and the way it was dealt with by . . . by . . . by people like you was far different. There were fewer female officers for one thing, and proving rape was by no means as easy. That much I did know. And as for telling him, all that would do would be to hand him yet another excuse for beating me. Eventually, of course, I had to tell him, and the result was even worse than I feared.'

'Why did you have to tell him?'

'Because I found out I was pregnant. He would have known the child couldn't have been his because we hadn't had sex for months, even before the rape. But of course he didn't believe me, and I suppose the fact that I'd delayed telling him only made him more convinced I was lying. His reaction was to call me a slut and a whore. That I must have been doing it with other men, because his friends would never do anything like that. He went on and on, trying to force me to give him the name of the father, of a man who didn't exist. The more I denied it, the more convinced he became that the reason I couldn't or wouldn't tell him was because I'd been with so many different men that choosing the right one to name as the baby's father would have been impossible.

'That was the prelude to the worst beating he'd ever given me. He punched and kicked me in the belly and the head until I passed out. I honestly think he was trying to force me to miscarry, but that didn't work. I almost wish it had. I was unconscious for several hours. Eventually, I came round. By that time he'd walked out, and I never saw him again. I heard later that he went on a bender that lasted for days and got into a pub brawl that turned nasty. He ended up in prison for six months.'

'What did you do?'

'I sat there all night and cried and cried. The following morning I rang the only friend I'd made at work. Girl friend, I mean. It was the best move I could have made. With hindsight I wish I'd spoken to her much earlier. She came round immediately, taking no notice of my warnings about what he might do if he found her there. That was very brave of her, but as I found out later she was no stranger to that sort of situation. She had helped several other women who had been the victims of abusive partners. As soon as she saw the state I was in and found out that I was pregnant, she called her brother, who was the vicar in a local parish. He came to the house and moved me out of there. Gathering my things didn't take long, because I wanted nothing that I could associate with him.'

'Where did you go?'

'They were going to try for the women's refuge but I was in such a state physically, she put me up at her place until the baby was due. I'd had to give up work, both because of my pregnancy and because I'd be at risk if I went back. It was a relief when I found out he was in prison. It was only after the baby was born that I was advised to adopt another name, to protect me for when he was released. I chose one at random.' Margaret smiled faintly. 'Fawcett was off a local butcher's van, I seem to remember.'

'What did you live off?'

'My parents had died a couple of years earlier. As well as the cottage at Kirk Bolton, they left me quite a lot of money. Money he didn't know about. It was enough to see me through.'

Clara frowned. 'Why didn't you move into the cottage to live? Or did he know about that?'

'No, I kept that secret as well. I would have told him after a while, had things been different. But when I found out what he was like, I knew he'd force me to part with the money to fund his boozing. I couldn't go to the cottage at that time. It wasn't safe.'

Both Nash and Mironova sensed that Margaret was keeping something back. Both of them thought they could guess what that was, but neither was certain how to broach the subject. Instead, Nash spoke for the first time, and the question he asked provided a lot more answers than Margaret realized when she replied.

'What did you do for a living, before you had to give up work?' Nash asked.

'I was a midwife at the local hospital where he was an electrician. After I left Harrogate, I heard via my friend that he'd eventually committed suicide. That might have seemed to be the end of it, but several of his friends blamed me for what had happened, and were heard uttering threats about what they'd do if they found me. That's why I maintained the false identity.'

'Why wasn't it safe to go to the cottage? If he didn't know anything about it, neither would his friends.' Clara's question was followed by a long silence, before Margaret replied. The silence was perhaps more informative than her answer.

'I can't tell you that. I promised I'd never speak about it; to anyone.'

Mironova looked at Nash before asking her next question. He nodded, anticipating what it would be. 'Was that because the cottage was already occupied? Was that where your sister Francesca was hiding out?'

Margaret gasped, then looked wildly from one to the other of the detectives, clearly appalled by the depth of their knowledge. Even then, she was unprepared for the extent of what they knew about events from that time. Clara left it to Nash to begin the process of enlightenment.

'My guess is that when Frankie's child was born, you delivered it. A home birth is allowed, I believe, when a registered midwife is present. Was your baby due at around the same time, and did Frankie ask you to look after her child as well as your own?'

'I . . . how did you know that? Frankie told me there was something she had to do, something she'd promised someone and it was very important. She went off three weeks after the baby was born, leaving me strict instructions in the event that she didn't return.'

'When she did fail to return, you must have been really worried. Did you know why she was in hiding?'

'She told me a little about the people she was scared of. But that wasn't all that worried me. Early on in her pregnancy, Frankie started to feel really unwell. Far more than just morning sickness. She rang me for advice and I told her to go for a check up. The tests showed she had a heart defect and she was advised to opt for a termination.' Margaret shook her head sadly. 'They underestimated Frankie's determination and spirit. She would never have succumbed to the sort of treatment I put up with; she would have fought back, whatever the cost. And so it was with the baby. Frankie was head over heels in love with the father and she thanked the medical people for their advice, but refused to consider an abortion at any price.'

'When you say Frankie was in love with the baby's father, I assume you mean Ray Perry?'

Margaret looked at Nash, her expression one of mild surprise. 'Of course, who else? I met him once and Frankie told me he'd been under a bad influence and had done some pretty wicked things. But to me he seemed a very nice bloke.' She shrugged. 'But I'm clearly not the best judge of men, given my track record. I don't think either Frankie or I was particularly good in our choice.'

'What about when Frankie failed to return?'

'What could I do? I couldn't go looking for her, not with two babies in tow. All I could do was wait and hope – and pray. I did a lot of praying, but I don't think anyone was listening.'

'What did you think had happened to her?'

'I wasn't sure. I didn't know if she had decided to go on the run again from the people who were after her, or whether they had caught up with her, or if her heart had given out. The childbirth had taken a lot out of her and she was still very weak, but she was determined to finish what she'd started. I did all I could, which wasn't very much. For a long time after she went, I listened to every news bulletin I could, read every paper from cover to cover trying to find some news of her. I didn't see anything to tell me what had happened.'

'I believe you might have been right on both your suspicions,' Nash told her. 'It's only guesswork, but we think she might have fallen into the hands of the people who were looking for her and the trauma that would have caused could have brought on a heart attack.'

'I don't know, as I said, once she left I never heard from her again.'

'Apart from the letter, perhaps,' Nash suggested.

Margaret looked at him, startled. 'How did you know? About the letter, I mean? I've never mentioned that to anyone, not even to Tina.'

'Not in so many words, but you did tell her someone might come to the cottage asking for something. That something had to be a letter,' Nash paused, 'or the diamonds.'

Margaret gasped. 'Diamonds,' she stammered. 'You know. . . .'

Nash smiled. 'We know. It had to be a letter giving a clue as to where the diamonds were hidden. Either that or the diamonds themselves, but if she'd left them with you, I'm not sure you'd have been able to resist the temptation to sell all or some of them, especially with two youngsters to feed and a limited income at your disposal.'

Margaret looked revolted by the suggestion. 'I would never have touched them.' Both detectives could hear the anger in her tone. 'Not once I learned where they came from. I knew about the wars that were fought because of them. I'd read about what the women who got caught up in those wars had suffered, brutality far worse than what I'd had to endure. It was the knowledge of what those diamonds represented that caused Ray and Frankie to take them. I would never have betrayed their trust.'

'So a couple of years later, when you read about the woman's body that was found in the woods near Bishops Cross, did you think that might have been Frankie?' Clara asked.

'I wondered if it might be, but I couldn't go to the police with my suspicions, for obvious reasons.'

Nash stared at Margaret for a moment, his thoughts on the DNA link between Frankie Da Silva and Graham Nattrass. That, together with the striking likeness of Tina to Frankie prompted his next question. 'How long was it after Frankie's disappearance that you decided to switch babies? And how did you manage the registration? Was it difficult to give your son up for adoption and keep Frankie's daughter?'

Margaret stared at Nash, her fear evident. 'What makes you think Tina isn't my daughter?' she asked, her tone weak and defeated.

'Sadly, I have to tell you that we are currently investigating the murder of a young man who was found battered to death in Helmsdale, a young man of about the same age as Tina. His DNA profile is a close familial match to that of the woman whose body was found in the woods. Close, but not that of mother and son.

Aunt and nephew would be nearer the mark, according to our forensic experts.'

The interview had to be suspended for a few minutes, as Margaret was too distressed to continue. She refused Nash's offer of tea or coffee, but gratefully accepted a drink of water. When she was ready, Nash asked his question about the babies again.

'Even without Tina to look after I wouldn't have wanted anything to do with the boy. I didn't even give him a name until I'd to register him. I couldn't stand the sight of him, didn't want him near me. My skin crawled even when I'd to touch him, to change him, bath or feed him. I know it isn't logical, and I know it wasn't his fault, but all I could see was that man's face; all I could remember was the attack. To be honest, Inspector Nash, if I hadn't given him up for adoption, I'm not sure that I'd have been able to resist the temptation to smother him.'

She paused and took a deep swig from the water. 'It was easy. I had to register both the births. I had the documents, so as the attending midwife I was able to certify that Frankie's child was a boy on the paperwork I wrote for her delivery. On mine I added "fe" in front of the word "male". Having said that, I wouldn't have wished him to come to any harm. Was he a good person, or did his death come as a result of his way of life?'

'We know absolutely nothing bad about him,' Nash reassured her, 'but we do think the people who are searching for those diamonds believed him to be Frankie's son. That's because we suspect that they stole the adoption papers. He was tortured in a fairly horrible way, presumably to extract information from him; information he didn't have.'

chapter twenty

Despite Margaret's statement about the loathing she had felt for the son she had given birth to, she was clearly shocked by the news of what had happened to him, and during the first part of the journey to Netherdale Hospital to see Tina, there was complete silence in the car. Nash had insisted that Clara accompany them. He felt Margaret would be far more comfortable with another woman present. He concentrated on the road ahead, his thoughts occupied with how easy it had been for Margaret to assume a new identity and live under that assumed name for years without questions being asked, and how easy it had been for her to claim her sister's child as her own.

'What will happen now? To me, I mean?'

Nash glanced in the rear-view mirror. Margaret was leaning forward, her question clearly addressed to him as much as to Mironova. 'That's a very good question. You've clearly broken some law or other, but I can't be sure exactly what, or whether you'll be prosecuted. It isn't the sort of thing I come across every day.'

Margaret smiled fleetingly. 'Will Tina have to know that she isn't my daughter?'

'I think she must. There are other people to consider in this, one in particular.'

'How did you work out that Tina was Frankie's child?'

'She told us so – or as good as. She said her full name is Christina Evangeline Silver. Evangeline is the name of Ray Perry's mother. Once we knew that, the rest was easy.'

'Please, can I be the one who tells her?'

'I think the least we can do is to allow that. And perhaps whilst you are telling her, it might help if you explain both why you did it, and that in doing so you actually saved her life, saved her from what her cousin, your son Graham, had to suffer.'

Out of the corner of his eye Nash saw Clara wince, but knew this had to be said. 'He died in place of Tina. She must be made aware of that. It might help her cope with the deception. And I have to say, you seem to have done a very good job of raising her. Tina is a very beautiful young woman.'

Mironova turned her head to look out of the window. That way neither of the others saw her smile.

'In the meantime,' Nash continued, 'you can help us, and by doing that, you'll help bring the people who killed your son and murdered your sister to justice.'

'I'll do whatever I can. For Frankie's sake, and the boy I never gave a chance to.'

'OK, do you know what was in the envelope Frankie sent to you?'

'No, I always assumed it held the location where the diamonds had been hidden, but I never opened it.'

'That's a shame; it would have been very useful to know exactly what that envelope contained. And now the thieves have got it, and have a head start at getting the stones.'

'The solicitor might know.'

'Sorry, what solicitor?'

'Frankie posted the envelope to me inside another one, and included a handwritten note, asking me to keep it safe, and only let it out of my possession if someone came along who could answer the password question, which she set in that note. The question was to give Tina's full name. I knew that person would have to be either Ray or someone acting for him, because no one else could have answered the question correctly. Both the note and the outer envelope were on stationery with a solicitor's name on them. It was a firm in Helmsdale. I see their offices every time I go down the market place. It's a permanent reminder,' – Margaret grimaced – 'one I would rather be without sometimes.'

'I know the firm you mean.' Nash glanced at the clock display on his dashboard. 'They'll be open by now. I must speak to that solicitor – as a matter of extreme urgency.'

When they reached Netherdale General, Nash phoned Pearce and asked for the solicitor's phone number. As he was waiting, he gestured towards the entrance. 'You go in. I'll join you when I've dealt with this.'

On the ward, Clara thought Tina looked subdued. She greeted her mother – or aunt, as she supposed she should now think of Margaret – but without much enthusiasm. Clara wondered if that was usual, or if relations between the two were strained – and if so, what would the revelation of Margaret's deception do to that?

Clara thought Tina's lacklustre and less than enthusiastic greeting might be a result of her ordeal or a side effect of the pain-killers she had been given. Those, combined with jet lag, would have subdued even the bubbliest personality.

Her question was answered a few minutes later when Tina's attitude changed markedly. She noticed Tina glance towards the door and saw her smile, so reminiscent of the photo of Frankie Da Silva. Nash was walking down the ward. If it had been his entrance that had caused the change in Tina's expression – and if she smiled at Mike that way – Clara thought he would be as powerless to resist Tina, as an alcoholic would of refusing a free drink.

'How did it go? Were you too late?' Clara asked when Nash reached the bedside.

He turned from greeting Tina, smiling broadly. 'No, I spoke to the solicitor's secretary.' He guided Clara out of earshot. 'She did have a phone call this morning from a woman passing herself off as Frankie Da Silva's sister. She's booked her an interview for tomorrow morning, because the solicitor isn't in the office today.'

'That was a stroke of luck.'

Nash's smile became a grin. 'You don't know how appropriate your choice of words is.'

'I don't suppose you found out where he is so we can contact him beforehand, did you?'

'I certainly did. The stroke of luck is that he's playing golf in something they call the Monthly Midweek Medal. We're going there as soon as we leave here.'

'I bet he'll be really surprised when we turn up at the nineteenth hole.'

'Not half as surprised as his partner will be. He's partnered with Tom Pratt.'

Nash turned and looked at the patient, who was seated in the chair alongside the bed. Even in the unflattering gown supplied by the hospital she looked highly attractive. 'Have you had word from the medics?' he asked.

'Yes, they came and did all sorts of tests, peering into my eyes and asking a lot of silly questions. The upshot is that they're sure I haven't got concussion and as they can't keep me here against my will, I've decided to sign myself out. I quite understand that you don't want us to return to the cottage in view of what's happened there, but will you take us back to Helmsdale, or should I order a taxi?'

Nash smiled at her. 'Don't worry about that, we'll get you back to your hotel, no problem.' His gaze switched momentarily towards Margaret, who was watching him apprehensively. 'Clara and I have to go and interview someone, which hopefully won't take too long. Then we'll come back here and collect you, if you'll be ready by then. Say in about an hour and a half? In the meantime, I think your mother has something to tell you.'

As he and Mironova turned to leave, Clara saw panic flare in Margaret's eyes. Once clear of the ward, Clara said, 'You were pushing things a bit, weren't you? With Margaret, I mean.'

'I had to, because if I hadn't, I reckon Margaret would have kept stalling. We're so close, and it's bound to come out soon. In which case, it would be far messier than telling the truth now. Anything that reduces the chances of a satisfactory outcome should be avoided, don't you agree?'

'Yes, I suppose so. What would you class as a totally satisfactory outcome, Mike?"

'Phil and Corinna behind bars serving life sentences for the murders they've committed, and justice for as many of their victims and those closest to them as possible would be a good start. That's the only way that Tina and others can feel safe.'

'Ah yes, and Tina's safety is important to you, isn't it?'

'Of course it is. What's wrong with that?'

'Nothing, except that you seem to be taking a very personal interest in this young woman's welfare. Very commendable – especially as she's so plain and unattractive.'

'Oh, very funny.'

'Of course, the fact that her face lights up every time you walk into the room might have something to do with it, too.'

Nash thought of several ways he could answer the allegation, all of which he rejected. In the end, he opted for silence, which was probably wise.

Having talked to the solicitor in the presence of Tom Pratt, whose surprise had been as great as Nash had predicted, they headed back to the hospital. Before leaving the golf club, Nash asked Pratt to phone him at home that evening. 'I've a job I want you to handle for me. All being well, I should have confirmation by tonight that it's all going ahead the day after tomorrow.'

He explained to Mironova what he had in mind on the drive back to Netherdale General. 'When we get back to Helmsdale, I'll drop you at the station first. I'd like you to get hold of Sister Evangeline and make arrangements with her. Whilst you've got her, ask her another question.'

'What's that?'

'Ask her if she ever met Phil Miller. If the answer's no, ask Viv to try to contact our doctor friend in California. He should be back from his surfing by now.'

'Is that still necessary?'

Nash thought about it. 'No, I don't suppose it is, really. But it will provide valuable confirmation – and we won't have to wait. After that, phone the chief, if she's available, and bring her up to speed with developments and warn HQ we'll need an ARU to be on hand as backup. Oh, and get me the number of Dales Bank in Netherdale. I'll phone their manager as soon as I get back from dropping Tina and Mrs Fawcett at the hotel.'

Tina and Margaret were waiting outside the hospital entrance when Nash pulled in. Clara noticed that both women looked upset and it was easy to tell that they had been crying. The journey to

Helmsdale was conducted in an uncomfortable silence. Mironova was relieved to be out of the car, clear of the oppressive atmosphere. Even Nash, who was normally able to lift the gloom, seemed to be affected by the tension between the two women.

Nash took Margaret's case from the boot of the car and carried it inside, where she was already in the process of booking in. Tina had remained outside, watching the detective in silence. Nash might have been flattered by the attention, but he wasn't deceived by it. Once Margaret had her room key, Nash escorted them upstairs, and as Margaret opened her door, he turned to leave, only to be detained by Tina, who put her hand on his arm.

'Mike, I know how busy you are, and I know I've taken up a lot of your time and caused you a great deal of trouble, but I really need to talk to you. If you could spare me just a few minutes, I'd be really grateful.'

Nash guessed that Margaret might already have an inkling of what Tina wanted to talk about, because she closed the door after thanking him for his assistance. He followed Tina down the corridor towards her room, staring admiringly at the long shapely curve of her legs, her neat figure and lustrous black hair.

Tina struggled to open the door one-handed then stood aside to let him enter first. Once inside, she closed the door and leaned against it, preventing Nash from leaving – in the unlikely event that he wanted to. 'My . . . Margaret told me the truth,' Tina began falteringly. 'About my parents, I mean. I don't know why, but somehow it wasn't as big a shock as she might have thought. The problem is, I don't know what to think. Part of me wants to hate her for misleading me and part of me wants to thank her because if she hadn't done that horrid thing, I would have been dead by now. I've always been uncomfortable with her because I've never felt as I ought to. I mean, I've never had the sort of love for her that a daughter should have. I thought perhaps that I was unnatural and cold.

'I know this is sounding all mixed up, and you'll probably think I'm overreacting, but I have no idea how to handle it. From what Margaret told me, I now have to brace myself for the fact that my real mother is dead, has been since soon after I was born, and my father was a criminal. Is that right? Margaret said I should ask you.'

Nash took her hand and led her across to the bed, where he sat down on one edge, patting the duvet. 'Sit here and I'll tell you what I can.'

Tina did as she was asked, aware that Nash was still holding her hand.

'If the facts we have uncovered prove to be true,' he began, 'then everything Margaret has told you did happen.'

'I dread to think what Margaret must have gone through,' Tina said.

'I watched her as she told Clara about it, and it was clear that even speaking about it was a terrible ordeal.' Nash paused and added, 'The worst thing is, I feel pretty certain that even then she didn't tell us all she'd suffered. There were parts of the story that she skimmed over. I'm not saying we ought to have heard them, but knowing what she endured helps to understand her. I hope you can forgive her. Look at it this way, she raised you when there was no one else around to do that, and kept you safe as you were growing up. Believe me, speaking as a father, that's no easy thing to do, and the worry is constant. You may have lost your mother, but look what you've gained. I can't say any more for the time being, but I assure you as soon as we have finished our inquiry you will understand.'

'Thank you, Mike, you've put everything into perspective for me. Strangely, I feel closer to Margaret now and once again I've you to thank for that. Thank you for everything you've done for me.'

Tina released her hand from his, leaned over and kissed him gently on the cheek. Nash stood up. 'I have to go,' he told her. 'I'm just glad what I've said has been a help.'

Clara confirmed she had spoken with Sister Evangeline. 'She's all set to come down as you asked. In the circumstances I had a word with Northumbria Police and they'll make arrangements for the train journey, but we need someone to meet her at Netherdale. I thought it best to have a word with you before fixing anything, as we're likely to be fairly busy.'

'No problem, I've already warned Tom. He can take my car. Did Sister Evangeline say whether she's met Phil Miller or not?'

'She's never set eyes on him, or so she said. She told me that after Max died and Frankie disappeared, she never even saw Corinna again. I got Viv to do the necessary, and we should hear back from California by tomorrow.'

'Excellent. Anything else?'

'I spoke to the chief, gave her a quick update and told her you'd fill her in with the detail once the operation is over.'

Nash waited a few minutes before making a phone call. When he was connected, Nash quoted an extension and was put straight through.

'Is DI Shaw there, please? Brian, Mike Nash. I need another favour.'

'Another? Don't you think we've any crime of our own to solve?'

'Come off it, Brian, we both know you've been sitting around swilling coffee and eating bacon butties, waiting for me to give you something to do.'

Shaw's initial response was unprintable. 'What is it this time?' he asked with mock weariness.

'I need to know what motors Phil Miller and Corinna are driving. My lad's done a DVLA search and they've five cars between them. I wonder if someone could have a quiet squint at the place they keep them and see what's missing. I need to know tomorrow if you can – so I can arrest them.'

'Really! That might not be as easy as you make it sound. But leave it with me. I'll see what we can do.'

The next morning, the solicitor phoned to say that he had met with Frankie Da Silver's alleged sister and gave Nash the woman's description. Viv was despatched to take his statement. Mironova told him that DI Shaw had rung back and supplied them with the details of the cars to watch out for.

Five minutes later Nash's phone rang. 'That was the bank. It's all set,' he told Clara. 'The securities clerk has made the appointment as we arranged. Someone claiming to be Frankie Da Silva rang. Apparently the caller made all the right noises. She apologized for failing to pay the annual service charge for the safety deposit box and asked how much she owed. She's been out of the country, or so she said.' Nash paused and reflected. 'Actually, that part's almost true. Anyway, she's promised to rectify the error tomorrow morning, after which she told the securities clerk she wants to go through the contents of the box. I'll bet she does.' He grinned, but Clara found it about as comforting as the snarl of a tiger.

chapter twenty-one

Before 8 a.m. next morning the team was assembled in the CID suite in Netherdale. The room was larger than the one in Helmsdale and as most of the morning's action was going to take place nearby, it was the obvious choice. The armed response unit members were clustered in a group at one end of the room, the bags containing their weapons a sinister reminder of the potentially dangerous operation ahead.

'As soon as Sergeant Binns arrives, I'll start the briefing,' Nash told them. He glanced at the wall clock. 'I'd like everyone in position by 9.30.'

'Can't we begin without Jack?' Mironova asked. 'After all, he won't be coming with us.'

'I know that, but I've asked Jack to take charge of things here when we leave, and I want him to be fully in the picture in case anything goes wrong.'

As Nash finished speaking, the outer door opened. Everyone looked, expecting to see Binns. Instead it was Tom Pratt whose ample form filled the doorway. 'Come in, Tom,' Nash gestured to the newcomer. 'We're just waiting for Jack.'

'He's on his way now. He had to field a couple of phone calls first.'

'Take a seat, Tom.' Nash turned to his colleagues. 'Tom and Jack have been involved in this case from the beginning, twenty-five years ago, so I felt it was only fair they should be in at the death.'

Binns hurried in. 'Sorry, Mike, I couldn't get off the phone,' he apologized. 'One RTA to deal with, then a bloke from the Health and Safety Executive who wanted to carry out an inspection today.

He took some getting rid of, but I put him off.'

'How did you manage that?'

Binns smiled. 'I told him we're about to arrest a couple of highly dangerous homicidal maniacs and we've the building crawling with armed officers.' He grinned at the ARU team. 'When I told him one of these characters made Jack the Ripper look like Paddington Bear he decided to postpone the visit.'

'Right, let's get on with it.' Nash turned to the sergeant from the ARU. 'I'm not anticipating this ending in a shoot-out, but the people we're about to detain are ruthless, determined career criminals. Furthermore, they've everything to lose, so we can't afford to take any chances. Fortunately for us, the location should work in our favour. The building they're going to visit is halfway along a cul-de-sac. That means we should be able to block the one exit and seal off their escape route, whether they're using their vehicle or on foot.

'Added to which, I hope we're going to catch them unawares. As far as they're concerned, they think everything is going to plan.' Nash paused. 'Their plan, that is; not ours. They're away from their normal territory, which means not only are they out of their comfort zone, but they've no chance of picking up rumours of what's about to go down. They've no reason to suspect we know they even exist.'

'What you're saying is, we're a sort of belt-and-braces option?' the officer suggested.

'Partly.' Nash smiled grimly. 'But for the most part, you're here in the devout hope that you won't be needed.' Twenty minutes later, when Nash was satisfied everyone had the facts clear, he signalled an end to the briefing. 'OK, I want you to make your way to the site and take up your positions. I'll be along in a few minutes. I just want a word with Jack and Tom before I leave.'

He watched the others file out of the room before turning to Binns. 'I've a job I want you to see to whilst I'm out. I'm expecting some visitors' – he glanced at the clock – 'who should be here in half an hour or so. Tom knows the details and he's going to collect them, but I want you to make sure they're comfortable and have everything they need. Here's what I want you to do.'

*

207

The Porsche slowed to a halt. Not, as Nash had anticipated, in the cul-de-sac itself, but on the main road that crossed its end. Parking was at a premium. The only space available required the driver to manoeuvre in a tight three-point turn. Luckily, the action gave Pearce, who was nearest, opportunity to read the number plate. He checked the registration against the ones written on his pad and lifted his radio. 'They're here,' he told Nash. 'Red Porsche, parking on Cross Lane.'

'I see it,' Nash acknowledged. 'Hold your positions, everyone. Let's see what they do before anybody moves.'

They waited, tension mounting. Nash glanced at the time on his dashboard display. 'Ten minutes to go,' he said into his radio. 'Everything ready inside, Clara?'

As she replied, her signal was broken up by static, caused by the fabric of the building, Nash guessed. Nevertheless, he made out her message: 'All set in here, Mike.'

'Passenger leaving the car,' Pearce reported. 'It's the woman. Hang on; let's see if the driver comes with her.' They waited. 'No, looks as if she's going alone.'

'Get that, Clara?' Nash asked.

'OK, Mike.'

'It's what we expected,' Nash told the listeners. 'Everyone remain in place until she enters the building. We don't want to spook the driver.' Nash was conscious that most of the ARU team, apart from their driver, would be inside the body of the Transit, and unable to see what was going on.

He watched in his rear-view mirror as the woman walked confidently down the cul-de-sac towards and then past him. He transferred his gaze to the Porsche. There had been no further movement from within the car. 'Looks as if her partner's leaving it to her. Everyone wait for my signal.'

Two minutes passed slowly, time the waiting men would have sworn was much longer; especially those blind to what was going on. 'Right, she's safely inside,' they heard Nash report at last. 'Pull the van down that alley opposite the end of the cul-de-sac, just beyond their car. Once you're clear of the driver's line of sight get out of the van and wait there, ready to move at a moment's notice.

Whatever you do, don't show yourselves until we've sorted things out inside. Viv, you're our eyes and ears outside, OK?'

'No problem, Mike.' Pearce watched Nash get out of his car and enter the building, before returning his gaze to the Porsche, whose driver was still visible, even through the tinted glass window.

The interior of the bank was deceptively spacious, especially for so small a town. The woman ignored the four cashier positions and headed for the reception desk set at right angles to the tills where it formed a barrier to the administration section of the branch.

'Good morning,' the receptionist greeted her. 'How may I help you?'

'I have an appointment with Mrs Simmons.'

'What name is it, please?'

'My name is Da Silva, Francesca Da Silva.'

'Please take a seat. I'll get Mrs Simmons for you. I believe she was on the phone a few seconds ago.'

The woman rose from her desk and entered the second office on her right. A minute passed before she emerged, accompanied by a tall, good-looking young woman with blonde curly hair. The receptionist returned to her seat, and the woman approached the visitor and held out her hand. 'Francesca Da Silva? I'm sorry, I don't know if it's Mrs, Miss or Ms.'

The visitor smiled as they shook hands. 'Just call me Frankie, everyone else does.'

'Very well, do you have the documents I asked for?'

The visitor took an envelope from her handbag. 'There's my driving licence and the receipt you need. I also put the overdue money for the safety deposit box in with them. I'll need a receipt for that' – she smiled – 'for the Inland Revenue, you understand. It's not all plain sailing, being a tax exile.'

'Of course, no problem.' Mrs Simmons studied the paperwork. After a moment she nodded. 'This all appears to be in order. Would you care to follow me? I'll get one of the cashiers to process the payment and get your receipt whilst I'm retrieving the box for you.'

She led the visitor into a windowless room which contained nothing apart from a table, two chairs and a telephone. 'Take a seat; I'll be back as soon as I can. It'll take a few minutes, I'm afraid.'

Left on her own, the time dragged. There was nothing to look at but the box key in her hand, four drab walls and a door that remained stubbornly closed. Eventually, however, the door opened and the blonde woman returned carrying the box. The customer's attention was distracted when she realized someone else had also come into the room. She frowned. This wasn't right, surely?

'I'm sorry about this,' the blonde told her, 'but my colleague needs to be along, and he has a couple of questions to ask. For security, you understand.'

Her momentary alarm eased, she nodded graciously. 'Of course.' Bloody red tape, she thought.

The man smiled encouragingly. 'Only one question, to be exact,' he told her, his tone relaxed. 'I need to know how you managed to get here today. I mean, it must have been difficult, when, to my certain knowledge, the rightful owner of that safety deposit box has been dead over twenty years. That is, of course, if you really are Frankie Da Silva, and you've returned from beyond the grave. Because if not, I'd say your real name is Corinna Perry, and you're under arrest for conspiracy to murder.'

Corinna reached for the pistol in her handbag, but halfway there she felt her wrist gripped firmly. As the handcuff was snapped in place she looked up at the woman. 'My name is Detective Sergeant Mironova, North Yorkshire Police,' she told Corinna. 'Seems as if nobody's who they say they are this morning, doesn't it?'

'And the morning's only just begun,' the male detective added.

Corinna watched, numb with shock, as the handcuffs were fastened round her other wrist.

'Right, Clara, you administer the caution. I'll send the bank security guard to join you while we deal with her partner in crime.'

Corinna's eyes flew to his face. So they knew about Phil. Then she relaxed; they might be able to get her for trying to steal the contents of the box, but they didn't know the rest of it. And even if they did, they'd never be able to prove it. The detective paused by the door and looked back. He nodded towards the table. 'Whatever you do, don't forget that box and key. The damned thing's caused enough trouble already.'

Nash walked out of the bank and down the cul-de-sac. Pearce

watched him pass, then spoke into his radio. Nash glanced to left and right, made sure the road was clear and crossed. He passed the front of the Porsche and stopped by the driver's window. The occupant's first hint of alarm came then, as the man outside gestured for him to lower his window. 'Are you waiting for a lady who's inside the bank?' the man asked.

'Yes, why?'

'I've been sent to tell you she's been detained – and so are you.' As he spoke, the man leaned forward and added, 'My name's Detective Inspector Mike Nash. You're under arrest.'

Too late, Miller saw the ring of armed police officers who seemed to have appeared from nowhere. Too late he felt the handcuffs tighten on his wrists.

Nash watched the prisoners loaded into the police cars before turning to Pearce. He handed the DC the keys to the Porsche. 'Drive that back to the station, and make the most of the experience. On police salaries it's the closest you're likely to get, barring a lottery win.'

Once they were back at headquarters, Pearce appeared brandishing a door key. 'This was in the glove box of the Porsche. Fortunately, it's got the agent's address on it. I rang them. Lilac Cottage, Bishops Cross.'

'Good work, Viv. Tell Clara and get the SOCO team organized. We'll have a ride out there.'

Their search of the cottage revealed little of interest until Pearce opened the larder door. Nash was reading a brochure from the company who leased the premises. Something about their name, Wilson Dream Holidays, should have rung a bell. He was trying to work out why when his attention was distracted. It was a mistake he would later remember – and regret in years to come.

'Mike,' Pearce called out, 'come and have a look here.'

There was little in the way of food in the larder. Somehow, Nash couldn't picture Corinna going in much for home cooking. Pearce pointed. Leaning against the wall was a sledgehammer. Nash picked up the weapon and pointed a gloved hand at the head. Pearce saw the stains and a couple of hairs that were stuck to what he guessed was blood. 'I assume that's Graham Nattrass's blood and hair. Otherwise, it could belong to either Thornton or his henchman,' Nash suggested.

Nash and Mironova left Pearce in charge at the cottage while she drove him back to Netherdale. 'What now?' she asked.

'Now we interview the prisoners.'

'Put Corinna Perry in one of the interview rooms, please,' Nash instructed the custody sergeant. He turned to Binns. 'Whilst we're talking to her, I want you to set up another camcorder and tape machine in the conference room.'

Nash stared at Corinna as Mironova switched on the recording equipment. He waited, even after Clara had finished delivering the introductory message. Corinna stared back, her look, her body language shouting defiant arrogance louder than any words could achieve. She'll be a tough nut to crack, Nash thought. He smiled to himself. He enjoyed a challenge.

Eventually, Nash spoke. 'It must have seemed like the perfect opportunity' – he paused – 'to get rid of poor old Max, who'd become such an embarrassing liability; so you could shack up with your lover. What was the problem with Max? I mean, there were a few problems to choose from, weren't there? Which one made you decide to do away with him? Was it the fact that so many people were after him? The people he swindled, for one thing. And there was Callaghan, and a few more, trying to muscle in on his territory. Or was it more than that? Max no longer any good in the bed department, perhaps? I mean, you're a handsome, red-blooded woman. I bet you'd take some satisfying. Wasn't Max up to it any more? No Viagra or crystal meth in those days. Nothing to give him the stamina you'd need. Or did you simply fancy a bit of fresh meat in your sandwich? I bet that was it. A new lover, a bit of excitement, someone who could do more for you than poor, tired old Max. Was that it, Corinna? Was that why Max had to go?'

Whatever Corinna had been expecting, this line of questioning was a long way from it. Nash was aware of that. Even as he was speaking, he saw her relax, saw the quiet smile. 'If that's what you want to think, carry on. It's all nonsense of course. But even if there had been a grain of truth in your wild accusations, you'd never be able to prove any of it.'

'But then everything went pear-shaped on you, didn't it?' Nash continued as if Corinna hadn't spoken. 'First of all Ray and Frankie found out what you were planning; or part of it at least. Then Frankie disappeared. That wouldn't have mattered, but for the fact that she took Max's stash of diamonds with her. That must have seemed disastrous.'

Corinna's smile had vanished; her pose had changed as well. Instead of lounging in the chair perfectly at ease, she was now sitting bolt upright, a frown replacing the smile. Nevertheless, she achieved a shrug. 'Think what you like, you can't prove it.'

Nash smiled. 'I might not have to; you might end up telling me everything. Especially when we throw your more recent crimes into the pot. Let me see, what have we got? Conspiracy to murder, attempted murder, carrying a firearm, obtaining goods by false pretences; that should do for a start. Even if I can't pin all your crimes on you, Corinna, I'm sure I can get you convicted of enough to keep you inside until you're an old woman. Yes, I'm confident we can send you both down for a long time.'

Nash signalled to Clara. 'That's enough for now. Put her back in a cell and let her stew for a bit.'

Unlike Corinna, Phil Miller didn't make eye contact with Nash. Not to begin with, at least. 'We've got you in the frame for murder, Phil,' Nash began. 'To be accurate: murder, attempted murder, burglary and deception. And that's just for starters. Tell me something. How long do you reckon it'll be until Corinna gives you up? Not long, I bet. I mean, she's not exactly the faithful type, is she?'

Clara was watching Miller closely. She saw that Nash had got the prisoner's attention. More than that, he'd riled the man. She saw the glitter of rage in Miller's eyes and smiled approvingly. This was more like it. This was the Mike Nash she knew.

'Let's look at the evidence. She ditched Max when he became a millstone. If she's capable of doing it once, she's sure to do it again, mark my words. Somebody told me she was devoted to Max. That made me laugh because I knew she'd hopped into your bed as soon as he was out of the way. Or was that before he was killed? Were you already at it? Was that why Max had to be got rid of? Or was it so you could get your hands on his fortune, get control of those precious diamonds and bed the lovely widow into the bargain?

'OK, so you didn't achieve all the objectives you'd planned for, but you still didn't do too badly, did you? Admittedly you missed out on the diamonds, but you still ended up ruling Max's empire, and renting the sexy widow all these years. I hope it was worth the trouble and effort. I suppose at least you'll have the memories. I mean, whilst you're serving a life sentence in a cell with a roommate suffering from BO and halitosis and only you in mind as a playmate. Shut your eyes and you'll be able to forget that Corinna's on the outside, having it off with her latest. Because deep down, you know that's how she is, how it'll end up, don't you? Once a slut always a slut, don't you think? That's just another worry to add to your list, isn't it? And we're the least of them, aren't we? I think we both know those diamonds are beyond your control forever. And from what I hear, that means some really evil men will be wanting a word with you.'

Miller hadn't spoken throughout Nash's tirade. He still didn't speak, but if looks could kill, Nash would have withered on the spot. Much to Mironova's astonishment, instead of pressing home his advantage Nash signalled the end of the interview. As the uniformed officer took the prisoner back to the cells, Clara still wasn't sure what the last three-quarters of an hour had achieved, if anything. Neither prisoner had volunteered any information, nor did they seem likely to. So why was Nash looking so cheerful? Then it dawned on her. Nash was toying with them. He hadn't revealed one single fact, hadn't shared any of what they knew. 'You're making them suffer,' she accused him.

Nash smiled. 'A little bit, maybe. But when you think how much misery and suffering they've inflicted, I reckon they've earned it.'

chapter twenty-two

Pearce was waiting for them, talking to Jack Binns; their conversation being listened to with interest by the Netherdale civilian receptionist. 'SOCO have finished at the cottage. They didn't find anything more. But the prints will prove they were living there, as well as the bloody great Merc parked round the back.'

'Good, how about you, Jack? Everything ready?' Nash gestured towards the first floor.

Binns nodded. 'The recording equipment's all set up. I tested it, too, just to be on the safe side. Your visitors arrived earlier. Tom and I got them settled and Tom's sitting with them.'

Nash smiled. 'Thanks, Jack. Wait here until I ring down, will you? Then bring the prisoners upstairs. I'll want you in on the interviews.'

Binns looked surprised. 'You're doing them both together? That's a bit unusual, isn't it? Are you sure you don't want them separated?'

Nash shook his head. 'That won't be necessary.' He turned to Pearce. 'Viv, will you wait here until my other visitor arrives and bring her up?'

Nash walked slowly, mentally rehearsing what he would say to the prisoners, what he wanted out of them and how he was going to set about getting it. The next hour or so would be critical to their case. Much of their evidence was circumstantial at this stage, but he thought that would be enough.

Clara, who had gone ahead to check the room, saw the expression on Nash's face as he entered. 'You're looking particularly devious,' she told him. 'I take it that means that your plans are all starting to come together? The puppet master has arranged the show, and now he's waiting for the marionettes to dance when he pulls their strings, is that it?'

'How very eloquently put, Clara. Yes, I suppose it does seem a bit that way, but given what we know about the suspects, I think we need to nail them.'

'I guess you're right. By the way, did Viv tell you we got a reply back from California?'

'No, perhaps he thought you'd already told me.'

'Well the good news is that the answer is "yes".'

'I thought it would be. That makes today's work even easier.'

He looked round. Binns had not only set up the tape machine and camcorder, but Clara had set out a water jug and glasses, more as if they were expecting visitors than arrested prisoners. Nash smiled approvingly. The scene had been set for the benefit of the camera so there could be no later allegation of mistreatment.

'Have we missed anything?' Clara asked.

'Not a thing. I like the water, that's a good touch. They can't complain about water. Whatever you do, though, don't offer to make them any of your coffee, Clara. We don't want complaints about police brutality.'

Two minutes later, Pearce entered. 'She's here,' he told Nash. 'Where do you want me to put her?'

'We'll introduce her to the others and they can all wait in the next room.'

Nash signalled Clara to come with him as they followed Pearce. It was almost fifteen minutes later when they returned to the make-shift interview room via a connecting door, leaving Pearce along with Tom Pratt to care for Nash's guests. Both Nash and Mironova looked subdued after the meeting they had witnessed.

'Ring Jack and ask him to bring them up from the cells, please, Clara. Let's get this over and done with,' Nash said as he left the adjoining door slightly ajar.

As soon as the prisoners were led into the room, Clara switched on the camcorder. When they were seated at the table, Nash asked her to perform the formalities for the tape.

He turned to the woman. 'You were arrested when you

attempted to remove the contents of Frankie Da Silva's safety deposit box from the bank, using the receipt you obtained from her solicitor, who gave it to you on the strength of the letter of authority stolen from Mrs Margaret Fawcett's house.'

His gaze switched to Corinna's partner. 'Unfortunately for you, we've managed to identify remains found near Bishops Cross village as those of Frankie Da Silva. I must tell you that in addition to her death, we are also investigating the murder of Graham Nattrass. Given the savagery of the blows that killed him, and the strength required to subdue him, even after he'd been sedated, we reckon Corinna couldn't have done it. Which leads us directly to you. Apart from Nattrass's murder, we are also investigating two other attacks. Plus, the murders of two men found in a burnt-out car, one of whom we believe to have been an acquaintance of yours by the name of Trevor Thornton. The Met have also reopened the inquiry into the earlier murder of Tony Callaghan, known as Dirty Harry. Other charges relating to further matters under investigation might also be forthcoming.'

Miller had remained impassive until that moment, but at the mention of Callaghan's name he looked up. Shock drained a little of the colour from his suntanned complexion. 'I'm not saying anything,' he muttered in a low tone. 'You can't prove anything. You've no evidence.'

'Actually, we have. We've searched your cottage.'

'Don't say a word, Phil.' Corinna spoke for the first time.

'Don't worry, I've no intention of saying anything. This lot can't prove a thing, despite all their bluster.'

Nash walked across to the open door and spoke. 'Have you heard enough? Would you care to join our little party?' he asked.

Everyone turned to look as Tom Pratt emerged from the adjacent room, pushing a wheelchair. Seated in the chair was a frail-looking man. Alongside it was Sister Evangeline. As he closed the door Nash announced for the tape. 'Civilian Support Officer Pratt has just entered the room, accompanied by Mrs Evangeline Perry – and Mr Raymond Perry.'

Both Evangeline and her son looked as if they had been crying. Hardly surprising in the circumstances, Clara thought, and wondered how many more tears would be shed before the day was out.

Shock held the prisoners speechless for a moment, then Miller burst out, 'It can't be! You're dead!'

'Really? Why do you think that? Mr Perry needed specialist treatment. We also wanted to make sure he was clear of danger so we had him moved to the Freeman Hospital in Newcastle. There, he could be given the treatment to help him recover and be close to his mother; close enough for her to visit him as he was recuperating.'

Nash turned to the man in the wheelchair. 'Do you recognize anyone in this room, Ray?'

'I recognize Corinna' – Ray nodded in her direction – 'although I haven't seen her for a long time. I don't recognize him,' he pointed to Miller. 'I don't think I've ever seen him before in my life. The odd thing is, though, when I was waiting next door I thought his voice sounded vaguely familiar.'

'Funny, I thought that as well,' Ray's mother chipped in.

Both prisoners remained silent, their eyes averted from Ray Perry and his mother. Nash looked at Clara and nodded towards the door. She walked across and took hold of the handle.

'I have someone else here I'd like you to meet,' Nash told them. As he spoke, Clara opened the connecting door and gestured to Pearce.

'For those of you who haven't had the pleasure of meeting her, allow me to introduce Frankie Da Silva—'

Corinna's scream cut across Nash's voice before he finished his sentence. Strangely, it was she who was more shocked than Phil by the apparent entrance of the woman they thought was dead.

'As I was saying, this is Frankie Da Silva's daughter, Christina.'

Corinna was white and shaking, her hand clasped to her mouth, her eyes fixed on Tina's face. She didn't seem to have taken in what Nash had said.

Although Nash had warned Ray and his mother what was going to happen, when he had introduced Tina to her father and grand-mother a little earlier, Clara could see that they, too, were moved by the similarity to Frankie.

The sudden appearance of Raymond Perry, followed by the girl who so uncannily resembled Frankie seemed to knock the last semblance of fight from Phil. 'All right,' he said, his tone heavy with the weariness of defeat. 'I'll tell you.'

'Yes, but will you tell us everything?' Mironova interrupted. 'Or will we have to prompt you?'

Corinna saw the glance that passed between Nash and his deputy and her heart sank. That glance told her the game was up. They didn't need to be told. They already knew it all.

'There was one unanswered question that had us puzzled,' Nash continued. 'Who would benefit from the death of Max Perry? Who stood to gain – apart from Corinna, that is? Certainly not the people whose diamonds had been stolen – they were hard-headed business men. Killing Max would have achieved nothing; it wouldn't have got their diamonds back. Nor did Callaghan stand to gain. He was having more trouble with the triads than Max.'

'Excuse me,' Clara said. 'Do you want to take their statements before or after we charge them?'

'Good question. We've only charged them with the attempted robbery of the diamonds from the bank this morning. Will you read out the other possible charges please, Clara? It will help to refresh the memory.'

Clara took a sheet of paper from a file and began to read. 'There's the murder of Graham Nattrass, the attempted murder of Raymond Perry, the assault on Tina Silver, the murders of Frankie Da Silva, Trevor Thornton, one as yet unidentified male and Tony Callaghan.' Clara paused and looked at Nash.

'Thank you, Clara, I think that should do for starters.'

Ray Perry interrupted. 'But what about Max's murder? Why haven't you mentioned that? Don't you think they should be charged with that? Wasn't Max their first victim?'

Corinna's heart sank as she saw Nash look at his deputy once more and realized the full extent of their knowledge. As if in a dream, she heard him say, 'I think it's very touching of you to be concerned that the killers of Max are brought to justice,' Nash told him. As he was speaking, he turned to look at Phil Miller. 'However, I believe that would be very difficult to prove. Impossible, I reckon.' His tone was almost conversational. 'It would have its comical side though, don't you agree? Being charged with your own murder, Max?'

There was stunned silence for a long moment. 'What did you say?' Evangeline asked.

'I was suggesting to Max that it would be funny if he was charged with having murdered himself, that's all.'

'Max? You think this is Max? But he's been dead over twenty-five years,' Evangeline persisted.

'Correction, everyone believed him to have been dead over twenty-five years,' Nash told her.

'That isn't Max,' Raymond chimed in. 'Max was killed. You know he was. Besides, that man doesn't look at all like Max.'

'No, he doesn't now, but he still sounds like Max.' He turned to Evangeline. 'Remember what you said about his voice sounding familiar? How could it, when you've never met Phil Miller? Unless of course, Phil Miller is actually Max Perry, your brother-in-law. Then you would think the voice familiar.'

'But what about his appearance?' Ray objected.

Nash was still looking at Sister Evangeline. 'Remember when you told me where Corinna worked as a nurse?'

'Yes; it was in Coventry.'

'We checked it out. You were right when you said the name was somehow connected to Captain Cook. It was the Endeavour Clinic that burned down, killing three people. One of them was a plastic surgeon who operated there. We managed to trace the anaesthetist who assisted. He now lives in California. He remembered a patient by the name of Phil Miller. He confirmed the identity via a photo we emailed him of Max Perry. So, Clara, I suggest you charge our friend here under his real name. And if he still insists he isn't Max Perry, a simple DNA test will confirm it. We've his nephew's DNA already on file.' Nash gestured to Ray.

Nash signalled to Clara to stop the tape. He looked at Max and Corinna. Both of them appeared to be stunned, defeated, deflated almost.

'Sergeant Binns, take them back down to the cells. Get them a solicitor if they want one. They might need legal aid,' he added wickedly, 'as they're up to their ears in debt.'

When the visitors had been supplied with refreshments, Nash turned to Ray. 'Tell me about Callaghan, what happened when he was killed?'

'I was framed. I got a call from him.' Ray explained how he'd been summoned to the car showroom on some pretext of a meeting and had only just arrived when the police showed up.

'Who set the meeting up?' Nash asked.

'Callaghan rang me.'

'Are you sure it was him?' Nash asked.

'Of course I'm sure. Who else could it have been?'

'Someone good at impersonations, perhaps? Someone with theatrical experience?'

'You mean. . . ?'

'There seems to have been more than one conversation attributed to a person that couldn't be verified.' Nash said. 'But tell me, why did you keep quiet all the time you were inside?'

'I got a message,' Ray explained. 'It was when I was on remand. Another convict passed it.' He shrugged. 'I thought it was genuine, because that's the way things happened inside. Still do' – he smiled – 'despite your lot trying to put a stop to it. The message was from Frankie, or so they reckoned. Now, I realize it was simply designed to shut me up. It said that she'd done what we planned, but in order to make sure she was safe, I had to keep quiet. I couldn't risk anything happening to Frankie, what with the baby and all,' he said with a deal of sadness in his voice, 'so I complied. Much later, as the years passed with no contact whatsoever, I began to have my doubts, but what could I do? I had no one to contact, no money to launch an appeal, and as far as I could tell, no grounds for one.'

'You knew about the baby?' Nash asked.

Perry nodded. 'We even discussed names – devised a password from it, either boy or girl, in case of emergency.'

'What about your mother?' Clara asked. 'Didn't you think of trying to contact her?'

'I did, once I started to wonder if that message was true, but then I heard that she'd died. You may think I'm simple for believing these rumours, but I'd no means of checking them out. All the news

I got was that a homeless alcoholic had been fished out of the river near Rotherhithe. What convinced me was I knew my mother used to go there a bit when she was . . . ill.'

'What did you think about the rumour that Frankie was involved with Callaghan?' Mironova asked.

'I heard that, and told Frankie about it. We laughed so much I thought she was going to wet herself. We both knew that Callaghan was queer. He used to visit a boy who lived in the same apartment block and that's how rumours start.'

'Tell me about the diamonds. How did you get hold of them? They would have been somewhere secure, I'd have thought.'

'Not from me,' Ray smiled, and Nash realized with some surprise that it was almost the first time he'd seen him look cheerful. 'I stole them,' Ray confessed. 'The lock-up had a safe in the corner, one that was cemented into the floor. I was good with safes, so I simply broke in and took the diamonds.'

'What did you intend to do with them?'

'First of all, we wanted to deny Max the use of them. We knew their history, the misery and bloodshed they had already caused to thousands, possibly millions of people. Frankie was passionate about it, and when I heard the rumour that Max had got hold of them, I was sure the men who had brought them to this country had been murdered. That, more than anything, convinced me she was right. After I got the stones, Frankie was going to come back to Yorkshire so that Margaret could look after her, as she was nearly ready for the baby to be born. She brought the diamonds with her. Our long-term aim was to contact one of the human rights organizations and explain how we'd come by them, in the hope that they could be sold and the money used to help some of the original victims. Whose was the body, by the way? The fake Max, I mean?' Ray asked.

'We believe the man was a South African private investigator who specialized in tracing stolen diamonds. There has always been a big trade in them in South Africa, so much so that there used to be a specific offence, called illicit diamond buying, for anyone caught in possession of them. The private detective's name was Karl Reikert, and he was reported missing soon after Max's "murder", so that tallies. They only had to invite Reikert to Max's place and his fingerprints would be easily matched. Who would question it?'

Nash looked at Ray. 'You've had a long day. I think we should leave you to spend some time with your family.'

Perry's eyes glistened with tears. 'Family – that's a word I thought I'd never use again, Inspector. Thank you.'

Tina asked, 'How many people have they killed in order to get their hands on those diamonds?'

'We can't be certain, but we believe there were two couriers who brought the stones from Holland, the fake Max, Callaghan and his bodyguard, who your father was convicted of killing, and the three victims of the fire at the clinic where Max had his plastic surgery done. Then we believe your mother, Frankie, died in their company too, but whether that was murder, we can't be sure. More recently, we know they killed Graham Nattrass, Trevor Thornton plus his minder and an underworld informant called Freddie Perkins.'

'Dear Heaven, so much evil,' Evangeline muttered.

'What I don't understand is why they waited all this time to get hold of the diamonds if they were so desperate?' Tina asked.

'That's a good question, and there's no simple answer to it. In fact, we believe there are a number of contributory reasons. One is that, with Ray out of circulation, Max had control all to himself. He entered the highly lucrative drugs trade, which Ray had always been dead against, and so he wasn't short of money.

'Added to that, they'd no idea how to get hold of the diamonds. The only people with any knowledge were Frankie, who was dead, and Ray, who was serving a life sentence. They'd been desperate to get Ray locked up because they feared that he was the one person who would be able to see through the "Phil Miller" fraud, and in doing that they'd put the stones out of reach until such time as he was released.'

Nash paused before continuing, 'Above all, they needed the money desperately now. Although they'd made a huge fortune from their various illicit activities, they'd invested it all, and borrowed more to put into a scheme that at first seemed highly lucrative. It was run by an American investment counsellor, and when the financial meltdown happened recently, it was found to be what's known as a "Ponzi scheme". The man behind the scheme was in the news afterwards; he was the one who made off with billions of pounds of investors' money. Phil and Corinna are broke, all their property has been re-mortgaged up to the hilt and with prices on the slide, they're having trouble keeping up with the repayments. Added to all that, we understand there are what's euphemistically known as "collectors" after them, regarding some of the money they owe to some disreputable lenders. Also, diamonds have appreciated in value enormously over the years. I think the collection we've taken possession of is worth somewhere around fifteen million today.'

'I don't know how you managed to work all that out,' Evangeline told him.

Nash gestured to Mironova and Pearce. 'They're the ones who did most of the work. I'm very lucky. I've a brilliant team, and they contributed just as much, if not more. Unfortunately, whatever we do, we can't put right all the evil things that were done, just get a little bit of justice for those who have suffered.' Nash frowned. 'I believe there are superstitions that say those blood diamonds are cursed. When you think of the number of people who have died because of them, that's easy to believe. Any pleasure at solving this case vanishes when I think of the victims we know of – and the untold number of whom we're unaware. All for the sake of some glittering bits of carbon.'